THE FRENCHMAN

USA TODAY & WSJ BESTSELLING AUTHOR
giana darling

Copyright 2024 Giana Darling
Published by Giana Darling
Edited by Jenny Sims of Editing4indies
Cover Photo by Stefan Rappo
Cover Model: Christophe Leitner

This book is licensed for your personal enjoyment only. This book may not be resold or given away to other people. If you would like to share this book with another person, please purchase an additional copy for each recipient. If you're reading this book and did not purchase it, or it was not purchased for your enjoyment only, then please return to your favorite retailer and purchase your own copy. Thank you for respecting the hard work of this author.

Without in any way limiting the author's exclusive rights under copyright, any use of this publication to "train" generative artificial intelligence (AI) technologies is expressly prohibited. The author reserves all rights to license uses of this work for generative AI training and development of machine learning language models.

This book is a work of fiction, created without use of AI technology. Any similarities to persons living or dead, events or places is purely coincidental.

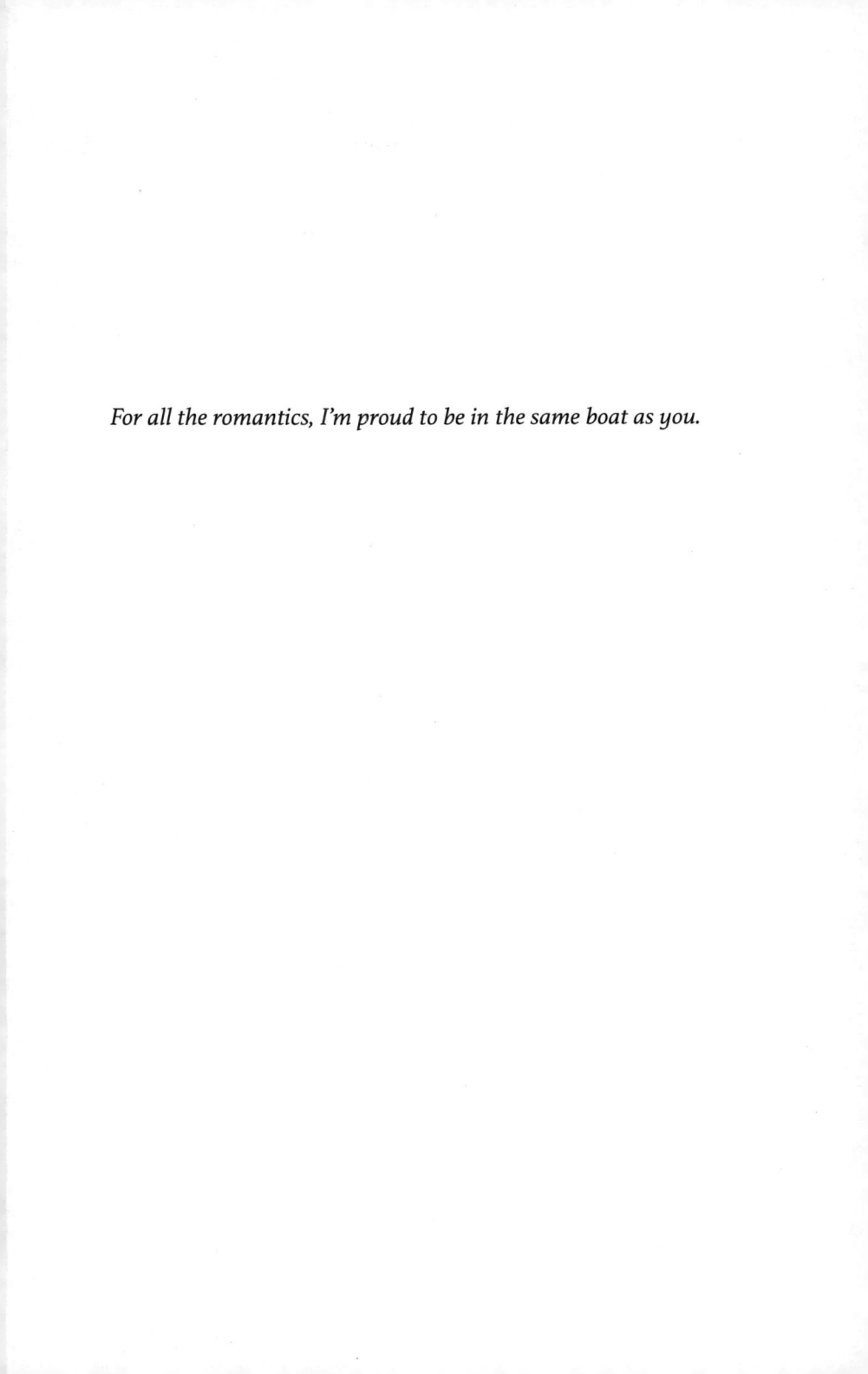

For all the romantics, I'm proud to be in the same boat as you.

"Take a lover who looks at you like maybe you are magic."

Frida Kahlo

Playlist

"The Night We Met" — Lord Huron
"Come Fly With Me" – Frank Sinatra
"Lover Undercover" — Melody Gardot
"Mar De Suenos" — Mark Barnwell
"Sinnerman" — Nina Simone
"Black Mambo" — Glass Animals
"Le lac" – Julien Dore
"Pleasure This Pain" — Kwamie Liv, Angel Haze
"Open" — Rhye
"Can't Help Falling In Love" — Ingrid Michaelson
"New Amsterdam" — Pink Martini
"Transformation" — The Cinematic Orchestra
"This Is What It Feels Like" — BANKS
"Le Vie En Rose" — Edith Piaf
"Leave Your Lover" – Sam Smith
"One Last Night" — Vaults
"Ne me quitte pas" — Carla Bruni

"Non, Je Ne Regrette Rien" – Edith Piaf
"Bleeding Love" —Leona Lewis
"Broken Strings" — James Morrison, Nelly Furtado
"Are You Hurting The One You Love?" — Florence + The Machine
"I Get Along Without You"— Chet Baker
"Dead Hearts" – Stars
"Baby I'm A Fool" — Melody Gardot
"Come Together" – The Beatles
"Anchor" – Novo Amor
"Painter Song" – Norah Jones
"Toes" — Glass Animals
"Late Night" – Foushee
"Love Love Love" – Of Monsters and Men
"Piano Sonata No. 16 in C" – Mozart
"Let it Be Me" – Ray LaMontagne
"All About That Bass" – Meghan Trainor
"Desparado" —Diana Krall
"To Love Somebody"— Lindi Ortega
"Quelqu'un M'a Dit" – Carla Bruni
"For Your Precious Love" – Otis Redding
"I Don't Wanna Love Somebody Else" – A Great Big World
"Generique " – Miles Davis
"Only You—Matthew Perryman Jones
"Exile Vilify" – The National
"Setlla By Starlight" – Miles Davis, John Coltrane
"Make You Feel My Love" – Adele
"It's Always You" – Chet Baker
"Turn Me On" – Norah Jones
"Fix You" – Coldplay
"I'll Be Good" – Jaymes Young
"Fever" –Peggy Lee
"Perfect" – Ed Sheeran

"All I Want" – Kodaline
"Often" – The Weeknd
"I Do" – Susie Suh

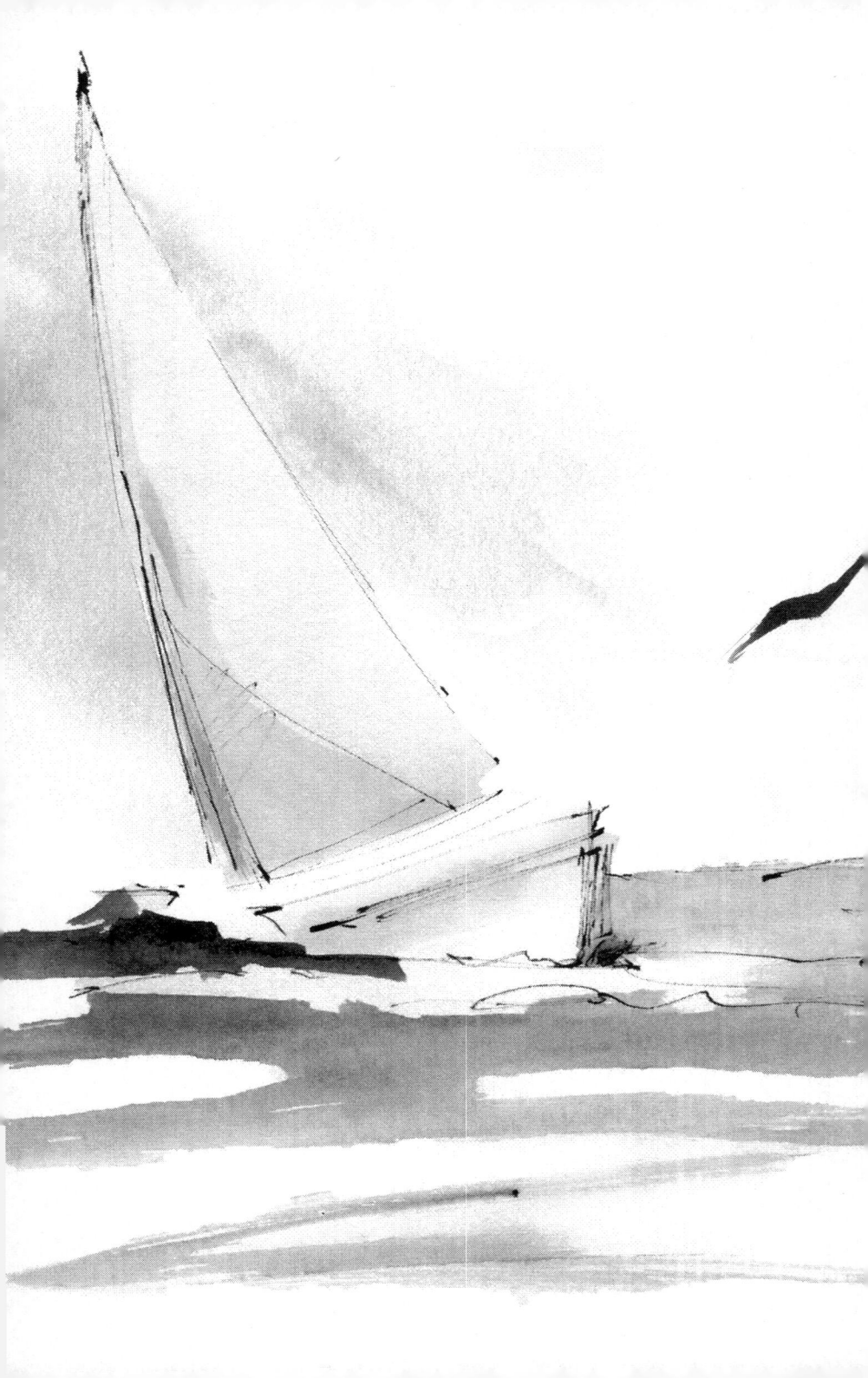

Chapter One

Rain pounded against the steaming tarmac, and the force of the wind slapped each raindrop against the oval window beside my head so that the gray of the runway, the rolling clouds, and the Vancouver skyline blurred into one. The rain calmed my nerves, and I closed my eyes to better hear the tap and whistle of the weather outside the tin machine that had —somewhat precariously—carried me from Paris to Vancouver in just fewer than seven and a half hours. We were deplaning a third of the passengers, then refueling to make the last leg of the journey to my final destination of Los Cabos, Mexico.

I took a deep breath and tried to focus on my happy place while the economy passengers filed off the plane. The flight was necessary, and after twenty-four years of traveling, I should have been used to the bump and grind of air travel.

In theory, I was. Before every flight, I waited calmly in the endlessly snaking line to check my bags, greeted the attendant with a genuine smile, and agreed that yes, I would have a pleasant flight. It wasn't until I was on the plane, secured in my seat by the tenuous hold of the belt, that my fear kicked into supercharge. I was intensely grateful to my younger brother Sebastian for loaning me the money for the first-class flight. At least now, if the plane went down, I would have a bigger seat to cushion the fall.

"You still look a bit green, *chérie*." The middle-aged gentleman beside me leaned forward and offered me his unopened water bottle. "The worst is over, though. I hope someone is picking you up in Mexico. You are in no shape to drive after all of..." He waved politely at the remaining travel sickness bags the flight attendant had passed to me twenty minutes into our flight.

I managed a weak smile for Pierre. He was a fifty-year-old bachelor, quite distinguished really, with steel gray hair and cunning brown eyes. And maybe, under different circumstances, he would have propositioned me. As it was, he had offered to pay someone to switch seats with him when he discovered how sick I was. Failing that, he had settled in with relatively good grace and lectured me on the tricks of international trade law to distract me. Everything considered—I had managed to drool on his Hugo Boss blazer while I dozed between throwing up—I was grateful to him.

"No, but I'll catch a taxi to the resort." At the moment, I wasn't looking forward to my enforced vacation. All I wanted was to step off the plane back in my familiar Paris and slip into the small wrought iron bed in my studio apartment in *St-Germain-des-Prés*.

Pierre nodded and shot me a sidelong look. "Are you going to be all right now?"

He was getting off now to visit his daughter and newborn grandson. He didn't like North America, and I got the feeling he was lingering just to eke out a few more words in his native tongue before switching to English.

I nodded meekly, but before I could respond, the deeper voice of someone behind us spoke. "If you will allow me, I think you are leaving her in capable hands."

I opened my eyes when Pierre nudged me indelicately with his elbow and cleared his throat. Immediately, I blinked.

The man who stood before us dominated the entire aisle. His dusky golden skin stretched taut over his strong features, almost brutally constructed of steeply angled cheekbones and a bladed nose. I had only the vague impression that he was tall and lean because his eyes, a deep and electric blue like the night sky during a lightning storm, held me arrested. The way he held himself, the power of his lean build, and the look in those eyes reminded me of a wolf caged within the confines of civility but eternally savage.

"I'm sure she would be delighted." Pierre sent me a barely concealed look telling me to pull it together.

I smiled hesitantly at the gorgeous stranger, aware that I was a mess of clammy skin and melted makeup. "I'm fine, really."

He nodded curtly, his eyes devoid of any real sympathy. "You will be."

Pierre hesitated as his eyes searched my face for reluctance. I smiled at him and took one of his hands between my clammy palms. "*Merci beaucoup pour votre aide. J'espère que vous passez un bon temps avec votre fille.*"

I was rewarded with a broad grin before he hastily collected his things and moved toward the front of the plane. I watched him go instead of focusing on the stranger as he took Pierre's abandoned seat, but after a few moments with his eyes hot on my face, I turned to him uneasily.

His thick hair was the color of polished mahogany and appeared overdue for a trim as it curled at the base of his neck. My fingers itched to run through the silken mass, but instead, I smiled.

"There really is no need to look after me, monsieur," I continued in French. "I am quite well now."

I squirmed in my seat when he didn't immediately reply. "It's silly, really. I've been afraid of planes since I was young."

"Oh?" He clasped his hands, and I noticed that he didn't wear a watch, that his fingers were long and nimble. The freckles on the back of those strong hands surprised me, and I found them strangely appealing. I wanted badly to dig into the bag at my feet for my sketchpad.

Because I was uncomfortable, I nodded empathetically. "I was four when we moved to Puglia for a year, and I don't remember the logistics of the move very well, but I remember the plane." I looked at him from the corner of my eye, and he nodded for me to continue with his hands steepled in front of his beautifully drawn lips. "It was with some budget airline, and the plane itself was barely held together by rusty bolts. I think the captain might have been drunk because we dropped and dipped the whole way through."

"Which airline?" His voice was silky and cool, like the brush of a tie against my skin.

"I don't remember now." I frowned at him. "Why?"

He waved my question out of the air with those deep blue eyes focused on my face. "Tell me more."

Those are magic words to hear from a man, I think. It unfurls something hidden deep within a woman, something that is habitually scared and insecure. *Tell me more.* It was somehow intimate to hear those words, even from a stranger, *especially* from this stranger.

"My father was in debt, so we were basically fleeing." I shrugged, but the sharp ache of terror still resounded in my chest when I thought of my mother's despair and my brother's desolation. "Maybe I had caught the flu, or maybe I was scared, but I spent most of the flight losing the contents of my stomach. Needless to say, it wasn't a pleasant trip. Since then, I've traveled a lot, but the feeling never goes away."

"Ah, but flying is a pleasure." He did not smile, and I had the sense he rarely did, but his eyes grew dark with pleasure. "Close your eyes."

"Excuse me?"

"Close your eyes."

I pressed back in my chair when he leaned into me slightly in order to reach the button on my armrest. My chair tilted back, and I found myself looking up into his lean face, his shoulder still warm against my front.

"Close your eyes," he repeated firmly.

I swallowed twice before doing so. I didn't know his name, where he came from, or anything personal to mark him with. But somehow, it was thrilling. To be in the hands of a perfect stranger and trust him enough to surrender my sight and allow him to make even the simplest decision for me.

So I hardly flinched when a blanket covered my chilled feet and was pulled up under my chin. His fingers, ridged with slight calluses, brushed against the tender skin of my neck as he tucked me in.

"You are flying," he said quietly, but it felt as though he spoke the words against my ear. "And if you relax, let every muscle loosen and breathe deeply. Nothing is more soothing than being in the air."

Instead, the pit of my stomach coiled, and I found myself wishing I was another kind of person. Someone who flirted with handsome strangers, who would lean into that firm mouth and take it without any qualms.

"We aren't in the air," I pointed out. "We are in a machine made of metal that has no business being in the sky."

"Ah, it is the machine that frightens you." I wondered where he sat and if he remained leaning over me. "Let it be a bird then, a swan."

"Okay," I mumbled, suddenly exhausted. "But only because swans are mean."

I smiled at his husky chuckle but fell asleep before he could say anything else.

When I woke up, it was to the delicate tapping of rain against the window and the brisk click of fingers on a keyboard. Deeply rested and disorientated, I moaned and stretched across my seat before righting it. Blinking away the sleep, I looked up and met the searing eyes of my stranger.

"You had a good rest," he noted, and for some reason, I flushed.

He was even more handsome than before if that was possible. In the darkening night, his hair was mostly black, kissed red by the artificial overhead lights. He seemed like some creature of the night, something dark and too sexy to be true.

"Yes, thank you." We spoke in English now, and I couldn't remember if we had switched over before I fell asleep. His voice was smooth and cool, enunciated perfectly with just a hint of French charm.

"We land in twenty minutes." He watched my surprise and handed me a plastic cup of sparkling liquid. Our fingers brushed as he passed it off, and a current of electricity made my grip on the cup shaky. Quickly, he righted it with his other hand and pressed both of my hands to the plastic. "You've got it?"

I nodded and flexed my fingers under his hold, but he continued to hold my hands against the cup for a beat too long. He stared at me with a slight frown between his thick brows, but I couldn't begin to discern if it was out of displeasure or surprise. I had never been so attracted to a man in my life, and I wondered if I imagined the tension between us. My tongue darted out to coat my dry lips, and his eyes followed its path intently. Then suddenly, his hands were gone, and he sat back in his seat, his fingers flying on the keyboard of his phone.

I blinked and slowly sank back into my chair. Obviously, I had misread the signs. I took a sip of the sparkling liquid and discovered with delight that it was ginger ale. Sipping it slowly to savor the sweet pop of bubbles on my tongue, I turned my attention to the early evening turning into twilight the color of a bruise outside my window. The sparkling lights of Los Cabos could already be seen ahead of us, and instead of wondering about the intrepid stranger beside me, I focused on my excitement. I had one week of paradise before I met with reality in New York City.

After five years in Paris and only a handful of visits in that time, I would finally be reunited with my family. The last time we all lived under the same roof, I was nineteen years old. My twin siblings, Cosima and Sebastian, had been the first to leave. Cosima when she was eighteen in order to model in Milan, and Sebastian just months later to England with Cosima's money in his pocket and a fierce determination to become an actor. I had lived with my mother and eldest sister Elena after that.

I squeezed my eyes shut and refused to think about those

years. It had been nearly five now since I had left our small life in Napoli to attend *L'École des Beaux-Arts* in Paris. Though I was close to my family, it had been good for me to spend those years apart from them. I returned home a better person than when I had hastily fled, and I was both excited and anxious for them to see the new me.

"What are you smiling at?"

His question was faintly brusque as if he was irritated with me. When I turned to him, though, his eyes were on the glowing screen of his phone.

"I haven't been home in a long time, and I'm looking forward to seeing my family again."

"Your husband?" he asked tersely.

I laughed, and it felt so delightful after hours of sickness and sleep that I laughed some more. He watched me with twisted lips as if he wanted to smile but couldn't understand why. "Was that funny?"

"Oh, not really." I leaned forward conspiratorially. "But one needs a boyfriend to get married, and I haven't had one of those in years."

"Now, that is funny." He put his phone back in his pocket, and I felt a flash of triumph when he once more focused on me. "It is incomprehensible to me that you would be single." His eyes sparkled as he leaned forward, and a lock of hair fell across his golden forehead. "Tell me, other than your obvious fear of flying, what's wrong with you?"

I laughed. "We're almost in Los Cabos. I don't have time to list all my flaws."

"I have a feeling there aren't many," he murmured and stared at me in that way I was discovering he had, looking through me and at me all at once. "But perhaps it's better that you don't tell me. A woman of mystery"—his voice was low and smooth, so captivating I didn't register the pilot preparing the plane for landing—"is a seductive thing."

"You had better tell me about yourself, then." I leaned back in my seat as the plane began its steep descent into the city. "You're handsome enough already."

His loud chuckle surprised us both. It was husky with disuse, and his expression, though inherently beautiful, was almost pained. When the sound tapered off, it left him frowning. "What would you like to know?"

"Something repellent," I demanded cheerfully.

"Repellent? That's a tall order." Though I usually was uncomfortable under the eyes of others, those baby blues against my skin invigorated me, and I beamed back at him as he spoke. "When I look at you, I can only think of lavender and honey."

His fingers found a lock of my auburn hair, and he rubbed it between his fingers to release the scent.

"Well." I cleared my throat. "Happily, we are talking about you."

His grin was wolfish as he leaned back in his seat again. "I make a very good living."

"Ah, you're one of those." His silver cuff links shined even in the dim light of the descending plane. "That helps. I'm more the starving artist type."

"Hardly starving." His eyes raked over my curves even though I wore a modest cotton shift.

Despite myself, I flushed. "No, but an artist all the same. Let me guess, you work with money."

"In a sense," he said, and his eyes danced. "Is this twenty questions?"

I laughed. "I haven't played that since I was a kid."

"Not so long ago."

"Long enough," I corrected and shot a look at him from the corner of my eye. "How old are you?"

"Thirty-one. I'm also six foot one, and I've broken my right arm three times." His small smile was a boyish contrast to his sharp, almost aggressively drawn features. I wanted desperately to trace the exaggerated line of his jaw and dip a finger into the slight hollow beneath his cheekbone.

"Twenty-four." I pulled the bulk of my wavy hair to one side in order to show him the tattoo of color, making a whirlpool design behind my ear.

When I didn't explain its significance, he frowned. "What is it?"

"A mark," I said simply.

I jerked slightly when his fingers brushed over the swirled ink. "I like it."

"Thank you." My voice was breathy as I draped my hair once more over my shoulders.

"What brings you to Mexico? I take it your family doesn't live here." His finger ran down my arm lightly, highlighting the paleness of my skin.

"My family is much more exotic than I am." I thought of Mama and the twins with a slight grimace; years of hero worship were hard to completely eradicate. "My best friend booked the trip but couldn't make it. I was only too happy to take her place."

He nodded, his eyes intense as he contemplated me. The connection between us thickened and hummed like the air during an electrical storm. Disturbed, I shifted away from him to look out the window as we swooped low over the ground above the runway. Strangely, I didn't feel my usual apprehension as the plane tentatively brushed the tarmac once, then twice before landing smoothly.

We didn't speak as the pilot announced our arrival, and it was only when the plane came to a slow stop at the terminal that I turned back to him. He faced forward with a furrow etched deeply between his brows and his mouth firm in concentration. I wondered what he thought of me, of this strange meeting.

Sensing my gaze, he said, "I've been trying to decide if I should see you again."

"What makes you think I would want to?" His eyebrow

arched in response to my attempt at sassiness, and I gave in to his silent reproach with a little shrug. "What's stopping you?"

The seat belt sign turned off, and we both stood at the same time, suddenly almost touching; the slim space between us charged with electricity the color of his eyes. He looked down at me, his deep chestnut hair softening the dangerous edge of his features.

"I have never wanted someone the way I want you." His hand skimmed over my hip and sent a deep, throbbing shock through my system. "But I don't like the idea that you could very well change my life."

My heart clanged uncomfortably against my rib cage, and though I desperately wanted to say something, I couldn't find the words to untangle the jumble of hormones and desires I had been reduced to. So instead, I watched a serious smile tilt one side of his closed lips as his eyes scraped over my face one last time, and then, without a word, he left.

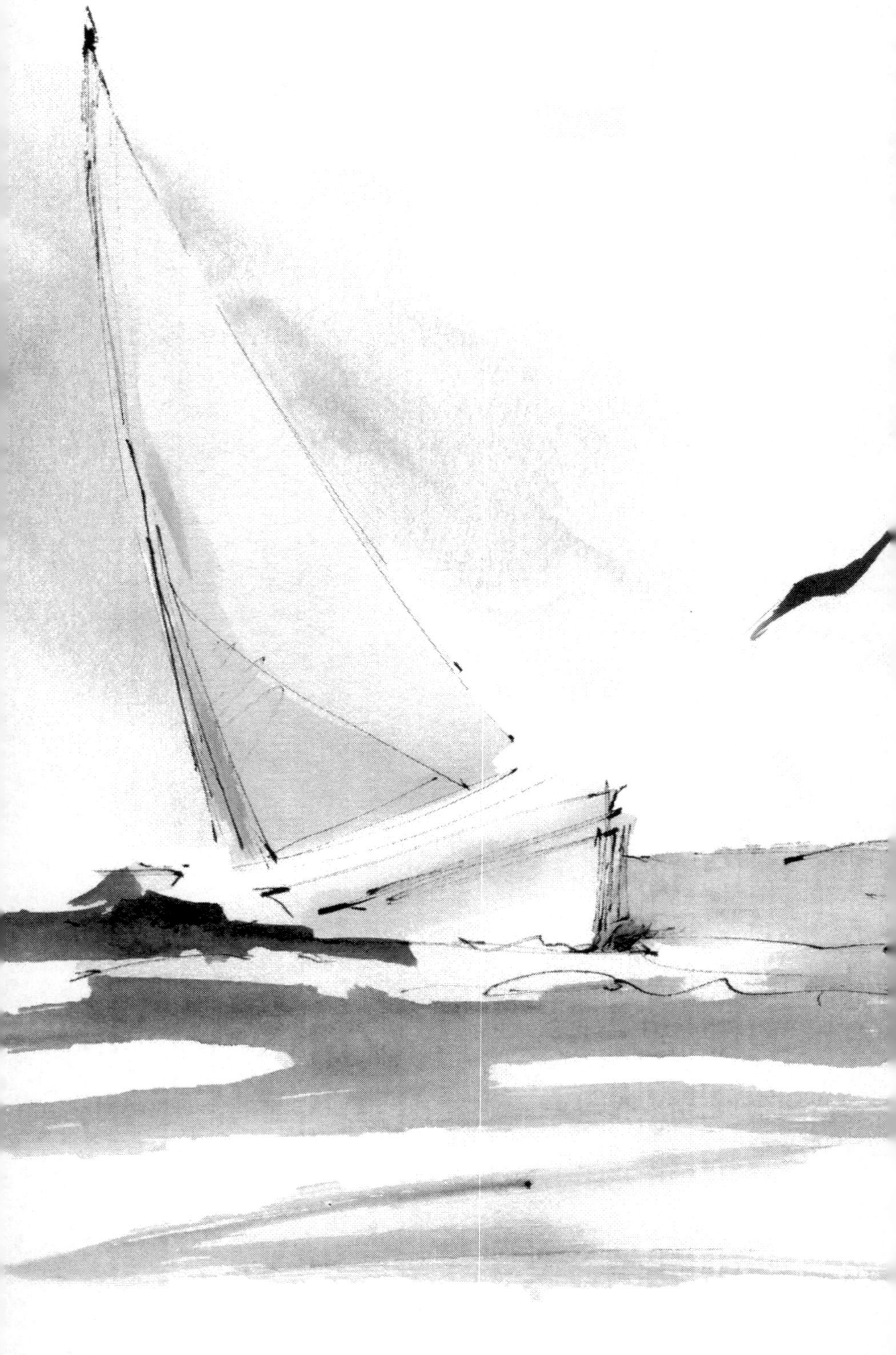

Chapter Two

My cell phone rang just as I emerged into the muggy Mexican heat to hail a taxi. I shook my head at the many men eager to help me with my suitcase for a few pesos and stuck my cell between my ear and shoulder.

"Giselle, darlin'." Brenna's husky Southern drawl warmed me. "How is the drug runner city treating you?"

I smiled and nodded enthusiastically at a sweet-faced Mexican man who pulled up in his beat-up yellow cab. "I just got off the plane, B, but so far no drug runners."

She laughed, but it wasn't the full-bodied sound I was used to. Brenna Buchanan was Hollywood royalty and my best friend from Paris. It was thanks to her that I was here in the first place, due to a scheduling conflict with an upcoming film. But something about her tone had me second-guessing that.

"How are things on set?"

There was a telling pause, and the creak and bang of an old door slamming shut. "Great."

"You must be in..." I paused and raked my foggy brain for the details. "Verona now?"

"Mmhmm." A whistle in the background sounded suspiciously like the call of a boiling kettle. "Listen, darlin', I don't have much time between scenes, but I just wanted to call to square away the details at the resort."

I sighed wearily as I got into the warm interior of the car. "You wouldn't be lying to me, would you, B?"

"No." Her own sigh echoed my own. "Maybe. I just needed to, um, take some time off from the fans."

"Don't let all this fame go to your head." I leaned my head back against the sticky leather and gave the driver directions to the resort. "I miss Brenna Buchanan, curvy misfit, not the Glamazon on red carpets in couture gowns."

She made a humming sound. "Fair enough, darlin', and for you, I will always be that girl. But admit it, I rock haute couture."

I rolled my eyes and laughed for the second time in weeks. "I wish you were here with me."

"I know." Her voice softened into a croon. "How are you holding up?"

"Fine," I murmured as the cab flew past brilliantly painted low buildings and old trucks lagging under the weight of debris in the peeling cabs. "I'm happy for the time to paint."

"It will be good for you to relax," she agreed before a cacophony of falling metal erupted in the background. "Listen, I should go. But don't worry about anything. I've got a handle on the situation over here, and I set up everything with the resort under my name. Just relax, drink the tequila, and find a man who makes your heart beat."

I smiled wryly as I thought of the handsome Frenchman I'd met on the plane. He had my heart racing the moment I caught sight of those electric eyes.

"Will do. Take care of you and your gowns."

She laughed and kissed me through the phone, but I held it to my ear for a minute after she hung up. Brenna had lived in Paris for the past three years with her husband, Franklin Robinson, a wealthy Brit with business in France. She had taken me under her wing as soon as I arrived, and she was the first one I had turned to when Christopher had shown up in Paris to destroy my life.

We pulled up to the Westin Resort and Spa in Los Cabos, and I was immediately blown away by the sheer size of the resort. The multistory tangerine building sprawled across a massive lot dotted with palm trees and dense green shrubbery. Women wearing expensive jewelry and small bathing suits wandered in and out of the hotel, and a group of men in exquisitely cut suits exited a huge black SUV ahead of me.

"Brenna," I muttered as a bellboy took my luggage with a smile.

"Ah, Brenna Buchanan." The man behind the grand marble desk smiled warmly at me. "Will Mr. Robinson be joining you later?"

I blushed at the mention of her handsome husband. "No, I'm here alone."

He frowned, and his fingers clattered across the keyboard ominously. "We have you booked into a deluxe suite with the couples package. I'm afraid it's nonrefundable."

Of course.

I smiled prettily. "I completely understand. Thank you."

He nodded briskly and printed out the necessary documents, but as he handed me the key cards, he winked. "I'm sure you'll find someone to share it with before the week is out."

I laughed lightly. "I don't think so. Have a nice day, *señor*."

Despite my disavowal, the Frenchman's silken voice wound through my thoughts as the swift elevator carried me to the twelfth floor. He had been so perfect that I doubted the reality of what had occurred between us. It felt like one of my childhood fantasies come to life.

It was just as well, though. I was in Mexico to relax before the inevitable rockiness of my family reunion. Just thinking about seeing them again made my heart race, so I was glad to open the door to my room to find the A/C cranked and the fan on. It was a lovely space echoing the soft colors of the sea with large French doors leading to a small patio overlooking the beach. I waited anxiously for the bellman to drop off my things, and then, with a squeal like a preteen girl, I jumped onto the brightly dressed bed.

Later that night, after an invigorating shower and a quick rest, I walked through the resort just as they were lighting the torches lining the walkways. The light south of the equator was different. Sunlight poured like honey, fragrant and gold across the brilliant tropical gardens, and as the sun brushed the horizon, gem-toned hues exploded across the sky. I raised my camera to my eye and allowed my instinct to take over, capturing shot after shot as I walked the darkening paths. Being somewhere so beautiful soothed my ragged heart, and though I was hyper-aware of the couples strolling past and scrutinizing my lack of a partner, I felt more at ease than in years. I had one week to unwind before my family reunion, and I intended to make the most of it.

There was a large outdoor dining room beside the beach with a mariachi band in full swing beside a roaring blue-green fire. A few couples swayed gracefully on the dance floor, but I was drawn to the quartet of men toiling away in the intense heat. As I drew closer, I saw one of them with his eyes closed, the body of his large guitar cradled against his round stomach. Sweat beaded on his forehead, the damp fabric of his thick cotton outfit clung to his chest, but there was pure rapture on his features as he swayed in time with his music.

I inched closer and took a picture of his passion.

"*Señorita!*" Another Mexican man, handsome and young with his glittering black hair slicked back, noticed me crouching awkwardly at the side of the stage and walked over with a large smile. "What is a beautiful woman doing on the ground? You must be dancing!"

"No, thank you," I demurred as the semicircle of well-dressed diners turned to look at me. Somehow, I had become a part of the evening entertainment.

"Come, *señorita*," he continued to coax, his hips swaying to the beat of the candle flames. "A beauty like you must dance."

I could feel a blush flame across my cheeks as I shook my head, mortified by the multitudes of paired diners staring at me.

"Maybe I can persuade you."

My breath left me in one long whoosh as I looked up at the man before me. The candlelight was at his back, illuminating his tall physique and casting shadows across his features. It could have been anyone really, and his English was flawless, but I knew who it was by the palpable energy pulsing between us.

A thrill ran up my spine, and I shuddered.

The Frenchman extended his hand, and the moment I took it, I was in his arms, pulled there seamlessly as I rose. I was overwhelmed by the smell of him and the strength of his body against mine. Unconsciously, my hands tense on his broad shoulders, mapping the shift of hard muscles between the silken fabric of his skirt.

His eyes gleamed in the shadows, night dark yet shining with predatory satisfaction as he whirled me away onto the middle of the dance floor with the other couples.

"The lady is dancing," the emcee cried, prompting a polite round of applause. "My job is done for the night, ladies and gentlemen. Please enjoy."

The music grew louder, filling the heavy night air with beats and vibrations. I felt them thrum through the soles of my feet, and I laughed when a couple beside us spun gracefully across the floor.

"It's good to see you again…" He waited for me to supply my name, and I realized with a start that he hadn't known it on the plane.

I bit my lip and considered my options. It was exciting, my interaction with the stranger, but I wasn't willing to give too much away. So with sudden confidence, even though no one had ever called me by the nickname, I said, "Elle."

He repeated the syllable, and the way he tasted my name was sinful, like biting into a slightly overripe fruit, sweetness bursting from his lips.

I looked up at him and smiled wryly. "I wouldn't have thought you'd be so happy to see me. You practically sprinted from the plane this morning."

A small smile twisted his lips, but his hands tightened, one in mine and the other on my hip. "Any man with sense runs from a siren."

"Good save." I looked up at him from under my lashes and was rewarded with his sparkling blue eyes. "I don't see you running now."

"No." He seemed just as perturbed by the idea as I was. "I'm here to work, and usually, I'm not the type of man to mix business and pleasure, but when I saw you standing there..." He shrugged, irritated by his lack of control even as he moved us masterfully across the dance floor. "I'm also not the type of man who denies himself when he wants something badly enough."

The music pulsed quickly now. I could feel the beat at my core, and any questions I might have voiced were lost to my breathless enthusiasm as the Frenchman spun me faster. We were doing some version of the tango. I had watched enough movies growing up to know that, but the more we moved together, the less formal it became. One strong hand hiked my leg up over his hip, and I slid inch by delicious inch down his steel thigh until he pulled me upright once again. With my arms on his chest, I undulated like the wavering flames low to the ground, his hands on my shoulders guiding me down. I was short of breath but not from dancing. I was moving intimately with a man I hardly knew, and I could have sworn nothing had ever been so erotic. The music reached its rapid-fire crescendo, and I was sent spinning across the floor in tight circles guided by his strong hand. It was only when the music suddenly slowed and ended on a breathless whimper that he stopped me with his body flush against my own.

He was basically unfazed by the most sensual experience of my life, cool and composed with not a gorgeous strand of hair out of place. But those electric eyes dilated as they stared down into mine, and his body was tense with unease. I melted further against his marble edges, and for a moment, I thought I might have had the courage to kiss the perfect stranger until hands descended on our shoulders, jarring us apart.

"Very beautiful couple, very beautiful!" the emcee cried, inspiring a round of applause. With his arms on both of us, he grinned at the crowd. "I think we have a winner for best couple tonight, *si?*"

There was some outcry and a smattering of agreement from

the other diners, and he taunted them to take the dance floor and show us up.

"And these two, they will dance again!"

A hand snatched his mic out of the air, and my Frenchman looked down into the much smaller man's face with inscrutable coolness. "No. We will not."

The emcee nodded and laughed nervously, but I was forced to mask a chortle as I was led from the dance floor.

His table pressed up against the beach, close to the fire but on the other side of the sweltering music. Its twangy refrains faded away as we approached, replaced by the gentle crash of waves on the shore. It was an utterly romantic setting, but I had a feeling my Frenchman could have made an industrial waste plant sexy.

"I have people joining me," he muttered almost petulantly even as he pulled out a chair for me.

I hesitated, awkwardly poised over my seat. "There is no need for me to join you."

Strangely, my coolness seemed to amuse him. Even in the wavering light, I could see a grin cut into his left cheek. "Excuse me, as I said before, I'm not used to mixing business and pleasure. My objection is to my pending associates, not you. Please, eat with me, Elle."

I bit the inside of my cheek but finally settled in my seat. I was silent as a waiter came to take our drink order even though I was usually very opinionated about wine. It was obvious when he began to order in heavy, polished Spanish that he knew what he was doing.

When we were alone again, he sat back in his chair languidly and stared at me with such carnality that heat flared across my skin, and my nipples puckered shamelessly against the frail fabric of my dress. He was so sleek and powerful it was hard not to relate him to a jungle cat, something dark and solitary stalking the woods at night looking for prey.

"You know..." I attempted to make casual conversation,

anything to lower the temperature between us. "I don't even know your name."

His mouth pursed, and his hands flattened on the table as if he was bracing himself. I shifted impatiently in my seat while I waited, but when he did look up, the desire in his eyes paralyzed me. "Have you ever had a holiday affair, Elle?"

I blinked and licked my lips nervously. "Would you believe me if I said yes?"

He smiled again, small and almost too fleeting to capture. "You are a stunning woman, so there can only be two reasons for your inexperience. Lack of opportunity or lack of gumption."

Even as I blushed, I tilted my chin and gazed down my nose at him. "I think we both know the answer to that."

"Yes." He leaned forward on his forearms, and his eyes caught the flame, glittering like sapphires caught in a fire. "The question is, now you have the opportunity, but do you have the gumption to take it?"

"Are you propositioning me?" I teased. My heart was racing, and my hands were damp as they tangled in my lap.

He nodded somberly. "I am."

"I see." I swallowed and tried to ignore the intensity in his eyes as our chemistry crackled in the hot air between us. "And if I say yes?"

"A girl who thinks ahead." He grinned, suddenly carefree. "Very good, Elle. You should always protect your interests."

I raised an eyebrow, prompting a short bark of laughter from him.

He held up his hands innocently. "You are here for the week?" When I nodded, one of his fingers began to trace the outline of my hand where it lay on the table. His eyes were hot on mine, and his voice dropped lower, smoke rubbing itself sensuously against my skin. "Well, I imagine we could find a number of things to do in seven whole days."

It was hard to believe this was happening. I had been such an ugly duckling my whole life, especially compared to my glamorous siblings, that I couldn't imagine what this beautiful Frenchman saw in me, but it was obvious he did see something. Something he liked very, very much.

My tongue darted out to wet my lips, and his eyes darkened as he followed its path. "One week with a perfect stranger, no complications, no surprises. Just..." He turned my hand over and feathered his fingers along the sensitive skin of my wrist where my pulse beat madly. "This."

"If I say yes, will you finally tell me your name?"

He blinked, and a slow smile spread across his hard features as he chuckled. "Yes, Elle, but I'll warn you now, you won't get much else."

I understood. If I entered into this holiday affair, as he so casually offered, he would remain a stranger. The only part of him I could know was his body. My eyes flickered over the strong width of his shoulders and the firmness of his hands on mine.

Was it enough?

My sister Cosima's voice rang out in my head; yes!

I opened my mouth to respond when a small group appeared at the entrance to the restaurant.

He leaned forward, an urgent desire in those blue eyes. "I want an answer by the end of this meal."

When I nodded mutely, still overwhelmed by the moment, he flashed me a genuine smile and traced one finger behind my ear and down my neck.

"You have beautiful hair," he murmured before sitting back in his chair, looking utterly unruffled and almost bored when his guests arrived at the table.

I stood to shake their hands when he introduced us and was met with surprised smiles. Cage Tracy lingered over our handshake with flagrant approval. I recognized him, of course, as the lead singer of Caged, the absurdly popular French band that was just becoming a phenomenon in America. He grinned down at me with gorgeous nearly black eyes and thick black hair he kept secured in a messy braid over his shoulder. I wondered how a rising rock star knew my French businessman.

"It's a pleasure to meet you," he said as he pulled out my chair for me and leaned forward familiarly when I sat down. "Sinclair always did have the most exquisite taste in women."

Sinclair. I tasted the name, rolling it on my tongue so that it split and reformed like mercury. It was an old-fashioned name, formal even, but dark too and inexplicably sexy. I looked over at him to find him staring at me, his eyes midnight blue in the darkness. A shudder rolled through my shoulders. *Oh yeah*, it suited him.

"She's only a friend, Cage," he said mildly as the other three men and a woman sat down around us.

"Of course," the woman––a plain brunette with slightly protruding front teeth––demurred. "Do stop interfering, Cage. You always hit on Sinclair's women. It does get boring, you know."

Cage smirked at me, but when Sinclair raised a cool eyebrow his way, his smile tripped and slid off his handsome face. I hid my smile behind my wineglass. Obviously, the Frenchman demanded obedience.

An older man, though no more than forty, with brilliant silver hair who introduced himself as Richard Denman leaned closer to Sinclair in order to politely inquire, "What happened to the other one, your girlfriend—"

Sinclair cut him off with a sharp glare before quickly looking at me. I feigned nonchalance, picking up my glass of water and smiling at Cage as he charmingly related his love for Mexico in his thick French accent, but I had heard.

Tension knotted the muscles between my shoulders.

I didn't know anything about this man I was considering sleeping with. And I *was* considering it. The idea of a holiday affair was not new to me—I'd read books and watched movies—

yet it went against every conservative bone in my body. Not to mention the addition of a girlfriend, a woman from his real life who probably expected his love and fidelity.

I snuck a glance at Sinclair and frowned. He didn't seem like the type of man to love easily, and I wondered about the nature of his relationship. Were they close, and, if so, how long had they dated? I bit my lip. It would drive me crazy to render a picture of the unknown girlfriend, so I resolved not to consider her any longer. It was cold of me, and I felt a pang as the idea rebounded off my morals, but I would do it.

I would do it for me because, for the first time in my life, I was faced with the possibility of something I wanted that was actually within my grasp to take. All it required of me was, as Sinclair had said, gumption.

I settled back in my seat while the wine was poured. When our waitress began to take dinner orders, Sinclair made eye contact with me as he ordered and raised one reddish brow. I understood his question, and though I raised both of my own eyebrows, I also nodded slightly, giving him full rein to order my meal. His eyes sparkled as he did so, and it gave me time to think over his proposal.

There was no doubt I was intensely attracted to him. Honestly, a woman would have to be dead not to be moved by his fierce looks. But I had never dated an overtly attractive man. In fact, I had only dated one man, and he had not been a hunk by any stretch of the imagination. Mark had been sweet-faced with thick-rimmed glasses and distinctly Canadian manners. We had dated a full month before he worked up the courage to even kiss me.

I watched Sinclair speak easily with one of his associates. After a moment, his posture changed infinitesimally, and I knew he was aware of my gaze. Immediately, heat pooled at the base of my stomach. I knew that saying yes to this man would rock my world, and honestly, I wasn't sure that I was sophisticated enough to deal with it. Catching my eye, he stared at me, desire blazing so brightly I was sure everyone at the table was aware of the fiery air between us.

"So, Elle..." Cage leaned over to me with a boyish grin on his exotic features. If I hadn't been so inextricably caught up in Sinclair, I'm sure I would have been bowled over by both his good looks and star power. "Tell me about yourself. What brings you to Mexico?"

My stomach fluttered, and I realized that my anxiety had been laid to bed by Sinclair's charm. I hadn't thought about the horror I had left behind in Paris or my family reunion in over an hour.

"I'm here to paint."

His eyebrows shot into his hairline, and a flicker of suspicion flashed across his face. "You're an artist. Would I know any of your work?"

I shrugged when I felt Sinclair's gaze on us. "Maybe."

"Well, where did you study? A friend of mine is one of the proprietors at MoMA." The woman beside him snorted derisively, but he ignored her. "I know quite a bit about art."

"European." Robert Corbett, the only man over sixty in the group, slapped his thick hand on the table and then pointed at me triumphantly. "Irish?"

"I thought French like Sinclair," Duncan Wright countered, his glasses iridescent in the candlelight.

"Not quite French, are you, *chérie*?" Cage frowned at me thoughtfully.

Before he could press me further, Sinclair chuckled darkly. "Elle is difficult to know. Leave her be."

It was said with good humor, but I knew it was a warning. No one was to press me for details, and I wasn't to offer any.

I should have been angry, or at the very least indignant over his privacy clause in our looming holiday affair, but I only felt a secret thrill of excitement. I wanted to know how his caramelized skin tasted and trace my fingers over the line of the muscles in his torso as it arrowed to his groin. If I could have that, I assured the more conservative part of my conscience, the personal details wouldn't matter.

"And what about you, Cage?" I spoke quietly as if I had a secret to share so that Sinclair could only wonder at our topic of conversation. *Let him worry*, I thought with an inner smile.

Cage threw his head back and laughed heartily, his glossy hair catching the candlelight and highlighting his heathen good looks. "Unless you've been living under a rock, I think you're playing dumb, Elle."

I smiled at him over the rim of my wineglass, pleased and surprised by my ease with the singer.

"And how do you know Sinclair?" I took a careful sip of my wine, savoring the robust flavors of the Cabernet Sauvignon he had ordered for me. It was delicious, and another current of arousal sparked through my system. The Italian in me loved a man who knew his wine.

"It's a long story. Let's just say we met through a mutual friend a very long time ago." His tone implied he and that friend had shared some very intimate times together, and once again, the woman beside him with the buck teeth rolled her eyes.

He laughed and winked at someone over my shoulder. "Isn't that right, Sin?"

I looked over my shoulder and up to find him standing behind me with a frown. Goose bumps rippled along my skin, and I rubbed my exposed arms even though the breeze off the ocean was tacky with warmth.

"If I remember correctly, I introduced you to our 'mutual friend,' and you took off with her," he said as he put a warm hand on my shoulder. The heat from his contact seared through the thin material of my dress and made me shudder.

Cage gasped in dramatic objection. "Me? Never. Elle, who do you believe? This French gypsy or the hunky rock star?"

I laughed, at ease with Cage's mock arrogance. It reminded me of my brother Sebastian's public persona, and unexpectedly, I felt a pang for home. "I'm not the right person to ask."

I tilted my head so that my eyes could meet Sinclair's over my shoulder. His were dark and troubled, his other hand clenched by his side as he fought to control the emotion in his features. I could sense his pain, his discomfort over Cage's carelessly worded humor.

"Oh?" he asked quietly.

"Because she clearly favors me," Cage declared smugly, leaning back in his chair like a king on his throne.

"No," I spoke softly and ran the fingers of my right hand gently down the outside of Sinclair's leg nearest to me. "Because I have a soft spot for gypsies."

His nostrils flared, and without looking at Cage, he said, "Trade places with me. Duncan has something he wants to discuss with you."

Cage looked at the man in question, who only shrugged, but Cage did as he was told with a roguish grin.

"Can't blame him for wanting you all to himself." He gave me a kiss on the cheek and chuckled when Sinclair took him by the shoulder to pull him firmly away.

"I liked him," I protested mildly as Sinclair settled in beside me.

"You'll like me more." His hand landed heavy and hot on my bare knee, branding me. "Now, are you done trying to distract me? I really do have business to discuss, and I want you to think long and hard about my proposal. Can you do that for me?"

His voice was so seductive. No one else I knew had such powerfully sexy speech. It might have been the undercurrent of French in his pronunciation or the depth of his baritone, the fact that he never spoke loudly, yet every word vibrated throughout my body. Whatever it was, I was almost certain I would do anything that voice commanded.

So I nodded mutely and watched a slow smile tip his firm lips.

"Good," he said and turned immediately to Richard Denman.

The sluggish ocean breeze carried his leather and smoke scent to my nose, and I sucked a lungful deep into my lungs. His hand on my bare thigh seemed to throb against my overheated skin, and when I squirmed slightly, he squeezed me into stillness.

"What brings you to Mexico, Elle?" The woman beside Sinclair leaned forward and smiled at me with closed lips. I wondered if she was self-conscious of her buck teeth.

"My best friend booked the room but was unable to make it." Brenna would have loved the luxurious resort, and I worried she was working too hard under the direction of her new manager.

"Lucky girl." She extended her hand. "Candy Kay."

My eyebrows rose by their own volition, but she was kind enough to laugh at my rudeness. "I know. It's misleading. I gave up introducing myself as Candace years ago. People refuse to call me anything but Candy."

"It's a lovely name," I offered politely, trying to recover from my earlier faux pas.

She laughed loudly, her teeth flashing in the candlelight. I found her rather beautiful actually when her features relaxed with good humor, and she forgot to pull her lips closed.

Her insecurities reminded me all too vividly of my own as I grew up. It was only recently that I had come to terms with myself, with the red hair and olive skin, the freckles and the lack of Italian spicing my speech. I was the only one in our family without a discernable accent, and though Elena shared my red hair, it was dark, almost black, and she had the long, lithe body of the twins while I remained stunted, shorter, and too curvy. For years, I had hidden behind baggy clothes and dyed my hair an unnatural black. I fingered a wavy lock of auburn hair nervously.

"Did I hear you say you're an artist?" she asked. "I'm hopeless with any form of creativity, but I so admire artists. You must have an awfully romantic life."

I laughed as I pictured the cramped apartment in an old servant's quarters where I had lived for the past five years. "Not exactly. But I do love what I do. I'm lucky to have had the opportunity to pursue it."

"I think it's wonderful when people follow their passions." Candy spoke in a low mumble, the better to hide her teeth, I thought, but Sinclair looked over abruptly as if she had yelled.

"Not everyone is so lucky," I agreed, thinking of my twin siblings toiling away in London and Milan for years; two young people alone in a foreign country trying to scrounge together enough money to support a family of five.

"That's why I respect Sinclair so much, of course," she said. "His passion is boundless."

He chose that moment to look over at me as Duncan Wright spoke animatedly to him about stock options. His eyes were dark, and the shadows cast his features in stark relief. The sharp jut of the bones in his face was almost cruel, and the intensity of his expression was near to savage with desire. A shiver trembled across my shoulders. *Boundless passion.* The look he gave me promised just that.

"I haven't known him for very long," I exaggerated smoothly; prying my eyes from his in order to smile at Candy. "Tell me about the work you do with him."

I watched her come alive, her lips pulled over her teeth, her eyes sparkling, and I knew she too shared a passion for her work. "I'm the vice president of the company, and while I love the thrill of closing a land deal, I won't lie to you. My favorite part is working with Romani International, Sinclair's charity. That's one of the reasons we are here."

"Oh?" I scoured my mind for any information on the Romani people but found I was sorely lacking in knowledge. I knew it was the politically correct term for gypsies and that they were nomadic people with somewhat vagabond lifestyles.

"He doesn't like to talk about it much." She cast a quick

glance at the man between us, but Sinclair was busy debating something animatedly with the other men. "But every year, he rewards his closest colleagues and associates with a week-long all-inclusive vacation. Of course, it's not really a vacation. We are here to close a deal on a resort while simultaneously milking our fellow travelers for donations to the Romani Foundation. Business never sleeps even when Cage crashes the party," she said with a sigh and a quick glance at Cage, who was leaning across the table shouting in faux outrage at an unfazed Sinclair.

So Sinclair was in real estate?

I was quiet as the food arrived, and a beautifully presented glass of fresh shrimp ceviche was placed before me. I looked over at Sinclair as I raised a spoonful to my mouth and hummed in delight as I took the first bite.

His hand tightened around my thigh, and his lips parted on a small gasp at my expression. I was dazzled by his desire, and emboldened by it, I deliberately swept my tongue across my bottom lip.

His blue eyes flashed. "I need you to say yes, Elle."

His smoky voice made me dizzy, but I shook my head slightly to clear it and smiled demurely at him as if I was used to this degree of male attention. "I'm still thinking."

"Well, stop talking and eat up then. I'm an impatient man."

I giggled quietly so as not to draw the attention of the other diners. "I would never have guessed."

His resulting smirk was self-mocking. "You are too observant for your own good."

"I'm an artist." I shrugged because, to me, that explained everything.

He stared at me intently for a moment, leaving his food untouched. "You look like a piece of art."

My eyebrows shot into my hair at the romantic thought, but Sinclair abruptly pulled his hand from my thigh and turned to Candy as he tucked into his chicken mole dish. I was almost glad for his dismissal as his words continued to ring in my head. No one had ever said something like that to me, and coupled with our electrifying chemistry, I was worried that despite my conservative upbringing and the fact that he obviously had a girlfriend back home, I was undoubtedly going to agree to the conditions of his holiday affair.

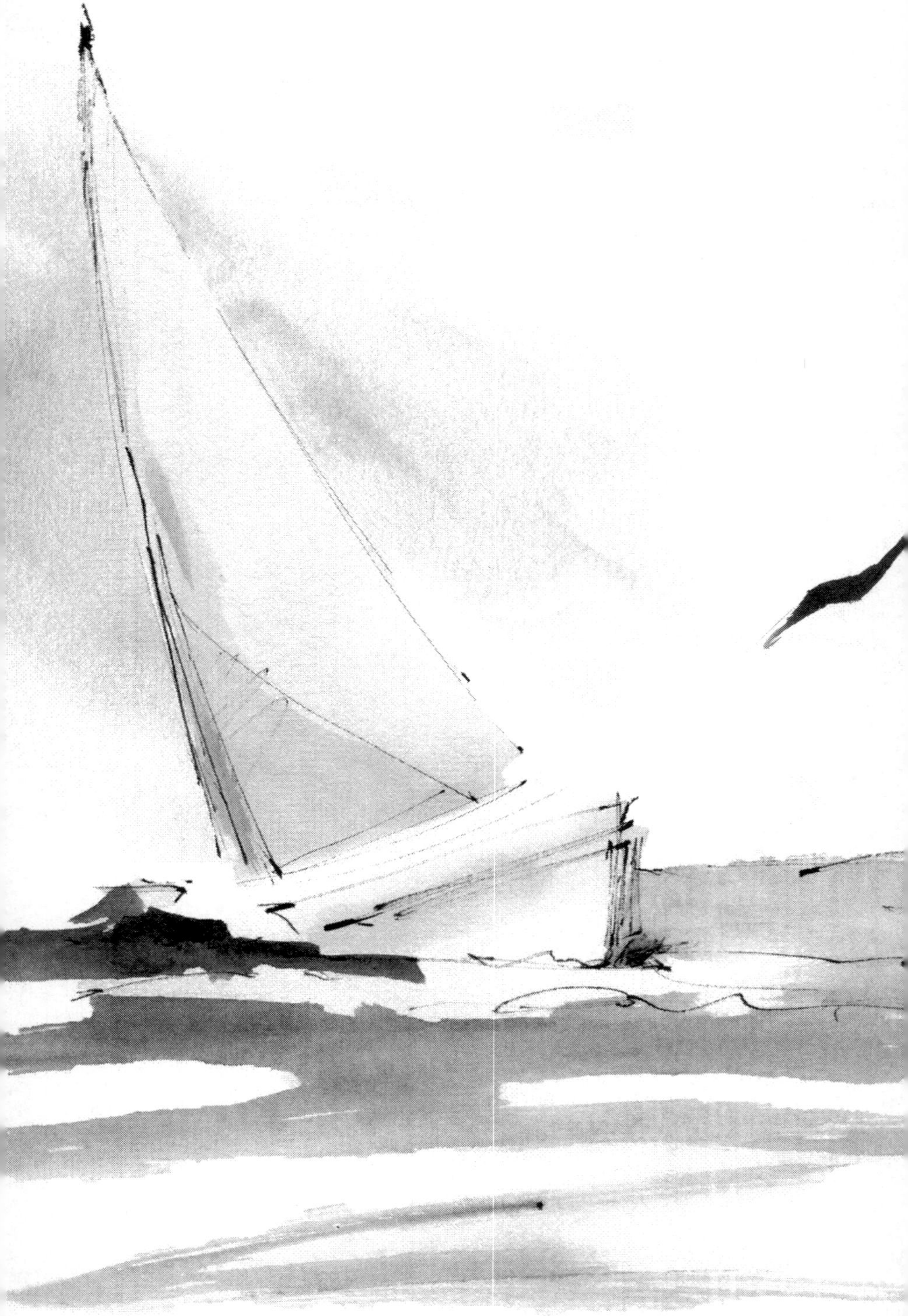

Chapter Three

"Did you enjoy your meal, Elle?" Sinclair's voice wrapped around me and tugged my focus from my conversation with Richard Denman, a fascinating man with his own architecture firm in New York, to the handsome Frenchman sitting on my other side.

For some reason, I blushed. "Yes, very much. Thank you."

We had made our way through four courses, ending in a rich Mexican chocolate mousse that had made me weak in the knees. I took the last decadent spoonful of sugar in my mouth and closed my eyes briefly as I savored it. When I opened my eyes, Sinclair's were blazing.

"Tell me," he gritted out between his teeth. "What will it be, Elle?"

It took me a moment to find my breath. He was so achingly handsome that I couldn't believe he was real, let alone that someone like him would be interested in me. His eyes narrowed at my hesitation, and I laughed breathlessly at his impatience.

I straightened my spine and looked him in the eye, trying to convey the weight of my answer. "Yes."

He blinked as if he had misheard. "Say it again."

"Yes."

The grin that split his face was the first unreserved expression I had seen on his hard features since meeting him, and it attracted the attention of Cage, who stopped his animated storytelling, which included an air guitar, to frown at his friend.

"What's cause for such a smile, Sin?"

"I've been smiling like that all night, and I'd wager it's for the same reason as Sinclair." Richard Denman slapped a powerful hand on my back. "This is one intriguing lady."

I tipped my head down in embarrassment, but Sinclair's hand found mine under the table and squeezed.

"Margot won't like her, that's for sure." Cage guffawed at the idea even as the rest of the table shot him disapproving looks.

"His personal assistant," Candy explained. "She's a bit... protective."

"Nothing will do it for that woman unless it's Sin. Not even me," Cage divulged with a wicked wink that made my heart sink farther.

And he had a girlfriend back home. I wondered what these people thought of the arrangement; if they knew Sinclair had decided to take me as a lover or if, perhaps, this was routine for him when abroad.

He must have caught the apprehension on my face because suddenly, he stood, pulling me with him. "Good night, everyone."

No one batted an eye at his rude farewell, and we were already walking away when they began to call their own goodbyes. I tried to wave at them and smile, but Sinclair's long legs ate up the ground, and I finally just gave up.

"That wasn't very nice," I pointed out as we emerged from the restaurant onto the torch-lined path to the rooms.

"I don't have the time to be nice," he said as we made our way swiftly through the lobby.

"Oh." I was struggling to keep up with his brisk pace, and my quip was slightly breathless as a result. "But you have time to cheat on your girlfriend?"

There was barely a hitch in his stride, but a muscle in his jaw clenched menacingly. He maintained an arctic silence as we took the elevator up to the top floor. I bit my lip, nervous that I had overstepped my bounds but angry with myself for succumbing to his charms. Whatever conflicting feelings I might have had fled when he opened the door to his room.

Glass doors dominated the entire far wall of the cream-colored living room, exposing the obsidian waves of the Pacific lacquered by the moonlight as they rolled gracefully onto the shore. I moved immediately to the sight, inexorably drawn to the power of the scene. Even as the beauty overwhelmed me, I was aware of Sinclair a step behind me. It felt almost like he was indulging me, allowing me to enjoy the view for a moment before the icy cold of the elevator ride descended once more.

"Are you ready to have a mature conversation about this now, Elle?" His voice was disarmingly soft, and the hand that skimmed down my arm was gentle, but when I turned slightly to face him, his deep blue eyes were frosted with censure.

"Mature?" I repeated, shocked by his rudeness.

He remained calm and grabbed my hands as they came up to push him away. "How old are you? Twenty-two?"

I glared at him, but he only raised one cool brow in the face of my defiance.

"Twenty-four," I muttered.

He kissed the center of one of my trapped palms. "That wasn't so hard, was it? Clearly, you have never had an affair before, of any kind, and I admit that is part of your considerable appeal." The way he stressed the word considerable, tilting his hips slightly so that they were pressed against mine, unraveled me. "And obviously, you have a problem with the idea of my infidelity. What would make you feel better about it? If I said that I had never cheated on her before? I haven't. That our relationship is rocky, that she is bitter, and we haven't slept together in months or years? Lies." His turbulent eyes locked onto mine with utter sincerity. "The truth is, she is steady and whip-smart, beautiful. I've been with her for a very long time."

I could feel my heart beating too slowly, too heavily. It knocked monotonously inside my chest like the dooming toll of an old clock.

He seized me suddenly, pressing me against the wall and lifting me slightly so that I was suspended between his warm body and the cool glass. One hand supported my back, and the other delved into the thick hair at the base of my neck so that I was completely entangled with him. Suddenly, I couldn't bear the idea of not being with him.

"But I want you. I want to know the flavor of the skin behind your knees and the way you smell when you're aroused by my touch. I've never wanted anything as badly as I want you against my skin."

I was flushed by the heat of his praise, of his steely body against mine, and I almost moaned with lust, but my resolve still wavered. Could I really do this?

He took a deep, almost frustrated breath, and for a moment, his handsome face was suspended in heart-wrenching uncertainty. "Don't say no. I don't think I could let you go."

Oh my.

That did it.

How could any woman resist such a powerful man genuinely yearning for her?

I brought my hand up to his strong face and placed my forehead against his. "I'll stay."

He stiffened and sucked in a ragged breath. "You don't have to."

"I know." I smiled, joy blooming in my chest. "I want to."

His mouth was on mine before I had finished speaking, hard and rough in his haste. I moaned as his tongue swept into my mouth and plundered. My hands sank into his thick hair and tugged him closer; my legs wrapped around his torso so that I was locked onto him.

His lips moved from my mouth to my neck, sucking lightly at the tender skin there as the hand in my hair tilted my head back.

"Ah," I breathed.

Urged on by my exclamation, he deftly undid the pearl buttons of my bodice to reveal my pale lacy bra. He groaned at the sight of me and bent his head to suck at my puckered nipple through the thin fabric. I arched into the wet heat of his mouth and groaned. The solid length of him pushed against the apex of my thighs, and I imagined what he would feel like inside me, stretching me and filling me until I burst with pleasure.

Suddenly desperate for the feel of his skin against mine, I fumbled with the buttons of his ivory shirt and pushed it from his shoulders. His skin was stretched tight across his lean cut muscles, and when I opened my mouth over the skin of his shoulder to bite down lightly, the manly, slightly salty taste of him exploded in my mouth.

With a growl, he reared up and trapped both of my hands in one of his, pinning them to the foggy glass so he had unfettered access to my breasts.

"God, you're beautiful," he rasped, his hot breath wafting over my nipple as he deftly undid my bra and plumped my breasts between his capable hands. "Keep your hands there. I have to taste you."

I almost choked on my sharp inhalation of surprise when he

dropped to his knees and tugged my dress to the floor. He grasped my hips in a vise-like grip and pressed his nose to the apex of my thighs, breathing deeply. It was unbearably erotic, seeing him on his knees before me, his dark head against my pale thighs. He ran his nose down the inside of my thigh, nipping the skin there so that I jerked. His soft chuckle fanned across my sex and further inflamed my arousal. I was quivering putty in his hands.

"What do you want?" he asked as he pressed his closed lips to my panty-covered clit and hummed lightly.

"You," I panted.

"Here?" He pressed an open-mouthed kiss to the inside of my thigh.

"No," I groaned in frustration. "Higher."

"What?" he practically purred, swirling his tongue in my belly button.

"Your mouth." I had never begged before for anything, but all reservations had melted off me at the first touch of his lips to my skin. "On me."

I groaned as he slowly began to peel off my underwear.

My head fell back against the glass, and I squeezed my eyes closed in anticipation. But instead of the lush feel of his mouth against me, the dull thud of vibrations against the wooden floor jolted me from my stupor.

With a vicious curse, Sinclair wrenched himself away from me and pulled his phone out of his pants pocket. He stared at the screen, taking tight, controlled breaths before looking up at me with rapidly cooling eyes. "I have to take this."

I nodded mutely.

He strode through the room into the adjacent bedroom as he answered the phone, "Hello."

It was her—the girlfriend—obviously. I took a shaky deep breath and closed my eyes. My sweat-dampened skin was stuck to the cool glass, and my underwear hung off me in disarray. I had never been this girl before, and the realization of what I had almost done shocked my system.

Suddenly freezing in the air-conditioned room, I pulled together my clothes and got dressed. I considered running away, but the thought of it chilled me, like a thief or a whore stealing away in the night.

Berating myself for not bringing a cardigan, I stepped through the glass door and onto the massive patio. The breeze was ribbon soft and smelled fresh, faintly of Mexican honeysuckle. I took a deep, bracing breath and leaned over the railing to gaze at the graceful sea.

I had never met anyone like the Frenchman. The moment I had laid eyes on him, I'd known something was inextricably compelling about him. I was in over my head. Sinclair was older, coupled off, and the head of an obviously successful company. But there was something else below all of it that called out to me. It might have been naïve of me, but I believed him when he said he hadn't cheated on his partner before. It didn't make the situation any better or worse, but maybe it was something.

"Have you been to Mexico before?"

I closed my eyes and didn't turn around to face him, but I could picture him leaning against the doorjamb with his arms crossed, protected and casual.

"No." My voice was quiet, but I had no doubt he could hear me. "I've lived in Europe all my life."

We lapsed into silence. I didn't think either of us really knew what to say, and it made me feel better to know that the sophisticated Frenchman was at a loss too.

"Look at me," he said softly. When I didn't, he repeated himself firmly, ordering me this time.

I turned around, and he stood exactly as I had imagined, propped against the doorframe with the light from inside silhouetting his mouthwatering physique. He looked cool and unruffled despite our almost lovemaking, but something in his silence was as vulnerable as me.

"Stay."

It wasn't a question or a plea, but I knew how badly he wanted me to stay because I felt the same inexplicable need.

I shrugged helplessly. "I don't know how to do this. I've never had a holiday affair or sex with a stranger, let alone someone in a relationship. I'd probably just screw it up and say something too intimate or do something to cross the boundaries."

"Try it," he coaxed, stepping forward into the moonlight.

His beauty caught me like a sucker punch to the gut. I braced on the railing to steady my resolve.

I couldn't find the words to refuse him, though. I knew that if I opened my mouth, I would say yes to this man, this man with the electric blue eyes and the ability to turn me into live nerve endings with only a look. So I smiled at him with my lips closed and my eyes downcast as I moved, carefully in a wide arc, away from him and back into the suite.

He didn't follow me as I crossed the palatial room to the front door, but when I turned around, unable to help myself as I opened the door to leave, he was standing in the darkness just outside the door, watching me with an impassive expression but for the telltale tightness in his jaw. Quickly, I stepped out of the room and closed the door behind me.

Only once I was in the elevator did I close my eyes, bang my head against the wall, and moan.

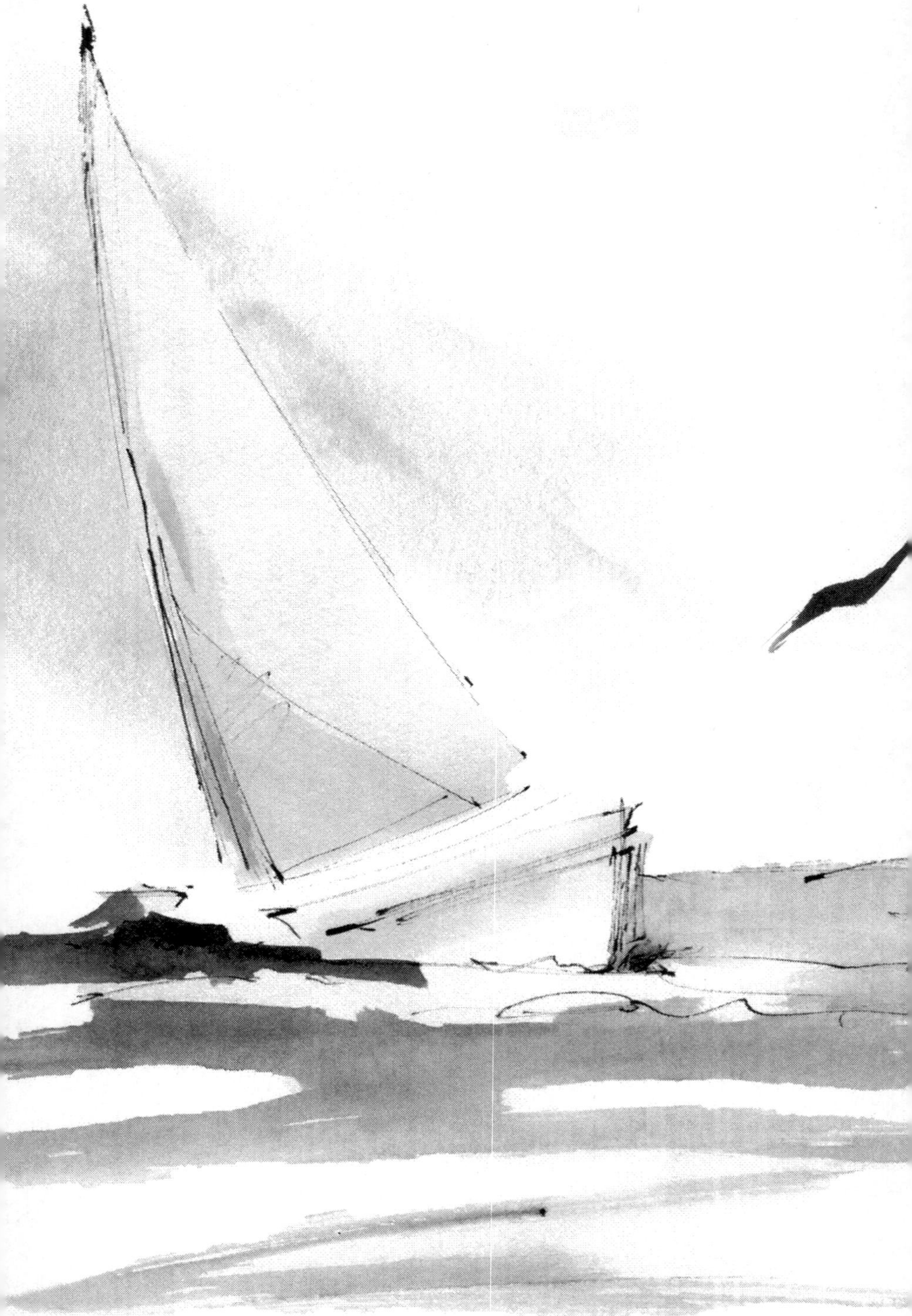

Chapter Four

I hadn't slept well. Hours after I returned to my room, I tossed and turned, tangled in my sheets, wishing they were Sinclair's sinewy limbs. Finally, around six thirty in the morning, I threw the covers off and dragged myself out of bed. I spent the morning creeping around the resort, swimming in the ocean instead of the pool, walking down the beach past other resorts so that if, by chance, he happened to be looking for me, it would be nearly impossible to find me.

When the sun began to blister in the midday sky, I retreated to my room for a siesta instead of finding a shady spot beneath a palapa on the sand. I woke up restless around four o'clock, too eager to catch the last of the sun's rays to continue my childish hiding. I was in Mexico to relax, and I wasn't going to let some inconsequential, albeit extremely gorgeous man, ruin it.

As I assembled my beach bag, I dialed the one person who could help me make sense of something like this.

"Cosima," I gushed when she answered the phone in her lilting accent. My youngest sister was the only woman on the planet who sounded just as gorgeous as she looked.

"*Bambina*, I miss you too much." The sound of city life interrupted her speech, and I could imagine her floating down the streets of New York on her way to a photo shoot. "I cannot wait for you to get here. How is Mexico? Any hot men come up to you on the beach?"

I blushed even though she couldn't see me.

She laughed delightedly at my pause, clapping in the background. "Oh, tell me everything. And I mean everything. People always skip the best parts without realizing it. Is he unbearably handsome?"

"Oh God, Cosi, he is the most beautiful man I've ever met." I sighed and flopped on the bed in my bathing suit and cover-up.

"Oh, don't let Sebastian hear that," she whispered, referring to our good-naturedly arrogant brother, her twin, who took his good looks very seriously.

I laughed but was too distracted with the thought of Sinclair to really mean it.

"Wow, he must be something," she murmured, picking up on my emotional state. "When did you meet him?"

"Just yesterday," I said, still incredulous that all of this could have happened in only one day of knowing someone.

I stood from the bed and grabbed my oversized bag, propping my sunglasses on my head as I left the room. "Listen, have you ever had a holiday affair?"

My little sister, only twenty-two and already light years ahead of me in the romance department, laughed her throaty chuckle. "Oh, Gigi, you surprise me! I highly recommend it."

I bit my lip as I walked down the four flights of stairs to the lobby. "Have you..." I hesitated. "Have you been with a committed man?"

She paused, and I could almost hear the cogs whirring in her head. "You mean like a married man?"

"Not exactly. Someone with a girlfriend, though, a long-term one."

"Hmm." She thought for a few moments, but it felt like hours before she finally said, " Never a married man. I demand a certain level of attention, and married men just can't provide that."

I smiled as she had intended, but I knew it was more than that. Cosima was one of the most honest people I knew; it would have been impossible for her to live a lie like that.

"But I have cheated with a man before. I didn't know until the deed was done, but I also tried to avoid him after that. As impossible a feat as it was..." She clucked her tongue, a habit she had inherited from our mother. "Why do you ask, *bambina*?"

"The man, he has a girlfriend back home." I smiled at one of the Mexican bartenders as I claimed a lounge chair and shed my cover-up.

It was a beautiful day with clear blue skies, and I settled down to get some sun on my pale limbs. I closed my eyes and allowed my sister's voice to counsel me, soothing me from my frenzied state of the night before.

"Listen, Gigi, normally I would say stay away from an attached man, especially for you. Given your lack of experience, I would urge you to think carefully about how far you are willing to go with a man you hardly know in a foreign land. But, at the same time, I think this could be good for you to have some fun with a handsome man. It won't be serious, and you won't get hurt. As far as the girlfriend is concerned..." Her voice was strained, her Italian accent much thicker, and I frowned with worry over her change in tone. "If he wants to cheat on her, then he will."

It wasn't exactly reassuring advice, but it was true, and I could always count on her for that. I took a deep breath and felt the sun soak into my skin like a balm.

"So you think I should do it? Have a holiday affair?"

"Gigi, from the sounds of him, I think you'd be crazy not to."

I smiled into the phone and accepted the acute pang of homesickness that pinged in my chest. It had been thirteen months since I last saw my sister, and before that, eighteen months since I had visited with any other member of my family. I was nervous about moving to a new city to rejoin my entire family after over five years of being separated from them, but hearing the familiar strains of Cosima's liquid voice reminded me why I was so desperate to see them.

"I love you," I said.

My little sister laughed loudly, no doubt stopping people on the street with the sight of her joy. "And I you, always."

I hung up feeling lighter than I had in a long time, and coupled with a brisk half an hour swim in the cool waters of the pool, I was happy and pleasantly lethargic when I emerged from the water to bask once again in the sun.

"Can I get you a drink, *señorita*?" a sweet-faced man asked.

"She'll have a sex on the beach," a strange voice answered for me.

I turned to my left to see a man stretched out on the lounge chair one over from me. His skin was the color of mahogany, and it rippled across his gym-toned body. He wore small black briefs and nothing else. I blushed and looked away quickly. The waiter nodded and left to place our orders.

"What if I don't drink?" I asked with soft reproach.

"Ah, but I am usually a very good judge of character." He swung into a seated position and leaned forward to offer me his hand. "Stefan Kilos."

I took his smooth palm in mine and smiled into his beautiful face. "Elle Moore."

He had startling green eyes in such a dark face, and his thick coffee-colored hair fell to his broad shoulders in glossy waves. I wondered briefly if he was gay, considering how beautifully maintained he was, but one flash of those perfect, pearly white teeth dissuaded me.

"You are the artist, yes?" He moved his lounge chair closer. "I saw your exhibit in Paris last month. In fact, I purchased one of your pieces, *Le Solitaire de Nuit*."

"You're kidding?"

It still astonished me that my art was becoming well-known, particularly in France. My mentor at *L'École des Beaux-Arts* had thought me crazy for moving out of the country just as my career was gaining momentum. I agreed with her, and it was only one of the many reasons I was nervous about New York.

"No." He shook his head and captured one of my hands in his. It was an overly familiar gesture, but it was something one of the twins would have done, and I beamed back at him. "I absolutely love it. It hangs in my bedroom at home in Greece. The light reflecting off the dome of Sacré-Cœur is masterfully done. I really am a big fan."

Pleasure unfurled in my stomach and sluiced through my veins like a drug. This wasn't the first time someone had approached me about my work, but it was the first time outside of France, and it gave me a flicker of hope for my artistic future in America. I allowed him to keep my hand and beamed into his face as I launched into my favorite kind of talk: the art world.

Thirty minutes and three sex on the beach cocktails later, a sharp prickle of foreboding tickled the base of my spine. I rolled my shoulders to rid myself of the teeth-gritting apprehension, but it remained for the next five minutes as Stefan made me howl with laughter over the antics of a mutual friend.

"Stop," I gasped, wiping the tears rolling down my cheeks. "Really, Stefan, you have to stop, or I'll die."

"Well, we can't have that." He chuckled then frowned at something over my shoulder, squinting into the high sun to discern the intruder. "Can I help you?"

"No." I closed my eyes briefly at the sound of Sinclair's smooth French-minted tone. "But I believe Elle can."

Stefan frowned, catching my weariness and Sinclair's obvious animosity. "I'm not sure if she can. We were just in the middle of sharing a drink, actually."

"One of many, it appears," he countered coolly.

I flushed at the collection of glasses on the plastic side table even though I was more than capable of holding my liquor.

"Listen." Stefan was getting irritated now, though he only rested back on his hands, exposing the mighty breadth of his chest like a gorilla sizing up his competition. "I don't know who you think you are—"

"Stop it," I said as I stood to face Sinclair.

I blinked hard at the sight of him. Though it had only been a few hours since I last saw him, his astonishing beauty took my breath away. He wore a white linen shirt and light gray swim shorts that exposed his muscular calves, and a pair of Ray-Ban aviators were propped casually in his mane of deep red-brown hair.

"Stop it," I repeated. "Sinclair, stop being such a bruiser."

"A bruiser?" His eyebrows rose almost comically into his hairline.

"Yes." I nodded adamantly. "A bruiser. I was having a delightful time with Stefan before you barged in, and I would like to return to it."

He stared at me for a moment with dangerously still blue eyes before directing his gaze to Stefan. "I think it best that you leave."

Stefan ran a hand down my arm, but it was more friendly than sexual, and I knew he only meant to reassure me. He would stay if I wanted him to and maybe even go so far as to tell Sinclair off. After half an hour of conversation, I had the distinct feeling that I had made a friend.

"You know my room number," he said softly in a way that conveyed undeniable intimacy, and I knew it was for Sinclair's sake. "Call me if you want to get a drink."

I nodded as he collected his things and left with a final wink even though I didn't really want to be alone with Sinclair. Cosima's advice had given me a new lease on the idea of a holiday affair, but I still wasn't sure if I could face sex without intimacy. Even with a man like Sinclair.

When I remained facing away from him for a few moments, and he didn't speak, I wondered if he had left. But two knuckles drew delicate lines down the bare skin of my back, and a second later, his front pressed into me. One hand pressed against my hip, pushing us gently together, and he placed a heartbreaking kiss where my neck met my shoulder.

"I've made a decision." I could feel him hard already against the small of my back, and a violent shudder wracked my frame. "Would you like to know what it is?"

His hand moved from my hip up over the curve of my waist between my breasts to my neck, where he wrapped his fingers one by one over my throat to tip it back for better access to his lips.

"Yes." I was too enraptured with him to be aware of my surroundings, but I was vaguely conscious of the fact that we stood in public beside a very crowded pool. When I tried to pull away, his hand tightened slightly around my neck.

"I've decided we are going to have an affair." He ran his nose up the side of my neck and gently nipped at my ear. "I know you want me, Elle; I can feel it in your lush body. I know you're scared that I'll ruin you for other men." His other hand made its way around my back and down over my rump to tickle the skin of my inner thigh. "It will be worth it."

Oh, I didn't doubt it. I was already damp with arousal and trembling with need. My mind was whirring with thoughts of his lean fingers on me, in me, how he would taste in my mouth and feel inside me.

"Do you believe me?" he crooned.

I nodded my head slightly and dropped it back against his shoulder. As I did so, I caught the eye of a tall, willowy woman walking by herself over to the bar. She was pretty, but it was the expression on her hard features that doused me like a bucket of ice water. Condemnation. Of course, she couldn't have known anything about our situation, who Sinclair or I was, but her look of disgust still quieted my lust, and I shoved away from Sinclair abruptly.

He stared at me expectantly as I swirled to face him, and when I glared, he lifted his palms in surrender. I almost laughed.

"I know the sex will be great," I said, surprised by my own boldness. He rewarded me with a slight smile. "But I told you last night, I just don't think I'm comfortable sleeping with someone I know nothing about."

He tucked his hands in his pockets and sighed heavily. "What do you want to know?"

I had so many questions that it took me a moment to make sense of my thoughts. I gestured for him to take the seat next to mine, and when he hesitated, I narrowed my eyes. With an exasperated shake of his head, he sat down, bracing his forearms on his knees so that he was still too close for me to think clearly.

"I don't need to know the specifics. In fact, I don't even want to." His eyebrows arched incredulously, but I ignored him. "I want you too badly to care if I know your last name or where you live. But I feel uncomfortable. Like if I ask you the wrong question, you'll be angry with me."

"You want boundaries," he confirmed, his eyes suddenly effervescent with intrigue. "Rules."

I nodded even though the look in his eyes gave me pause. "Exactly."

His slight smile was wicked, his voice like smoke. "Rules I can do. Number one: no personal specifics such as full names, location, family, etc. As we are both here for work, I think some discussion on the matter is acceptable."

I sat down across from him with a sigh. "So we can talk about business and sex?"

At my less than enthusiastic tone, he grinned. "Trust me, both are infinitely interesting. Number two: if we do this, we do it my way." Automatically, I frowned, but he placed one hand on my knee, lightly brushing the tender skin on the inside of my leg until I was soothed. "You belong to me for the next six days."

My mind protested loudly at such a possessive statement, but my body reacted positively, warming and liquefying until I was as pliant as warm dough.

"Before you argue with me, think about the practicalities." His fingers were moving softly, teasingly over the inside of my trembling thighs. "You don't have someone else in mind for a holiday affair, do you? No, I didn't think so. As you said, you don't have much experience with these things. But you're eager to learn, aren't you, Elle?"

I was too focused on his fingers—now at the apex of my thighs, lingering over my bikini-clad core—to answer. We were tucked into a reasonably unpopulated corner of the pool, and I was grateful for the rock formation concealing us from most of the swimmers.

"It turns you on," Sinclair continued in velvet tones, "to have me touch you here." His fingers slipped under the elastic of my bathing suit, and he hummed at finding me wet. "When anyone could walk by and catch us."

I shook my head, but I wasn't fooling anyone. My knees quivered slightly as the pad of his thumb feathered lightly over my clit.

"Be mine for the week, Elle. Let me show you how many ways I can make you come."

Without warning, two fingers plunged into my wet core, and I moaned involuntarily. He shifted slightly to block the view of me from across the pool and tilted his fingers to find my sweet spot while his thumb drew tight circles on my clit.

My orgasm descended quickly, a short, sharp burst of exquisite pleasure radiating from beneath Sinclair's skilled fingers. My knees quaked, and I let out a soft cry before slumping forward. He caught me on his shoulder and ran his free hand down my back soothingly. To anyone watching, we probably looked like a sweet couple embracing. No one could see his hand skillfully bringing me down from my high with delicate finesse. My nose was at his warm throat, and his scent, coupled with my post-orgasm state, made me dizzy.

After a minute or two, he gently pulled his hand away from between my thighs and righted me. I stared at him with drowsy half-lidded eyes as he brought his fingers to his mouth and sucked. A tremor sparked at the base of my spine, and I shivered.

"You taste like honey," he murmured. His eyes burned so bright a blue that I blinked.

I knew I should say something, but my mind was dumb with bliss, and when I opened my mouth, all I could find was, "Thank you."

His eyes widened, and one corner of his mouth rose in a smirk. "You are most welcome, Elle."

I laughed. "I'm sorry, I just don't normally do things like this. Not to mention, I've never orgasmed so quickly in my life, I think I'm a bit stupefied."

I closed my legs and reached for my cover-up. It was easier to concentrate when I was covered.

"But you'd like to, wouldn't you?" he asked darkly.

I licked my lips nervously and watched his eyes map the path of my tongue. My body was still soft and warm from coming, and while I couldn't believe he had just skillfully brought me to climax beside a very public pool, or that I had allowed it, there was no denying that it had been the most exciting experience of my life. *It was only a week*, I reminded myself, and nothing irrevocable could happen in such a short time.

"Yes."

He nodded, not surprised this time by my acquiescence. "Don't play with me. I need you to mean it."

"I do." I stared at him with earnest eyes and watched as his stern features relaxed into a slightly boyish grin.

"Good. Now, I'd like you to accompany me to a business party I have to attend tonight."

"Oh." I hadn't expected that.

Detecting my disappointment, he widened his grin. "Trust me, Elle, I would love nothing more than to spend the rest of the day in bed with you, but duty calls. I promise to make the wait up to you."

I blushed, embarrassed that he had discovered my eagerness, but his smoky laugh made me smile too.

"I have some work to do, and I realize I interrupted your sunbathing. I'll meet you in the lobby at eight." It wasn't really a question, but he waited for me to nod before he stood to leave.

He hesitated for a moment before leaning down to brush a swift kiss to my cheek. "Until then, siren."

I sat there after he left, stunned by the turn my vacation had taken. Brenna had sent me to Mexico to relax, the only person who knew why I was so hastily leaving my beloved Paris, and here I was, more stimulated than I had ever been in my life. With a large sigh, I flopped back against the chaise lounge and closed my eyes. I knew next to nothing about the devastatingly handsome Frenchman, but already, I was hooked.

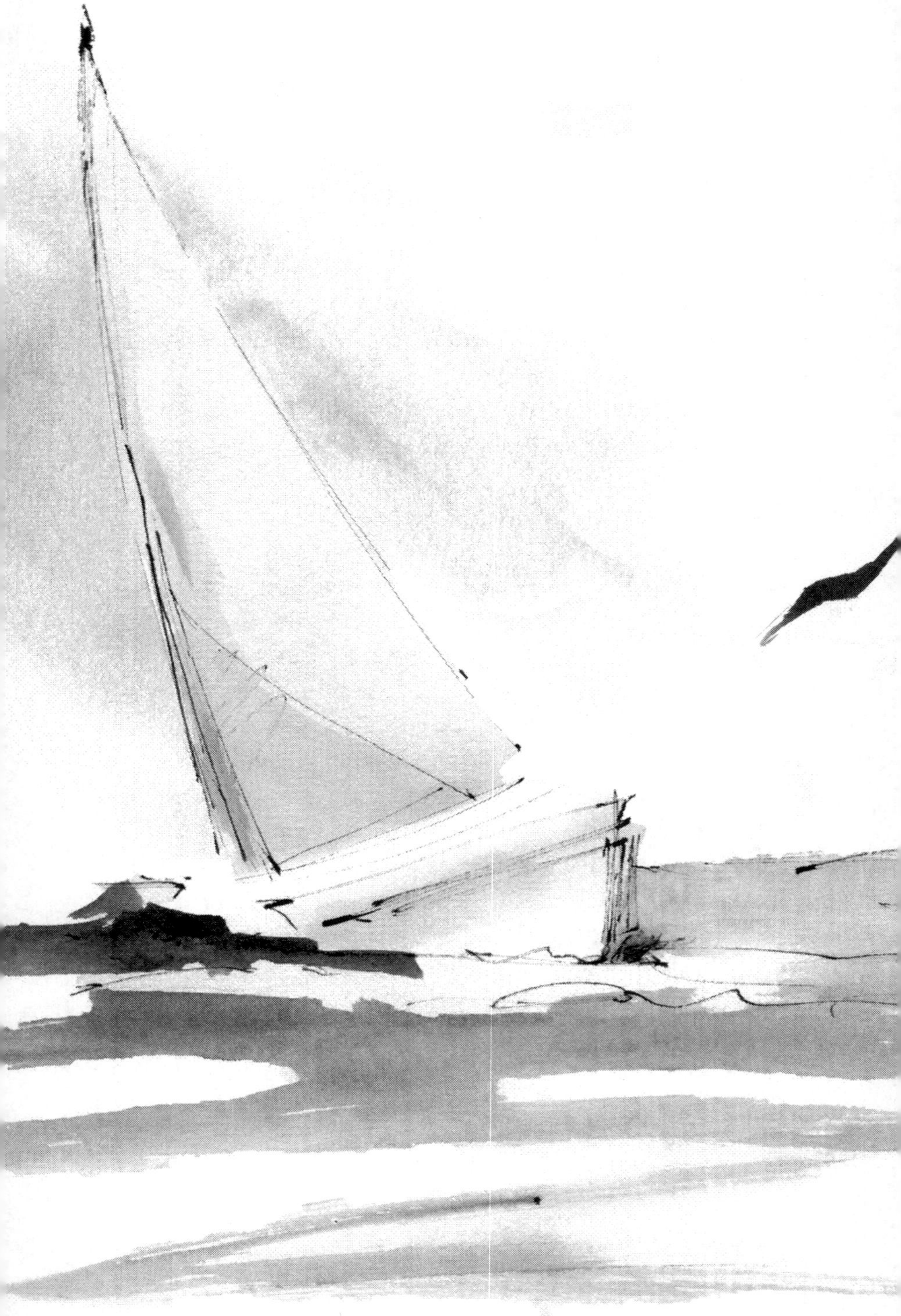

Chapter Five

The home of Santiago Herrera was the kind of place I had only ever seen in movies about drug cartels. It was a low sprawling building made of butter yellow stucco and roofed with the traditional red tiles, but that was where the classic Spanish style ended. The interior was modern-day opulence. The kitchen, which I had accidentally wandered into after getting lost on the way back to the reception from the bathroom, was larger than most restaurants, and the bathroom boasted a talking toilet. We had been at the party for two hours, and Candy had assured me I'd only seen one-quarter of the massive home. I found it all a little bit off-putting; the modernity was something out of a science fiction book, and by the time I found Sinclair, I was a little flustered.

It was hard to believe the movie star handsome man sitting at the bar was waiting for me. Sinclair wore light gray trousers and a deep blue dress shirt with a cobalt blue tie that matched his eyes. He had discarded his jacket at the door even though most of the men at the party were dressed more formally in suit jackets and tails. I preferred his look and so too, it seemed, did the slinky brunette leaning against the bar so close to him. He seemed unperturbed by her attention, but his expression was only politely interested, and he turned his head briefly to check the hallway leading back from the washrooms. I smiled, and as if he had sensed it, he froze, his glass suspended between his lips and the bar. I held my breath as he slowly turned his head, unerringly finding me across the large, crowded floor. I could feel his eyes scorch a path of fire across my body, and when his gaze finally met mine, it flared with desire.

I had worried the whole afternoon about what I should wear to a Mexican soiree, but the minute I saw Sinclair's reaction to the dress, I knew I had chosen well. The gossamer-thin fabric draped itself elegantly across my shoulders and crossed over my breasts, exposing a deep slice of plump cleavage. The soft lavender color suited my sun-kissed skin and auburn hair, which I had left simple, just curling softly down my back.

Sinclair strode forward without noticing the sour expression on the face of the now lonely brunette at the bar and brushed a chaste kiss against my cheek. "Have I mentioned yet that you look absolutely lovely, Elle?"

"So do you," I murmured after dragging in a deep lungful of his leathery scent.

His smile was small, his conservatism back in place after the more playful man I had seen by the pool that afternoon. "Thank you. I was worried you had run away when you didn't come back straight away."

"I got lost," I explained with a small laugh. "I don't have the best sense of direction, and this is a big house."

"Of course," he allowed smoothly, his hand on the small of my back as he moved us out of the way of foot traffic and into a more private corner of the room. "I should have texted you the floor plans."

I looked over at him sharply to see if he was teasing. "Would you have?"

His expression was practically inscrutable, but I was beginning to know where to look for telling signs of emotion in his sharply cut jaw and expressive brows. I was about to tease him when someone called his name from across the floor and started over to us.

My smile slipped slightly, but Sinclair pressed his palm to the small of my spine and leaned in to whisper, "Poor girl, you were hoping for a more exciting evening, weren't you?"

"This is delightful, Sinclair, really." I gestured to the opulent surroundings and the glittering Mexican magnates littering the hall like discarded jewels. "I've never been to an event like this before."

"I wish I could say the same." His hand was warm on my hip as he tucked me into his side, but his smile was gone, replaced with his normal implacable mask as the guest arrived at our side. "Santiago, it's good to see you again."

Santiago Herrera was younger than I had imagined, with thick black hair slicked back from his broad forehead to reveal large obsidian eyes. He wore a burgundy dinner jacket and shoes with tassels. Despite his obscene wealth, something was amazingly approachable about his demeanor.

"And the same to you, my friend." He took Sinclair's hand and turned immediately to me. "Please, introduce me to your lovely date. It's not often I have the pleasure of meeting a beautiful redhead."

"It's not often I have the pleasure of meeting a man brave enough to wear a velvet dinner jacket," I teased, surprised by my boldness. It must have had something to do with being next to Sinclair, who made me feel tingly with female power.

He guffawed, a strange chortle of amusement that made me giggle. "My last wife complained about my fashion sense." He flattened the lapels of his jacket carefully. "I divorced her over this jacket."

I looked up at Sinclair to validate the outrageous claim, but he was staring at me with a slight frown between his chestnut brows as if we were discussing complex physics.

"Well, I think you look dashing," I asserted.

Santiago beamed. "Tell me you speak Spanish, and you will be my next wife."

"Don't make promises you can't keep," I scolded lightly and watched him laugh again.

This time, Sinclair smiled slightly too, and that small expression of humor warmed me more than a room full of laughter. I wondered what had made Sinclair so reserved, but it was undoubtedly part of his appeal too. Every insight into his carefully concealed mind and spirit felt like a major victory.

"I'm sorry, Iago, not only is Elle French, but she's unavailable to you," Sinclair said smoothly, his hand still lightly resting on the swell of my hip.

I opened my mouth to correct him about my nationality before I remembered the rules. No personal details. And truth be told, being French and everything that represented—refined, contained, and witty—was preferable to me than the gritty, poverty-stricken image my Italian upbringing invoked.

"What a waste." The Mexican magnate spoke in flawless English, only slightly spiced with an accent. "You had the drop on me, though, Sinclair. It's hardly a fair playing field when you are French as well."

"American," he corrected with narrowed eyes, all amusement gone.

Santiago pursed his lips but nodded, obviously understanding the gravity of his tone. What was so wrong with being French?

"I saw Dylan Hernandez by the buffet. We should discuss business now rather than later so that you can enjoy your party," Sinclair said.

The feel of his hand smoothing down my back distracted me. With that simple touch, the desire that had lain tamely at the base of my belly all night flared to life.

"Of course." Santiago squinted at us, his lips still pursed, but finally, he nodded. "We'll go up to my study. Katarina can hold down the fort while I'm gone. You should meet her, Elle; her beauty is your only competition tonight." His grin flashed again. "She is my sister."

"Good idea. Kat will no doubt be on the patio on a clear night like this. She is an astronomer. You'll like her. But first," Sinclair turned to me, his gaze strangely intimate, "I was telling Elle about your remarkable collection of Frida Kahlo's work."

"Kat will show her," he said, with a dismissive wave of his hand as if such a collection was nothing to brag about.

Considering she was a longtime idol of mine, I couldn't believe that I had the opportunity to view her work outside of a museum. Sinclair noted my smile and matched it with a small one of his own.

"I thought you might enjoy that."

I nodded, my tongue tied with anticipation.

"If you'll excuse us for a minute, Iago, I will just show Elle the powder room, and then I'll meet you in the office."

I frowned slightly as I had just returned from the restroom, but his fingers stroked the skin at the base of my neck tantalizingly, and I forgot to protest.

"Of course." Santiago nodded and leaned forward to grasp my hands. "I wish Sinclair always visited me with such a beautiful companion. He never mixes business and pleasure. Such an awful separation, don't you think?"

"I'm not so sure. He hasn't been divorced three times," I joked.

He laughed and squeezed my hands. "Touché." After brushing a kiss against my cheek, he stepped back and looked at Sinclair. "Five minutes?"

"Better make it ten."

Santiago's thick brows raised, but he acquiesced with a shrug before turning away.

As soon as he did so, I turned fully to Sinclair with my own arched brow. "The powder room?"

Amusement and something darker sparked in his eyes. "Yes. You are bored with this party, and I'm sorry for it. Let me try to ease some of the tedium. Come."

With sure feet, he led me out of the main hall and through twisting, turning corridors. I had no idea how he could have known where he was going in such a maze.

"You made Iago laugh within thirty seconds of knowing him," Sinclair said, almost to himself. "I haven't seen him open up to a stranger like that in years."

I shrugged. "He seemed very friendly."

"Oh, he is. But he doesn't enjoy life much anymore." At my searching look, he explained, his hand warm in mine as he led me through the house. "His brother was killed two years ago, gang violence in Mexico City. He moved himself and Kat here soon after."

I felt sympathy pang in my stomach and shrugged off the brief thought of life without one of my siblings. Even my eldest sister, Elena, whom I had never been particularly close to, was vital to me.

We had stopped in the middle of a narrow room fronted in glass paneling, standing beside an open door in the gently rushing breeze. There was barely an inch separating our bodies, but Sinclair carefully maintained the distance.

"I didn't mean to make you frown," Sinclair said. "Santiago is a very rich man, with many things to take his mind off it."

Money couldn't erase heartache, I wanted to say but didn't. I had the feeling Sinclair would have argued with me, and I was too curious about why he had brought me to this room to fight with him.

"Enough of that," he said, somehow sensing the change of direction in my thoughts. "I have something much more enticing in mind at the moment. We only have a few minutes, so do as I say." He looked at me sternly, but I could tell he was amused and aroused. "Stand against the wall."

My belly was already fluttering with anticipation, and I hastened to do as he asked.

"Spread your legs and clasp your hands behind your back." His voice was like a physical caress. Instantly, I moved to do as he bid me. "Don't move."

He admired me for a moment.

"You really are the sexiest woman, Elle." Swiftly, he moved to stand in front of me, but frustratingly, he didn't touch me. "I've been hard all night thinking about what you are going to let me do to this sinful body of yours."

My nipples beaded against the thin material of my dress, and I arched forward slightly, willing him to notice. His lips twitched in acknowledgment, but he ignored them.

"Have you been thinking about it too?"

I nodded, wishing my legs were together so I could alleviate the throbbing in my core.

"What did you imagine me doing?" Finally, he touched me. He ran a finger down my chest between my breasts. "Touching you here?"

Lazily, he circled one breast with his finger, narrowing in closer and closer to my furled peak. My chest felt heavy with sensation, and even though he had only just started caressing me, I was panting. I jolted when his fingers found both aching nipples and pinched. The flare of painful pleasure made me moan.

Sinclair shifted on his feet uncomfortably, and I was grateful to find evidence of his own arousal.

"Or maybe here?" he murmured, running one hand up the inside of my left leg. His fingertips trailed like fire up my sensitive skin, and I whimpered slightly, begging him to touch me properly.

Heeding my silent plea, he crouched to his knees before me and lifted the front of my skirt to gaze at my lace-covered sex. I trembled when he pressed an open-mouthed kiss to the skin just to the left of my center.

"We were interrupted last time." His hot breath fanned over me, making me shiver. "I was going to wait until we got back to the resort, but I have to taste you."

His mouth closed over my clit through the flimsy cloth and suckled. I gasped and pressed my hands against the wall to support my shaking knees. Pulling aside my panties, he slicked his fingers across my wet flesh. He groaned against me, heightening the sensation of his tongue against my sensitive nub.

"You want this badly, don't you?" he questioned, sitting back on his haunches to look at me. "You want to give yourself up to me."

"Yes," I breathed, nudging my hips against the fingers circling my entrance. "Please."

I felt no embarrassment, only knee-weakening lust. At that moment, I would have done anything for the orgasm looming large in the distance.

He smiled triumphantly and lowered his head to me, once again finding my clit, but this time without the barrier of lace between us. His tongue laved at my bundle of nerves as two fingers entered me, twisting to reach my sweet spot. I was so incoherent with lust that it took me a moment to realize that he was pushing something inside me other than his fingers. I looked down abruptly, but his dark head blocked my view.

"Trust me," he ordered hoarsely as a small vibrator nestled inside me.

My legs tensed as I hesitated—I had never played with sex toys before—but his ministrations increased, the pace of his fingers devastating against my swollen flesh. The moment I relaxed, the device inside me switched on, buzzing softly within me. I cried out loudly as my orgasm came crashing down, and Sinclair reared up to swallow my loud cries, his fingers still strumming my clit. I had never tasted myself before, but I found it surprisingly erotic, and when he pulled away, I protested weakly before laying my head against his solid chest.

I squeezed my eyes against the overwhelming sensation, and I was grateful for Sinclair's large body holding me upright when he turned the toy off, and my legs turned to noodles. My love life with Mark had never been anything close to as mind-blowing as this, and Sinclair and I hadn't even had sex yet.

"Best. Party. I've. Ever. Been. To," I said between shallow breaths as I recovered.

Sinclair's dark chuckle ruffled my hair, and I could feel his solid length pressed to my hip. "I have to agree with you."

"I've never..." I hid my face against his chest, and murmured, "I've never done that before."

"Which part?" he asked dryly. "Had a tryst at a party? A man kiss you here?" His fingers gently swept over the curls between my thighs. "An orgasm?"

"All of the above," I whispered.

Gently, he pulled my face away from him and took my flaming cheeks between his palms. His blue eyes were darkly serious. "You are beautiful. I didn't realize how inexperienced you are."

It was a vague probe into the state of my virginity, I knew. I wondered if it would matter to him or if it would make him change his mind. I didn't take the bait.

"Oh." I squeezed his arousal in my hand, causing him to hiss loudly. "Do I have time to take care of this?"

He raised a brow, and I bit the inside of my cheek, wondering if I was being too bold, but he smiled reassuringly and smoothed my hair in a surprisingly tender gesture that seemed so at odds with the in-command man of minutes before.

"Unfortunately, our ten minutes are up; though, I'm sorely tempted to forget business and whisk you back to my hotel room right now."

I grinned and interlocked my hands behind his neck, pushing up against his erection. "Why don't you?"

His eyes were electric with suppressed desire.

"Another thirty minutes tops, and we will leave." He pulled his phone out to check the time and grimaced. "We've taken too long already." Swiftly, he leaned down to readjust my underwear and smooth the skirt of my dress. "Come on."

"But, um." The sex toy was still inside me. "Aren't you forgetting about, erm, something?"

One eyebrow rose coolly. "I don't believe so."

Oh, okay.

So he wanted me to walk around the party with a sex toy inside me?

I thought about arguing with him, but his aloof, almost daring expression and my warm glow dissuaded me.

"Okay, we should hurry to your meeting," I said, taking his hand to lead him out the door.

He might have chuckled, but as soon as I opened the door, the sounds of the party reanimated. After a minute of indecision at an oddly shaped corridor, he took the lead from me, gently guiding me to the kitchen where he thought we might find Katarina.

"I'll be in the room next to the library if you need me," he said as we paused to the side of the kitchen doors, out of the path of the hustling waitstaff. At my blank look, his lips twitched. "Kat will know the way."

I nodded, but the idea of being without Sinclair in the twisty-turvy house was unpleasant. Unlike my siblings, I had never been particularly good with large groups of people, and outside art showings and gallery openings, I rarely went to parties.

"You'll be fine," he assured me, reading my thoughts. "You and Kat will get along brilliantly. Think of me when I'm gone?"

There was a devastating twinkle in his eye as if he knew something I didn't. I narrowed my eyes at him suspiciously, but he only shrugged innocently and put his hands in his pockets. When he turned to leave, he started to whistle. I watched him move through the crowded room with the grace and power of a wild cat, his broad shoulders straight and his long legs eating up the space. Women turned to watch him, but he remained oblivious, and I knew few would approach him. His carefully controlled expression, almost cruel due to his hard features, would discourage even the most ballsy women.

With a sigh, I turned away from him. Sinclair was the sexiest man I had ever met, the kind of man who only inhabited women's darkest fantasies and Hollywood movies, yet he was here with me. It was enough to make any girl feel like a million dollars. Of course, my recent orgasm didn't hurt either.

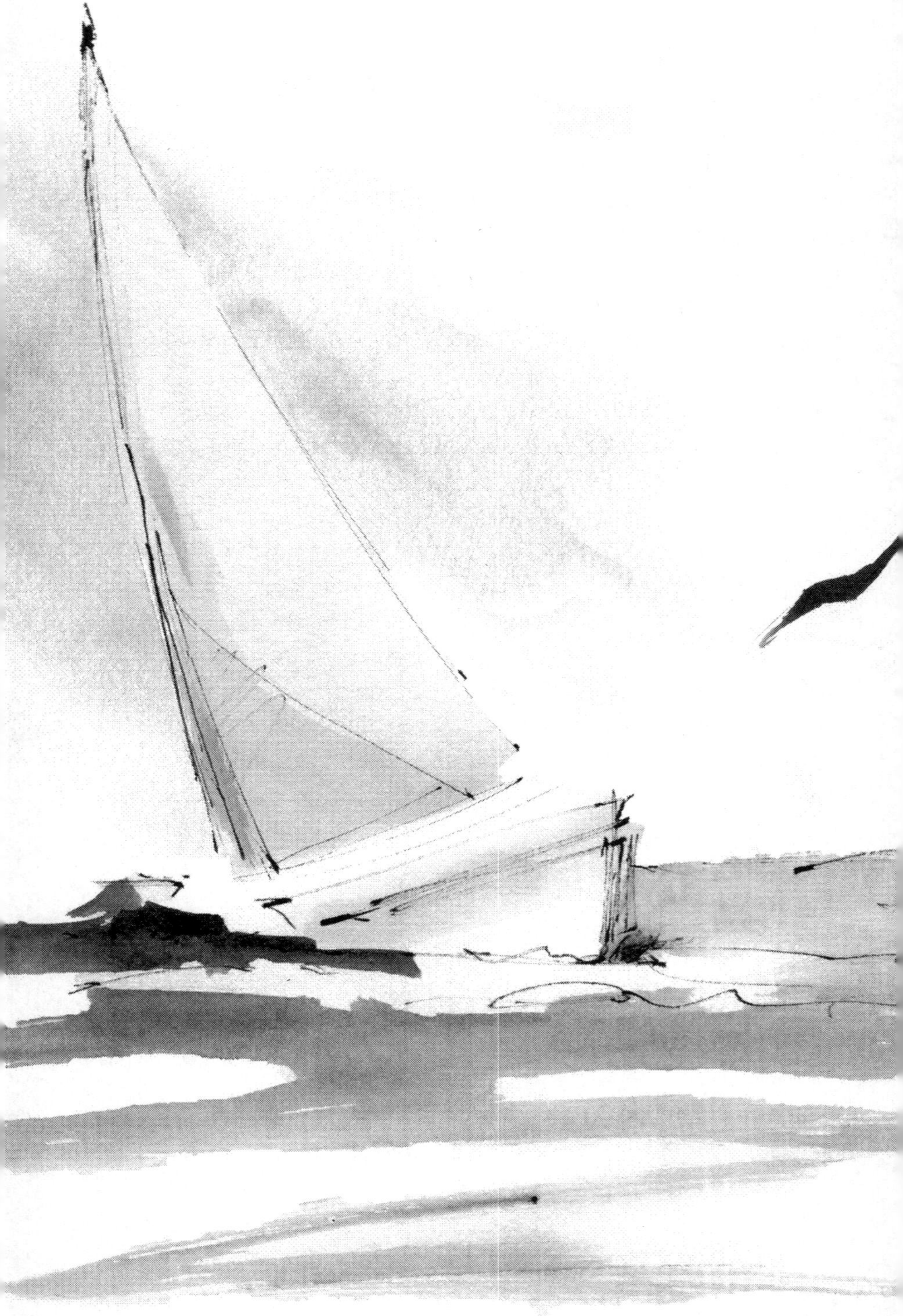

Chapter Six

Santiago's collection of art was staggeringly comprehensive and outrageously expensive. A room three times the size of my studio apartment in Paris was dedicated to the works of renowned Mexican painters like Diego Rivera and Frida Kahlo, but it also paid tribute to local artists and some contemporary American talents such as Julie Combal.

"I know I'm in the minority, but I find Kahlo's drawings almost more haunting than her paintings," I murmured as I took in her 1926 sketch *Accident*, which depicted the artist bound in a body cast besieged by images of the car accident that had left her with multiple broken bones and lifelong pain.

"Honestly?" Katarina's thicker accent made all her words run together like a song. "I prefer the American style."

I smiled at her, once again struck by her likeness to Cosima. Though Katarina was not particularly attractive, she shared the same effervescent spirit that kept me smiling and laughing.

"My brother is much more interested in the arts than I am." She shrugged. "I find it hard to understand the beauty in living things. Planets are much easier."

We moved along to another image, this one a satirical reimagining of a Del Monte ad by Minerva Cuevas, a contemporary Mexican artist.

Kat gave me a sidelong look. "I think we have been friends long enough now—what has it been, fifteen minutes?—for me to ask you about Sinclair."

"What about him?"

She laughed at my coyness and shrugged. "If you don't want to discuss him, I understand. But as I understand it, you are here alone. Sometimes it's just nice to talk to a fellow woman about a boy, no?"

So true. I had been itching to call Cosima all day, but there was no way she could really understand the magnitude of my holiday affair without knowing anything about the gorgeous, composed man who was Sinclair. Kat was a gift, really, given to me by the man himself. I wondered if he had thought about just that when he paired us together.

"We met on the plane coming down." I flushed, remembering it. "Planes make me nervous, to say the least, and I was making a fool of myself. Sinclair was nice enough to keep misery company."

She looked me up and down clinically with a critical eye that only women possess. "I would say he was only too happy to help."

"Trust me, it's the makeup." I laughed.

Katarina pursed her lips, a habit that she and her brother shared. "Beautiful and bashful. I can see the appeal."

"Oh, stop embarrassing her, Kat." Cage Tracy's familiar French melody had me turning around to face him.

He looked dashing in a white silk shirt that contrasted with his developing tan and impenetrable black hair, but it was his smile that made him so disarming, and I could tell from Katarina's startled little gasp that she thought so too. The murmur of voices around us spiked slightly at his arrival, but he was still relatively obscure enough that no one bothered him for autographs. I realized it was his ungodly beauty that drew their attention more than his fame.

Cage gave me a warm kiss on the cheek. "Though she does have a point. You look absolutely edible tonight, Elle."

I swatted his compliment out of the air, but the feel of the toy between my legs was a constant reminder of just how desirable Sinclair found me. "You are such a tease."

"Me?" He feigned horror. "How dare you? Kat, vouch for my character, please."

"I certainly will. Cage only ever acts like a bad boy if someone leads him astray, isn't that right?"

I looked over my shoulder as the statuesque blonde who had spoken came up beside Cage and took his arm. She was very beautiful but in a sharp, almost menacing way like something from a Grimm fairy tale. Her blond hair was so pale it was almost white, and her frosty eyes found mine instantly, regarding me with cool reserve.

"You must be Elle." She presented her hand to me as if it were a gift.

I was usually pretty easygoing with people, but something about the studied haughtier of this woman set my teeth on edge. I didn't take her hand, but I did smile at her, thinly. "I must be."

Cage guffawed, despite her withering look his way. "And this is Margot Silver, Sinclair's executive assistant."

She looked far too glamorous to be someone's assistant, but I let that slide. Katarina cast a furrowed glance at Margot's slim arm resting possessively on Cage.

"Margot, maybe you would like to look at Diego Rivera's works with me while we get to know each other better?" I asked, my voice carefully devoid of anything but sugar sweetness.

Her pale eyes widened slightly, but she bared her teeth in a semblance of a smile. "Of course."

I winked at Katarina as we walked away, and Cage turned to regale her with a funny story. She seemed surprised but quickly blushed and mouthed, "Thank you," over his shoulder. I didn't know what chance the sweet girl had with the rock star, but I was willing to do my part to foster the flames.

"So, Margot." I smiled demurely at her as we came to a stop out of hearing distance from the others. "Why don't you say what you have to say?"

Her large eyes widened, and my candor exposed a moment of vulnerability. It took her a second to bare her fangs. "Sinclair has a long-term partner."

She waited for me to react, but I only blinked at her and crossed my arms. If she had expected Sinclair to lie to me, then she didn't know him as well as she thought.

"Listen." She sighed sharply and adjusted her stance on her ridiculously high and absurdly lovely heels. "Despite what you may think, I'm not warning you off to be a bitch. I'm doing it because Sinclair, for all his coolness, is still a man, and a beautiful woman is any man's weakness. He's had a rough life, and the past few years have been good to him, so he doesn't need some random strumpet messing that up for him."

Okay, even though I objected to her use of the word strumpet, I had to admire her mettle and loyalty. Sinclair deserved people like this in his life, and even though Margot Silver was far too judgmental and cold for me to genuinely like, I tipped my hat to her.

"I appreciate that." I dropped my defensive pose and ran a

hand through my hair in frustration. "But I have no designs on Sinclair other than as a friend. Not that it's any of your business."

"A friend?" She snorted. "Sure."

Fair enough.

"Our friendship will end when the vacation does," I amended.

Margot stared at me for a long minute, seemingly taking note of everything from the color of my hair to the shape of my fingernails. "See that it does. Under other circumstances, we could have been friends."

I inclined my head even though I didn't really share her sentiments. It wasn't her fault, I thought as she walked away, that she had touched on those icky feelings within me, on the idea that I was being a whore and a home wrecker.

As I made my way back over to Cage and Katarina, I gasped. The egg inside me began to vibrate, jolting my dozing nerve endings with a burst of electricity.

"Are you okay, Elle?" Cage asked as I came to a sudden stop two feet away.

I nodded, my throat working past the moan in my throat. Surreptitiously, I searched the room for Sinclair, but he was nowhere to be found. How was he doing this?

"Did Margot put the fear of God into you?" Cage asked, hiding his smile behind his glass of whiskey. "She can be a fearsome woman."

"Evidently," I said dryly. "Thanks for the warning before I wandered off with her."

He laughed. "I had a feeling you knew what you were doing."

I smiled slightly and subtly rubbed my legs together, trying to ease the sensations at my core. The conservative side of me, the one that had always dominated, urged me to go to the bathroom and remove the toy while the other side, the one embraced by my more passionate twin siblings, delighted in the sensation of being teased unbeknownst to the crowd of people milling around the multi-million-dollar mansion. It was the cherry on top of an utterly decadent night. The only thing that would have made it complete was Sinclair.

As if summoned by my desire, a warm hand slid over my bare shoulder and down my back possessively. "Have you been thinking about me?" he whispered darkly in my ear as the vibrator ceased its motions.

Cage seemed taken aback by his friend's grin, but he recovered quickly with a wink at me. "It's a good thing you came when you did, Sin. I was just thinking about asking your date here to leave with me."

I rolled my eyes, but Sinclair remained unmoved, his voice cool. "I should have known you would find her tonight."

"In that dress? She's hard to miss."

I reached out to Kat, who had taken a step away from us, and lightly tugged her closer to me. "Katarina has been the most wonderful guide."

"Of course, she has." Cage squeezed her shoulder as a brother would. "Our Kat's a real gem."

She blushed, but Cage was too oblivious to notice how she reacted to him, and when I looked up at Sinclair to see if he noticed, his eyes were on mine, twinkling with mirth.

My mouth fell open when the vibrator started again, this time at a higher intensity. I wobbled slightly, and Sinclair smoothly tucked me under his arm.

"I think Elle has had too much to drink." I frowned at him as he spoke—I had only finished two glasses of wine—but he looked down at me with unmasked desire, and I bit my lip. "I should be getting her home."

"How did the meeting go?" Cage asked as he leaned forward to double kiss me on each cheek in farewell.

"As can be expected. Santiago assures me the deal will go forward as planned."

I tuned them out in order to say goodbye to Kat, but when I

tried to get out from under Sinclair's arm, he tightened his hold. He did stop the vibrator, though, and I was grateful when the thick fog of desire cleared slightly from my thoughts.

I shrugged at Kat helplessly, and she giggled.

"I've never seen him like this," she whispered in her lovely accent. "He is very interested in you, no?"

I shook my head. "We just met."

She waved my statement out of the air. "This is no problem. I just met you, and already, I know that we are friends."

I beamed at her. Yes, I had felt that instant connection as well, and I was sorry to be saying goodbye to her already.

"If you stay with him, I mean, after this vacation, then maybe I will see you again," she said, ignoring my look of doubt.

"Why don't you give me your email?" I suggested instead of hinging my hopes on something that would very likely never happen.

Kat grinned, and we exchanged information. Sinclair finished his conversation with Cage and patiently waited for me to hug her goodbye before tugging us away. Immediately, people converged on us to talk to Sinclair as we made our way from room to room and into the main reception hall. When the man walking swiftly beside me ignored a particularly adamant older gentleman, I frowned.

"Shouldn't you stay and talk to these people?"

He continued his brisk pace without looking at me. "No."

"Because you don't have time to be nice?"

"Exactly."

I assumed he had already said goodbye to Santiago, so I felt less guilty about leaving so hastily. But honestly, I was burning from the inside out because of the infernal toy, and now, with my hand in Sinclair's and the knowledge he was taking me to bed, that he simply couldn't wait, I was incoherent with lust.

I shivered as we stepped into the cool night air, and Sinclair took off his jacket without any hesitation to slip it onto my shoulders before he went to secure a car. The blazer smelled strongly of his musky, leathery scent, and I pressed my nose into the collar in order to get my fill. He caught me when he returned, but he only gave me a funny look as if he couldn't understand me. I shrugged and took his hand once more in mine. He tensed at first, but when I squeezed his large palm, he squeezed back.

I stared up at him as we waited for the car to come around. He was so dashing with the bright moonlight in his thick hair, burnishing his bladed nose and sharp cheekbones like a lacquered mask.

He sensed me staring at him and looked down at me with smoky eyes. We stared at each other, and my breath hitched as desire spiked down my spine straight to my sex. I'd never known a single look could spark an inferno of longing in my gut.

The chauffeured black car stopped in front of us, breaking the connection, and Sinclair helped me in before moving around to the other side. The moment we were settled and the car took off, the vibrator started again. I squirmed, but Sinclair stilled me with a firm hand on my knee.

We sat like that in silence for a few minutes while I struggled with the building sensations. Then, almost indiscernibly, his hand began to draw patterns on my knee, inching higher up my leg. I watched his tanned hand trace my paler skin and closed my eyes on a breathy sigh when he reached the junction of my thighs.

He hushed me as one finger pressed against my damp panties. "Did you enjoy the party, Elle?"

I nodded my head with my eyes squeezed shut.

"Open your eyes." He waited for me to do so before plunging two fingers into me, jostling the vibrating toy.

I gasped loudly, and my eyes flickered to the front, where the driver listened to soft classical guitar.

"Obviously, you can't stay quiet." He frowned at me and lightly slapped my sex.

I bit off my moan. "I'll be quiet."

"Too late," he whispered before taking his hand away from my heat and turning off the vibrator.

He pressed a button, and a partition slowly closed between the front and back of the car. His eyes were dark and serious as he stared at me, taking in my flushed cheeks and tumbled hair.

"Take my cock out," he ordered.

Desire rolled through me and made my mouth suddenly parched. "What?"

"Don't make me ask you again."

I swallowed rapidly and turned in my seat in order to reach his zipper. A sizable erection strained against the front, and I almost groaned again when I took it in my hand through his pants. His strong grip clutched my wandering fingers, and I understood that I had disobeyed him yet again. I took a deep breath to settle my nerves before I unzipped him and reached inside his boxers to grab his naked length. He was large and thick, the head plush and red. I licked my lips.

"Suck it," he commanded, but his voice was less demanding than it had been.

I took the crown slowly in my mouth, swirling my tongue along the sensitive underside. The taste of him was potent, musky, and all man. I moaned as he thrust forward, pressing the head against the entrance to my throat. I braced my hands on his thighs and tried to relax in order to take him deeper.

"You love this, don't you? Taking me in your mouth," he rasped as his strong fingers wove into my hair so he could hold me still while continuing to thrust gently into my mouth.

I leaned farther down, eager to feel all of him. It felt right to do this for him. A heady sense of power and arousal rushed through my blood, and when Sinclair suddenly pulled me away, I was disorientated.

He looked at me with electric blue eyes, his fingers on my chin. "We're here."

I blinked and nodded. "Right."

His chuckle followed me as I scrambled out of the car, suddenly embarrassed about going down on Sinclair with someone in the front seat. I kept a few feet between us as we walked into the lobby, and I didn't think he noticed. But the moment we got into the elevator, I was pressed hard against the wall.

His hand lifted one of my legs, curling it around his waist while the other took a fistful of my hair and tugged, forcing my chin back. He stared down at me with hard eyes.

"Don't pretend you don't want this, Elle. I can feel how you respond to me." His hand traveled up my thigh and over my hips and quivering belly until he could cup one of my breasts. My nipple was sharp against his palm, and I shuddered when he rolled it between his fingers. "I could see these puckered on the plane. Your breathing hitched just like this." I gasped when he lowered his head to nip my bottom lip. "And when I leaned over you, your eyes begged me to kiss you."

I remembered it vividly, how his charm had made even the dreaded plane ride feel sexy.

"Do you still want me to kiss you, Elle?" His breath fanned across my neck as he placed a kiss there and another at the edge of my jaw.

I moaned and pressed my hips against his, but he only laughed and lightly bit my chin. His tongue swept across my pouting lower lip. "Tell me."

"Kiss me," I begged shamelessly.

The elevator pinged, and before I could capture his lips, he was pulling me gently from the wall. My legs were less than steady as I followed him from the elevator into his palatial suite. He must have called ahead because the lights were dim and Latin music wafted through the room on the sweet-smelling breeze from the open French doors.

"I even get music?" I looked over my shoulder at him, where he lingered by the door. "I'm a lucky girl."

My teasing smile faltered slightly when I saw the depth of intensity in his eyes. He walked toward me slowly with long, predatory steps. I didn't realize I held my breath until he was in front of me, and his knuckles skimmed my cheek.

"You deserve much more than music." His voice was quiet and slightly forced as if the admission cost him. "Flowers, and jewels, and romance."

I pressed his lingering hand to my cheek, and murmured, "I just want you."

He stared at me intently, and for a moment, I wasn't sure if he would continue our holiday affair. It made me aware of how very much I wanted it.

"I'll hurt you."

He wasn't being arrogant, and honestly, I couldn't say that I would emerge completely unscathed from our romance. I wasn't the kind of woman to sleep around, and I had only ever been romantically involved with one very sweet man who was just as naïve as me. And Sinclair was not naïve. He was coolly confident, full of smoky secrets, and sexy as hell.

"I'll forgive you," I assured him, but he remained frozen before me, the only sign of his desire the burning light in his lightning blue eyes.

So, I took matters into my own shaky hands. I stepped closer until his arousal pressed into my belly. On my tiptoes, I planted an open-mouthed kiss on his fragrant neck, sucking lightly at the skin before scraping my teeth across it. His entire body tightened with need, and I smiled against his throat, emboldened by his reaction. Slowly, I worked my fingers against the buttons of his shirt, popping them open so that his torso was bared to me. My hands slid down his smooth stomach, trailing the deep V leading to my final destination. He sucked in a sharp breath when my fingers wrapped firmly around his fabric-covered erection. He was long and thick in my hand, and I wondered how he would react if I dropped to my knees to take him in my mouth again. Just remembering how he had tasted made heat unfurl deep in my belly. I squeezed him harder, and he groaned.

I squeaked when he moved suddenly, plucking me from the ground. Automatically, I wrapped my legs around his waist, and his hand cupped my bottom. He tilted my head in order to plunder my mouth with long, bold strokes of his tongue. His teeth gently nipped my bottom lip, but his tongue soothed over the small pain before I could register it.

He carried us to the bedroom and placed me on the edge of the bed. I watched from under my lashes as he crouched before me in order to slip off my shoes. His eyes found mine as he cradled my foot and ran his teeth along my instep, then placed a kiss below my ankle. I shivered and tried to reach for him, desperate to have him on me, in me, any part of him, but most specifically, the appendage straining violently against his gray trousers.

He tugged my hand so that I was standing and then turned me to face away from him. His fingers found the center zipper of my dress and slowly tugged it down. The sound of yielding fabric had never been so erotic, and when his tongue lightly traced the path of the parting dress, I sighed in warm arousal. Only when the dress pooled at my feet did he press himself against my back. His erection rested against the crest of my bottom, and I wiggled back against him. He nipped at my earlobe as a warning. This was his seduction, and with only a moment of hesitation, I yielded to his direction. When I became pliant against him, he growled his appreciation, and his hands trailed up my stomach to cup my breasts through my bra.

"You have amazing breasts." His voice was hot against my neck, and I dropped my head against his chest to give him full access to them. "You would blush if you knew all the things I wanted to do to these."

I did flush as one hand deftly undid my bra, and I shrugged my shoulders so that it slid down my arms. His warm palms against my bare flesh seared my delicate skin and made me gasp. His fingers circled my nipples, so close but not touching. I arched into his palms, but he only chuckled darkly. "You seem so quiet and prim, but I knew the moment I had you naked under my hands, you would come to life. My siren."

His fingers finally found my nipples and pinched firmly. I moaned and pressed my bum hard against his arousal. Too soon, his palms left me, trailing down my hips to grab the sides of my underwear. He pulled them down slowly, descending to his knees as he did so. I felt naked and vulnerable, faced away from him as I was. I could feel his eyes on my bare posterior, and the unadventurous Giselle protested.

"Bend over and place your forearms on the mattress." Sinclair's voice was hypnotic, and I swayed under his persuasion, his sinuous tone banishing my bashfulness.

I did as he asked without hesitation even though I was now open to him. Oddly, it didn't feel clinical or even embarrassing. It was sexy to present myself to his gaze, and I knew by the way his breath hitched that he was impacted by the display. One finger reached out and ran lightly from the top of my buttocks down to my wet sex. I shuddered at the forbidden sensation.

"You look gorgeous like this," he mumbled slightly as he leaned close to me. "Pink and wet and open for me. This is what you need."

I groaned my agreement and wiggled my backside slightly, encouraging him to explore further. His gentle laughter, more an exhalation than anything, fanned across my aching core before he pressed a chaste kiss to my right cheek. His hands caressed the round orbs firmly and moved down my thighs to lightly skim the backs of my knees. My legs shook and almost failed me.

He continued to plant open-mouthed kisses down the inside

of my thighs, closer and closer to my dripping core. I whimpered as he sucked on the tender skin beside the apex of my thighs.

"Sinclair." My voice was breathless, needy, and I barely recognized myself. "Please."

"Please what?" Cool air blew gently against my overheating sex, and I pushed my bottom backward, shamelessly hoping to connect with his mouth.

"Touch me." I knew what he wanted. He was pushing me to voice my desires, to explicitly describe my needs. It was terrifying and exhilarating at the same time to hear my voice beg him for contact. "Please, put your mouth on me."

"Good girl." The smile in his voice and the bold sweep of his tongue against my core soon overtook my excitement at pleasing him.

I cried out loudly, and my legs shook as he pushed two fingers inside me and began pumping them slowly in and out. One hand found my lower back and pushed it down so that I was arched up, even more exposed, my legs farther apart to balance. His lips found my clit and gently sucked.

I yelled into the duvet as my climax bloomed, building and building until I thought I would die.

"Sinclair, stop, it's, I ..." I said incoherently, but he ignored me, his fingers moving faster now as he added a third.

The blankets were clenched tight in my damp fists, and I bit into my thumb as the pleasure spiraled higher, and my womb clenched almost painfully with pleasure. I had never experienced anything so blinding, so beyond normal sense, and I was almost afraid to let go and dive into the deep well of bliss his fingers coaxed me toward.

"Come for me." His voice was tight with control. "Come for me now, Elle."

His demand pushed me over the edge, and as I went tumbling into the darkness, his voice kept me anchored to reality. The orgasm overwhelmed me, my legs shaking, sex convulsing, and it took all my strength just to stay conscious through the powerful onslaught.

"Are you okay?" he asked between gritted teeth as he stood behind me. His arousal brushed against my buttock, hard and pulsing, and I realized at some point while I recovered, he'd shed the rest of his clothes.

I was exhausted, but the feel of him against me spurred me on. "No, I need you. Inside me."

Anxiously, I waited as he recovered a condom from his discarded trousers. He groaned as he took my hips between his palms and brought himself to my drenched entrance. I gasped when he pressed forward slightly and moved his hips gently, just kissing the inside of my sex. Passion reignited violently in my belly, and I tried to push back against him, but his strong hands held me firmly. He planted a kiss on the middle of my back before placing his hand there, gently pressing me down once more so that my rump was raised in invitation. I tightened on the tip of him embedded in my core, causing his fingers to twitch on my hips.

"I want to feel you inside me," I almost whispered, embarrassed by my bold desires but too stimulated to ignore them.

His fingers tightened an instant before he thrust inside me, wrenching an animalistic moan from him and a cry of pleasure from me. He was so large inside me that, at first, despite my wetness, there was an uncomfortable stretch. I winced slightly, hoping that he wouldn't notice. He paused, and I held my breath until he began to slowly pull out. My breathy sigh must have satisfied him because he moved forward again. His strokes were slow and sure at first, pulling almost all the way out before thrusting inside my aching depths. The pain was gone, drowned in a tidal wave of pleasure as wave after wave of sensation coursed through my blood.

"You feel incredible," he rasped as he leaned over my back to play with my hanging breasts. His fingers rolled my taut nipples until I was breathless with pleasure.

"Come for me like this," he ordered, pressing an open-mouthed kiss to my damp shoulder. "With me deep inside you."

One hand dropped from my breast and unerringly found the sensitive nub at the top of my sex. His fingers circled it, mirroring the ministrations of his other hand on my right nipple. The tremors began at my core and vibrated through my entire body as my orgasm took me. I crested the wave on a broken cry, and my sex clenched tightly around Sinclair inside me, milking him until he groaned and climaxed too. I could feel the kick of his dick as he climaxed, and it drew out my orgasm. Minutes later, I was still panting and shaking slightly when we had both collapsed to the bed in exhaustion.

Sinclair rolled over, propping himself on his rippling arm to look down at me as I recovered. He was covered in a thin sheen of sweat that made him glow golden in the low yellow lights. "Please tell me you aren't a virgin, Elle."

It would have been too good to be true if he hadn't noticed.

I considered how to respond, fingering the white duvet as if I wasn't concerned with our conversation or my very exposed position.

"Not anymore."

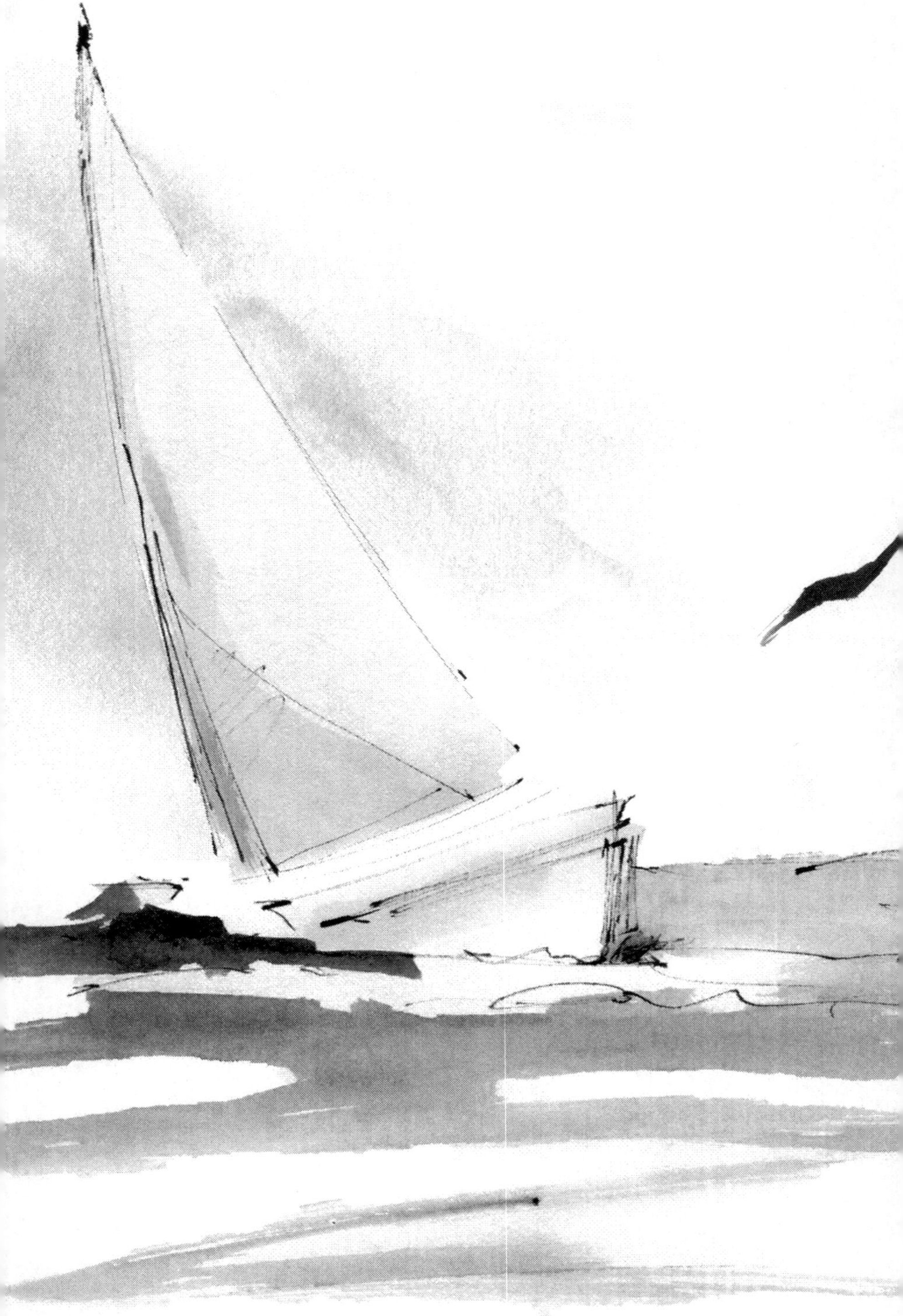

Chapter Seven

He cursed under his breath again and was silent for a few minutes. He flopped to the bed beside me and dragged an arm over his forehead as he stared at the ceiling. Tears pricked the backs of my eyes, but I reminded myself that I had wanted this. I had been completely naïve my entire life, and I didn't want to arrive in New York as the same meek girl I had been when I left to go to Paris years before.

"You should have told me," he said, not accusing but firm, as if he was scolding a wayward puppy.

"I thought this was supposed to be just physical."

I propped my head in my hands in order to look at him. He didn't sound very angry, and I was inordinately glad about it. I was still flushed and joyful from our lovemaking, and I wasn't ready to argue yet.

"An affair is an intimate thing, Elle. I didn't propose one night of sex with a stranger. As I told you on the plane, I've never been so drawn to a person in my life. I'm not interested in having sex with a stranger; I want to be with you. And that includes knowing pertinent information about you, like the state of your virginity."

I nodded. "I'm sorry. I realize it was deceitful of me."

His brow furrowed, and I somehow resisted the urge to smooth it with my fingers.

"I don't know if it would have changed anything," he admitted softly.

Joy unfurled in my chest, and I smiled at him prettily. "It doesn't have to change anything now. I quite liked it."

He lifted his head to raise a cool eyebrow at my attitude, but I only grinned at him.

"You quite liked it?" he repeated in a deceptively reserved voice.

I giggled as he leaned once more on his elbow to look at me. "Well, yes. Didn't you?"

He shook his head at me and ran his other hand through the tumbled mass of chestnut hair falling around his ears. "I more than liked it. Despite myself, I'm already thinking about all the other ways I can have you."

I noticed his frown, and this time, I didn't quell the urge to iron it away with my touch. He allowed me to touch him, though he tensed under the caress and grabbed my hand.

"I may have been a virgin, Sinclair, but I wasn't completely inexperienced. I have had a boyfriend before, and we did do things." It was not pleasant to think about my sexual encounters before Mark, but I wanted him to know. "And before that, I did things with a man. Things I'm not really proud of and would prefer not to talk about, but I just want you to know. I'm not pure or anything."

Sinclair rolled over me. Bracing his weight on his knees, he straddled my legs and bracketed my face with his forearms. His gaze was somber, but one hand played almost absently with a strand of my hair.

"Not pure? Regardless of whatever happened before and heedless of your conventional virginity, I noticed your purity right away." He pressed a finger to my lips when I tried to protest. "I don't mean you seemed young to me or naïve. I mean that there is a grace, a serenity to you that speaks of purity. It has nothing to do with sexuality." His grin was self-deprecating. "Though obviously, I noticed that too."

"You are just being nice." I squirmed beneath him, uncomfortable with his compliment.

"I don't have time to be nice," he reminded me curtly, but his eyes were dancing as I looked into them. When I smiled back, he sighed happily. "There. You are mine for five more days, Elle, and I fully expect you to smile and graciously receive my flattery whenever I desire it. Understood?"

I laughed. "Yes, sir."

His eyes darkened suddenly, and I felt him twitch against my thigh. "Are you sore?"

I mentally checked my erogenous zones for discomfort, but other than a slightly swollen, pleasantly achy sex, I felt fine, extraordinary even. "No."

I slid my arm around his neck, aware for the first time that he was naked in my arms. My fingers boldly explored the play of muscles in his back, my nails scratched lightly down his sides so that he hissed, and when I brought them between us to run my hand down his beautifully defined torso, he hummed with pleasure.

I squealed as he wrapped his arms around me and flipped over onto his back so that I straddled him. I blinked down at him a few times as he smiled and placed his arms behind his head.

"You wanted to explore," he reminded me. "Feel free."

I bit my lip, and he frowned, his voice hardening. "Do not be shy with me, Elle. We have six days together, and I assure you, this will be the tamest of those nights. There are so many things I want to do with you, for you, to you." His hand reached up and cupped my full breasts, his thumbs flicking my distended nipples.

Emboldened by his words, I leaned over and softly kissed the hollow at the base of his throat. I readjusted my position over him so that I could reach one of his small brown nipples with my lips. Sucking it into my mouth, I gently ran my teeth over it and was rewarded with his hands sliding into my hair, urging me on. As I trailed sweet kisses down his chest—my nails raking his skin harder now so that his breath came in pants—I realized how powerful sex could be. There was nothing in my world but Sinclair's body laid out like a dusky-skinned Adonis for me to worship.

My lips found his jutting erection, and I mirrored my other chaste kisses by my softly pursed mouth to the flared crown. A bead of moisture rested there, and as Sinclair looked down at me with fevered eyes, I deliberately licked the salty-sweet substance, smacking my lips as I hummed my approval. His hands tightened in my hair, but the mild pain only heightened the experience. I was his, to do with as he pleased, and the idea aroused me further. I moaned around him as I took his length past my lips and deep into the back of my mouth. His taste was intoxicating, tempting me to reach one of my hands down to play with my soaking sex, but I was too dedicated to his pleasure to do so. Instead, I wrapped one hand around the base of him, squeezing firmly each time my lips descended to my grip, and with the other, I cupped his soft sack drawn up with desire.

"Make me come this way," he said through his teeth.

I murmured my consent as I took him from my warm mouth to run my tongue along the length of him, wondering at his size and loving his girth. I hesitated at the root and wondered if he would like his balls touched in the same way. At the first tentative brush of my tongue, his muscles contracted, and when I rolled one in my mouth cautiously, his groan reverberated through my core.

"Yes," he hissed, and he tugged on my hair almost painfully, causing me to moan too.

I could feel my wetness trail down my leg, but I was so focused on Sinclair that I barely registered my own needs. His release would be better than my own.

Suddenly desperate for the taste of him spilling into my mouth, I took him swiftly to the back of my throat, relaxing so that I wouldn't gag as he began to pump back and forth in my mouth. I relaxed my jaw, flicking my tongue over his tip whenever he retreated and waited breathlessly for my reward. I could feel his climax the moment it shuddered through his body. The muscles in his legs and stomach grew taut, and his fingers twitched before clenching tightly in my hair. A feral groan ripped from his chest as he spent himself across my tongue. I quickly lapped up his release, surprised by how much I enjoyed it.

He lay exhausted as I straightened from my slightly uncomfortable position, but his arms tightened around me, and he brought me to his chest to press a kiss into my hair.

"You are magnificent," he murmured, and I wondered if I imagined the reverence in his words.

I closed my eyes and absorbed his praise. We lay silently for a time, and I wondered if he had perhaps fallen asleep. *Maybe I should leave*, I thought with sudden anxiety. This was a holiday affair; he wouldn't want to spend the night with me. I chewed the inside of my cheek as I considered my options, but his sleep-roughened voice interrupted my reverie.

"What are you thinking about so loudly?"

I sighed, deciding to tell him the truth. "I was wondering if I should leave now."

Instantly, his corded arms tightened like a vise around me, but his voice was casual as he said, "If you'd like."

My heart dropped into my stomach, but I nodded against my chest and tried to push from his embrace. "No problem."

"But," he continued mildly, and when I looked down at him, his eyes were still closed, "I would prefer it if you stayed."

Relief flooded me, reheating every place that he had spent the night coaxing to life inside me. My hand splayed across his chest, burrowing in his sparse chest hair. I could feel the calming beat of his heart against my palm.

"I'd like that too," I whispered, looking down at the most handsome man in the world.

His thick, dark eyelashes rested on his sharp cheeks, casting long shadows over his dusky gold skin. He wasn't too tanned yet, but there was a depth to the color of his skin that suggested his forefathers had been something other than white, and his hair was a richer shade of mahogany than I had ever seen. My throat ached from his beauty.

His eyes fluttered open, and I froze under his brilliant gaze. "What are you looking at?"

"You," I said simply. "I love the way you look."

His smile moved slowly across his face, tilting his firm lips and creasing the corners of his eyes with crow's feet. "Let me take you on an adventure tomorrow."

I laughed at his abrupt change of subject and the boyish glee in his eyes. "An adventure?"

"Yes."

"What kind of an adventure?"

"One that is a surprise."

I looked down at him with wide eyes, delighted by his carefree mood. "And if I don't like surprises?"

His shrug dislodged me slightly from the side of his body, and he was quick to tuck me back into his arm, pressing my head gently against his chest once more. "You'll like this one."

I didn't doubt it, and as an unattractive yawn completely

distorted my features, I wondered sleepily if it was possible for me to dislike anything about this man.

"Sleep," he encouraged, a hand smoothing over my hair. "I'll wake you up in the morning when it's time to go."

I snuggled closer to him and wondered if I had ever been happier. It was silly, I knew, to think such things when I only had another six days with him, but it was hard to ground myself in reality when Sinclair could show me such wicked fantasies. As sleep descended, I remembered the girlfriend waiting at home for him, and my heart jerked uncomfortably. It didn't matter if I was emotionally battered at the end of the affair. I would let him go back to his partner, and I would move to New York with no regrets. But even as dreams began to flicker behind my closed lids, I knew that wouldn't be the case.

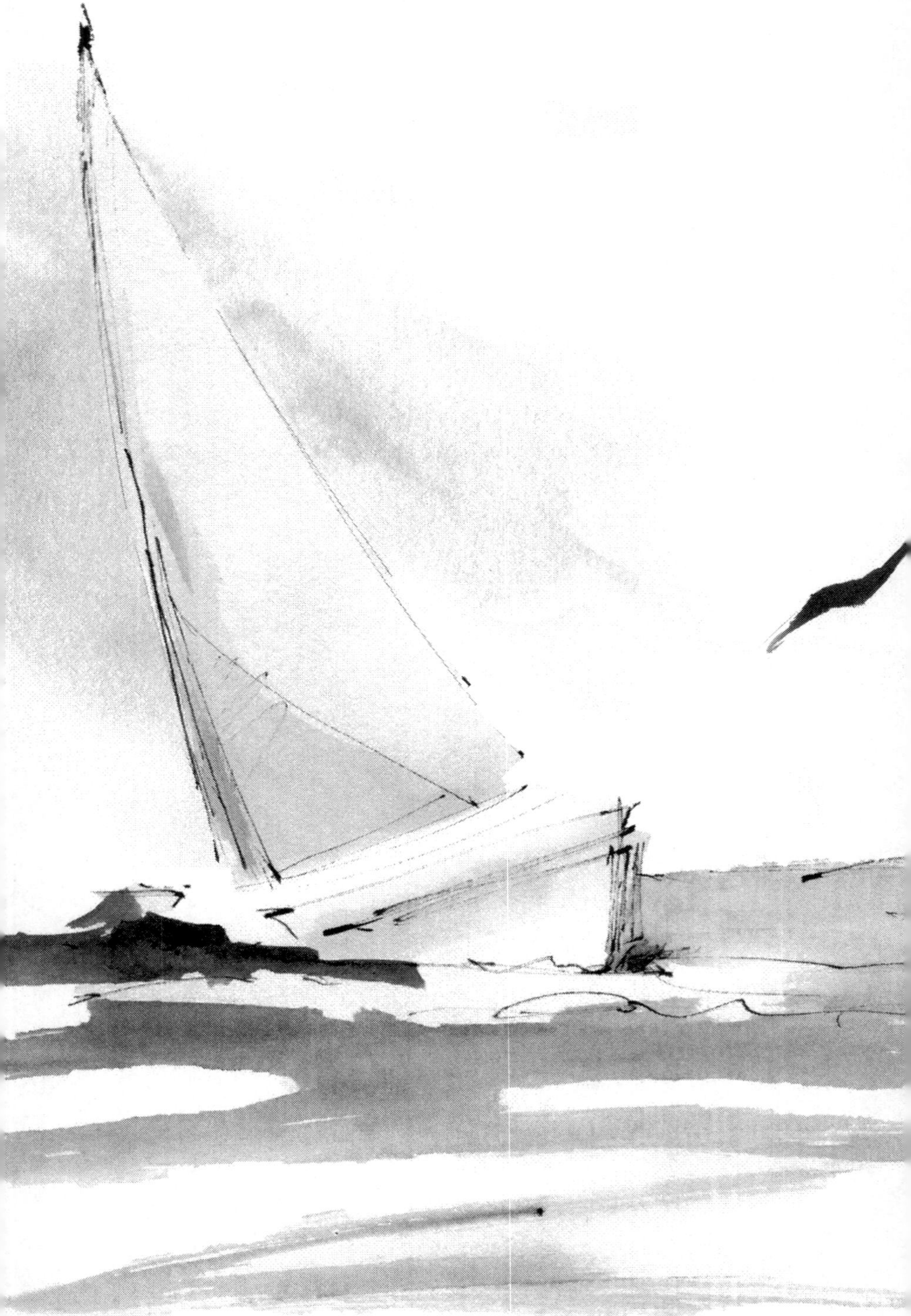

Chapter Eight

I woke up slowly, stretching my arms over my head and twisting my hips to work the kinks out of my lower body as I groaned into awareness. Without opening my eyes, I smiled because I knew what had awakened me.

"Hi," I said softly.

Rough tipped fingers traced the side of my face, and when I opened my eyes, Sinclair was looking down at me. "Elle, are you ready for our adventure?"

I smiled, gazing at him from under my lashes, and gently pushed the duvet back in order to expose my breasts, which instantly drew tight in the cool air. "I had a different adventure in mind."

He shook his head, and his voice was almost sad when he

replied, but I could tell he was pleased with me too. "I've unleashed a monster."

I pouted playfully. "That doesn't sound very flattering."

"A siren, then."

He sat on the edge of the bed, already fully dressed in a thickly knit, light blue sweater that complemented his eyes and white linen shorts. His overlong hair was still damp from the shower, and his rich and manly fragrance drifted over me.

My mouth watered, just looking at him. Though I was slightly sore, my sex clenched at the thought of being with him again. And again.

His eyes sparked on the fire in my gaze, but he only shook his head again and moved off the bed, walking away into the bathroom. "We have to leave in twenty minutes. You're welcome to have a shower here, and we can swing by your room on our way out."

As much as the idea of a shower in his room, preferably with him, appealed to me, it made more sense for me to return to my room to shower and change. When I told him so, he nodded and patted my bottom as I walked past him to dress.

"Meet me in the lobby in fifteen. Wear something comfortable," he ordered over his shoulder before leaving the bedroom.

I walked back to my room in a state of hyper-awareness as if my happiness magnified my senses. My bare feet kissed the cool marble floor of the lobby, and the soft skirt of my dress swished over my tingling thighs. Despite my lack of sleep, I was awake and eager for more.

Sinclair consumed my thoughts as I peeled off my party clothes and stepped into the shower. The hot water stung the sensitive skin between my legs, but the pounding spray massaged my aching muscles.

I was amazed by the way he had undressed my conservatism and laid bare the heart of my sexuality. With Mark, I had been awkward and bumbling under his sweetness, and it was a revelation to have someone so confident and experienced drive the action. I thought about the way he had ordered me to bend over and commanded me to orgasm. I shuddered at the memory as I lathered my hair with my honey-scented shampoo. His cool words echoed in my head, and a resulting tightness in my gut confirmed my attraction to his controlling nature.

I was also grateful for his reaction to my virginity. Really, I had been sexually active for years, and it had felt wrong to misled Sinclair by labeling me a novice. But I was also loath to validate those sexual experiences, the hands and face and acts of a man who had used me for years. I closed my eyes and pressed my forehead against the tiles, letting the water sluice down my head and back. Was it foolish to believe that Sinclair could erase those memories? I could still feel his hands on my skin, so it was easy to believe in their potential power to eradicate all touches before them.

Regardless, I had five more days with the man, and ignoring the shadow of foresight at the corner of my bliss, I vowed to enjoy every moment of it.

When I arrived in the lobby ten minutes later, Sinclair was frowning at the screen of his Blackberry. I stopped for a minute to study him, the way his gleaming chestnut hair fell over his forehead and the deliciously narrow set of his hips.

He looked up suddenly, straightening to his full height as if he was a hunter that had just scented his prey. The look that sparked in his blue eyes was just as feral, triumphant. If I could have torn my eyes away from the sight of him, I would have checked to make sure no one was staring. As he stalked toward me, I could feel my heartbeat kick up, and the absurd desire to flee seized me.

"Hi," I breathed when he came to a stop just before me. I had to tilt my head to continue looking into his vivid gaze, the only windows into his otherwise inscrutable expression.

"Hello, yourself." One of his fingers smoothed down my neck, tickling the heavy beat of my pulse there. "Nervous?"

My laugh was unusually shrill, but I rolled my shoulders and forced myself to relax. This man had just been inside me; why the hell was I behaving like an awkward stranger?

Sinclair's eyes narrowed, and his fingers threaded through my hair, tugging until my head was forced back and he towered over me. "Tell me what is going on behind those grays, Elle, or I'll take you over my knee, and we can forget all about the surprise adventure."

A shiver of excitement raced up my spine, and I bit my lip at the thought of being spread over his lap, exposed like I had been last night. He must have felt the shudder, and his brows rose in silent question, but I shook my head.

"I don't know why, but I feel shy around you this morning," I said.

His head tilted as he studied me, his fingers now firmly massaging my scalp. Each stroke of his fingers released one of the knots of tension pinching my shoulders together.

"We are no longer strangers, but we aren't lovers yet, not after one night. Normally, this might be awkward, but not for us, not when I own you." He marked the downward quirk of my mouth and responded with a sharp tug on the roots of my hair. "You are embarrassed because you liked being taken by a stranger and ordered to come."

I shifted restlessly on my sandaled feet as liquid desire pooled between my legs.

A slight smirk tilted his lips as he leaned forward to speak against my lips. "Are you wet now, Elle? Just from hearing my voice?"

I groaned, unwilling to admit the power he held over me.

A couple passed by us, talking happily as they dragged their suitcases into the lobby. The man, a short, older gentleman with a thick helmet of gray hair, turned to us sharply, and his nostrils flared as if he could smell me. Sinclair turned his head slightly to stare at him and used his free hand to tug my bottom until I was pressed against him. The gray-haired stranger smiled and winked at me before patting his own partner's bum affectionately.

When he was gone, I tried to push Sinclair away. "I can't believe you just did that."

His grip was firm, and the lines of his body against mine were made of steel. I wanted to rub up against him like a cat, scratch him and nuzzle him until he stroked me.

Somehow, he read my thoughts. "I can do whatever I want to you. The night you agreed to our holiday affair, you knowingly entered into my world."

I briefly remembered his words, *"You belong to me for the next six days,"* and my anxiety upped another notch.

I licked my parched lips. "That doesn't sound very fair."

"No," he mused. "It isn't. No mortal man should hold a siren in his arms, but you've given me the opportunity of a lifetime."

My heart tapped a quick dance against my rib cage, delighted and surprised by his poetry, but as I watched his eyes darken, the beat moved lower, pulsing now in my belly.

"I want to push you, Elle, see how far I can take you. By day seven, you'll be begging for me to take you in ways you can't even imagine now."

I gasped as my mind raced with possibilities. I was so preoccupied that I almost stumbled when he suddenly pulled away from me. He frowned at me, catching my hand and winding it around his arm.

"Sore?" he asked, and though there was no hint of emotion in his beautiful profile, he sounded a little amused, maybe even smug.

I blushed and tried to take my hand from him. "Not a bit."

Unable to even wriggle under his strong fingers, I sighed and allowed him to pull me outside the main doors to the front of the resort. The same long black car from the night before idled in front of us. Sinclair opened the door for me to slip in so that I faced him, backward to the momentum of the car. He was quiet for the duration of the drive, his eyes on the glowing screen of his phone as he read emails and conducted business, but I was glad for the reprieve.

I rested my head against the plush seat and stared out at the blurring colors of Los Cabos slipping by. My camera was strapped across my body, and without hesitation, I swung it into my hands to snap the abstract smear of Mexican scenery.

We stopped at a light beside a bus station where a young woman, only a few years younger than me, slouched against a pole, a soft roll of brown belly exposed by her small white shirt and tight blue jeans. Her skin was dewy with sweat, and her slightly unkempt hair stuck to the dampness between her breasts. She stared at me insolently with large eyes the color of molasses, and when I raised my camera to capture her strangely erotic sloth, her pale tongue poked out and caught a bead of sweat from the downy hairs of her top lip. My shutter clicked, and my heart palpitated with triumph as the car pulled into the traffic a second later. I recalled the photograph to the screen of my Canon and found exactly that moment of lazy sex, her belly exposed, sweaty breasts plumped up.

I wasn't sure if I would have normally found sexiness in the image, in the girl, but the darker recesses of my mind were cracking open. I wondered how many kinds of sultry there were, how many types of sex and fantasy.

I peeked up at Sinclair with my tongue unconsciously mimicking the slow lick the Mexican girl had stroked against her top lip. He was staring at me, his head still slightly bent to view his phone as if he had become entranced by something after briefly glancing up at me.

The electric heat in his eyes shocked something within me, and without really thinking about it, I scooted lower in my seat, spreading my thighs wider as I did so. It was cool in the car, but I could suddenly feel the Mexican heat press heavily against my body, warming my breasts until they ached and slowing my heart rate until it thumped lazily, only strong enough to pump languid arousal through my veins.

I stared at Sinclair from beneath lowered lids, my tongue caught between my teeth as my hand found my breasts and squeezed, stoking the fire there. He was completely still. I pressed on, following my own pleasure. My palms slicked down my smooth thighs and slowly pulled my legs farther apart until I was bared to him. Slipping off my flip-flops, I planted my feet on either side of him, my toes curling over the cool leather to steady myself. His Adam's apple bobbed as he swallowed, and I smiled slightly, my fingers lightly dancing over the ticklish skin of my inner thighs.

It was so unlike me to explore myself like this, even in the privacy of my own bed under the cloak of night, but Sinclair made me feel wanton, just as damp, and obviously as sexual as the woman at the bus stop.

I groaned when my hands finally found the edge of my swimsuit and slipped inside. I wanted to tell him how wet I was, but my voice was stuck somewhere around my toes, and I didn't want to push myself too far. Desperate for his involvement somehow, I pried my eyes open and looked up at him.

He was staring between my legs with burning eyes, but almost immediately, his gaze found mine and rapidly read what I had written there. His eyelids lowered, and his voice was rough with longing, so potent it arrowed desire straight to the wet place my fingers played over.

"Feel how wet you are, how ready you are to have my cock inside you. Circle yourself with your thumb, place two fingers at your entrance, and pretend they're my cock, pressing against you."

I struggled to keep my eyes open, but I wanted to look at him as I did this, as I touched myself for him.

"You look so sexy playing with yourself. I could watch you all day," he said.

I groaned, increasing the pressure of my fingers across the slick folds of my sex.

I could see the long, mouthwatering length of him press against his shorts and I imagined crawling between his knees to take it out, the feeling of him in my hands, against the roof of my mouth as I took him to the back of my throat. I shuddered.

"That's it." His voice was so deep it reverberated throughout my body, strumming me until I vibrated. "Push those fingers into your sweet pussy for me. Feel how tight you."

I could hear myself, the wet suck of my fingers plunging inside my aching core, but it only drove my pleasure higher.

"Do you think you can come like this, Elle? With only your fingers and the sound of my voice?"

I whimpered and finally closed my eyes against the growing pressure in my groin, but the snap of his words sliced across my flesh with the force of a whip. "Open your eyes." His firm lips moved sensuously, deliberately over his next words. "I own you. When you come, you will look at me. Add another finger."

The additional finger stretched me wide, reawakening the ache of last night. Now, I really could imagine his thickness inside me, sliding forcefully into my depths over and over again.

"Don't come yet," he said, and when my eyes flashed open in a panic, he hushed me. "You can't come without my permission."

I was desperate for it. My orgasm was so close I could taste it, metallic, at the back of my tongue. My blurry eyes watched as he grabbed himself through his shorts, and I wasn't sure which one of us groaned. Maybe it was both of us.

"Do you want me to take my cock out, Elle?"

I nodded, my head lolled back against the seat. My breath came in short, hard pants, and my chest was tender, heavy with sensation. But Sinclair was not unmoved by my display. His slashing cheeks were taut with control as he spoke through gritted teeth, fighting to keep his cool. I knew he was doing it for me, allowing me to explore, to discover how to pleasure myself, but it cost him.

My breath hitched when he exposed his erection, curved and severe with desire for me. I licked my lips and watched as he wrapped a strong fist around himself and pulled up. A pearl of liquid shimmered at his crown, and already, I knew how it would taste, remembering the unique flavor of him on my tongue.

"I want you in my mouth," I whispered, my dry mouth flooding with saliva as I thought about it.

"I know you do." His lids were heavy. Only thin slits of blue gazed at me. His thick lashes brushed his cheek. "Which would you prefer, Elle? To come on your hands or to have this"—he brandished his cock, his fist pumping it from root to tip and his thumb rolling over the slick head—"in your mouth."

His eyes widened slightly as I shivered, and a small smile warmed his mouth, his question answered. "On your knees."

Inelegantly in my haste, I dropped to my knees in the spacious town car and reached forward, eager for my prize. When he caught my hands in one of his, the other still on his throbbing length, I frowned up at him.

He looked so handsome staring down at me, his bottom lip lush beneath the firm top, his jaw tensed but his eyes sucking and hot with excitement. He was a paradox, my Frenchman, hot and cold, stern but poetic, mine but not mine.

"I don't want you to use your hands. Clasp them behind your back and take me with your mouth. I won't be easy on you. You have no idea what you do to me." His fingers threaded in my hair and slowly pulled my mouth toward him.

I tentatively licked the sensitive underside, and when he hissed, I opened my mouth, sheathing my teeth, and took the flared head of him inside. My tongue traced over his flesh, greedy for the taste of him, the saltiness of his fluid and the musky smell of his arousal. I breathed through my nose as I bore down on him and swallowed rapidly when he pushed through the back of my throat. I almost gagged on my triumph when my nose pressed into his groin, and a primal groan ripped from his lips.

He kept me firmly planted there for only a few seconds, lessening the pressure for my ascent long before I was uncomfortable, and after a brief circle of my tongue over the head, I opened my throat and took him all the way again. And again.

Heady on the pleasure, I could feel my own wetness slide down my thighs, and the orgasm that had receded with the absence of my fingers hovered over me. I knew I only had to press the pad of my thumb delicately to my pulsing clit to come, but I didn't.

Sinclair hadn't said I could.

He swelled in my mouth, and his strong legs tensed. I prepared for his orgasm, tipping my head to allow a deeper angle of penetration even as my eyes sought his face, desperate to see his expression as he spilled into my mouth. But his hands clenched my hair and pulled my face away roughly. His chest heaved as he breathed in and out through his mouth, trying to control his desire. I blinked at him in confusion, but after a moment, when he was under control, he rasped, "Are you very sore?"

I nodded. "I'm aching."

He detected the wantonness in my tone, and suddenly, he was lifting me and easily fit me on top of him with my knees straddling his legs and his pulsating erection at my entrance. His fingers found me drenched with desire, and he let out a long, ragged breath.

"So wet for me." He seemed awed by it, and the smokiness of his voice made me wriggle, rubbing against him. "Stop." His fingers bit into my curved hips, and his eyes bore into mine. "This is going to be quick. For both of us. Put your hands on my shoulders and hold on."

His dark promise thrilled me, and I grabbed his shoulders, clenching his sinewy muscles and the soft fabric of his shirt in my fists. As soon as I latched on, he breathed deeply like a warrior before a battle and thrust into me. I screamed, my head falling back on my shoulders, but he was already lifting me to slam back inside. He was so big that I couldn't take all of him. The size of him inside me ached as it was, but it was a delicious pain, and I began to throw my hips down as he manipulated me over his rigid length. I was moaning, babbling incoherently, so lost in the pleasure I momentarily forgot where I was.

His thumb shifted and found my needy clit, gently brushing it with the pad. My orgasm lay before me, and I was greedy for it, gagging for it, but he hadn't said the words, and after a few more battering thrusts, I was worried he wouldn't.

"Do you want to come, Elle?" His voice was somehow still cool and controlled, only slightly cracking through with desire.

I grated my hips against him, taking another inch, and heard him gasp with pleasure. "Please, I need it."

"I know you do. I can feel you milking me. Desperate for my cum, aren't you?"

I loved listening to his cultured voice speak such dirty words, they made me wetter somehow, and the next time he plunged into me, it was to the hilt.

"Oh God, please, please, please," I begged, quaking with the need to release.

"Yes," he hissed. His hands raced up my torso, holding my plump breasts between his hot palms and scraping both callused thumbs across my puckered nipples. "I am your god. Come hard for me. Now."

I shattered. Currents of pleasure raced over my body, undoing my particles and liquefying my bones. I was vaguely aware of Sinclair's bark of triumph, like a rutting animal, and the sound intensified my pleasure. The heat of him releasing inside me tipped me further over the edge so that I clawed at him with both hands and leaned forward to bite his shoulder. He shuddered at the contact and twitched inside me even after he had finished.

I lay exhausted on top of him for a minute before he lifted me gently off him and placed me on the seat beside him. My eyes were closed, but I could hear him fiddle with something in the side door, and then my lids sprung open when I felt the slightly abrasive cloth against my sloppy sex. He concentrated on his cleanup, a furrow marring his habitually smooth forehead. I reached up to touch it, and he flinched.

"What's wrong?" I asked, too fatigued to feel embarrassed by his sudden aloofness.

He shook his head, the reddish hairs at the back of his neck sticking there. "I shouldn't have lost control like that. You must have been in pain."

I snorted and shrugged when he stared at me with a cool raised brow. "I was overwhelmed with pleasure. When I'm with you, I, well, I feel electric, like there is a pulse between us."

He nodded curtly as if he understood. When he finished his gentle cleaning, he closed my legs and disposed of the damp napkin in the door garbage.

"I came inside you." A thrill punched me in the stomach, and I placed a hand there, shocked by my reaction. "And you obviously aren't on birth control." He shook his head, and a muscle in his jaw clenched. "There is a pharmacy near the resort. I'll get you something on the way back."

"I am," I whispered, suddenly embarrassed. "To regulate my, um, periods."

"Good." He nodded curtly. "I am tested regularly, and I assume you are clean, but that won't happen again."

My lips pursed, but I nodded, unable to speak past the constriction in my throat. It was stupid of me to be so emotional, but I was wrung out, physically and mentally, by the lack of sleep and the whirlwind nature of being with Sinclair. I closed my eyes and sighed.

"Hey." His hand was on my chin, turning it to look me in the eye. "You should know, I've never seen anything sexier than you touching yourself like that for me, except maybe the sight of you on your knees or the excitement in your eyes as you took me in your sweet mouth."

It was hardly romantic, but his words ignited joy deep within my chest. I was proud, so proud of having pleased him and having pleased myself. Despite what my first sexual partner had said, I was capable of doing it right, and the knowledge gave me new life. I beamed at him and watched as he blinked as though he was staring at the noon sun.

"Magnificent," he murmured before shaking his head slightly, his features once again stone cold. "Now, are you ready for the adventure?"

I continued to grin at him. "Hell yes."

His eyes narrowed. "A simple yes would have sufficed."

"Yes, master," I teased and watched as his eyes turned molten. I couldn't believe I had such power over him, and I giggled.

He relaxed; a small grin tucked into the left corner of his cheek. "Siren."

Yes, I thought, leaning back against the seat, allowing my bones to liquefy, *your* siren.

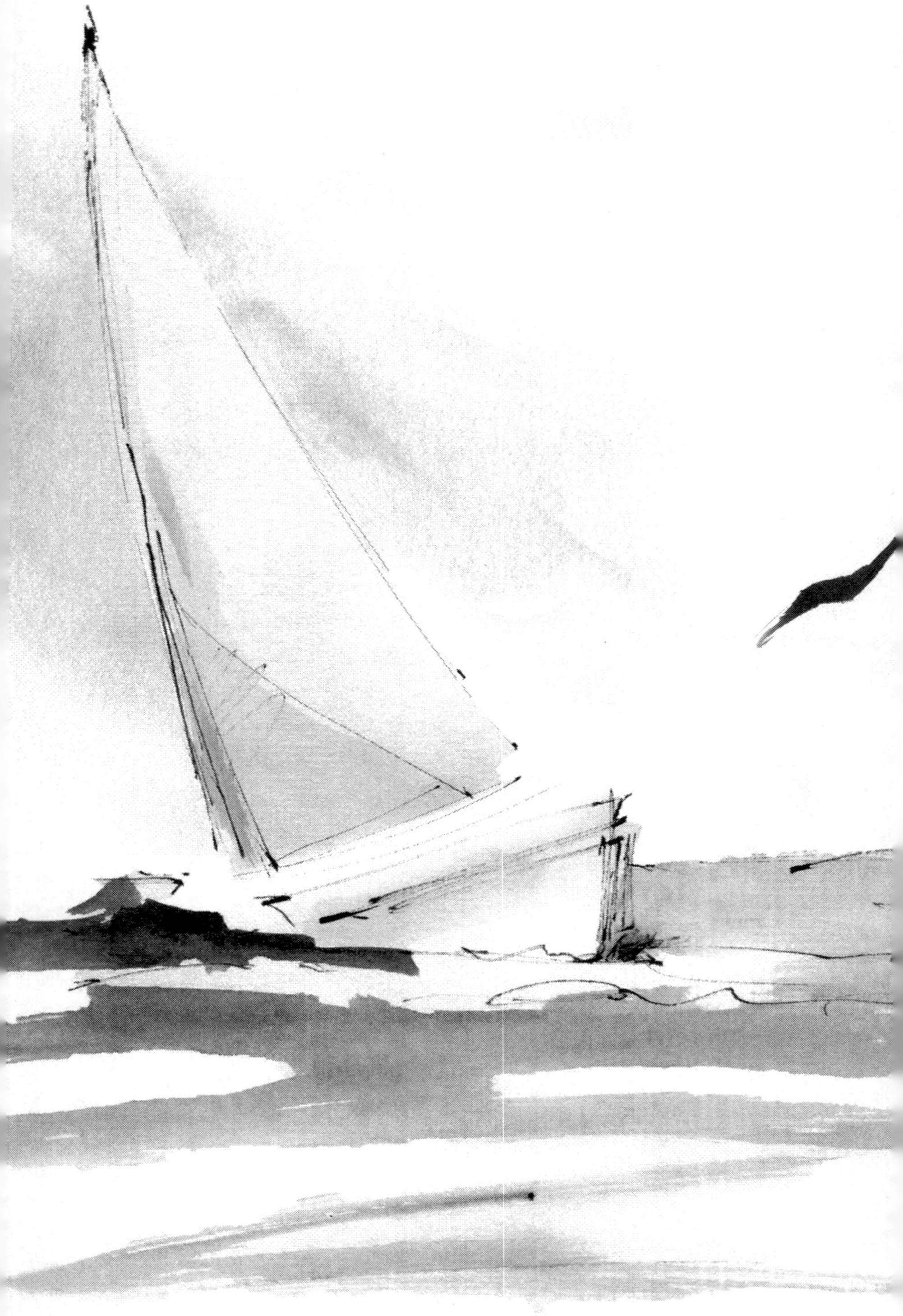

Chapter Nine

I don't know how he did it, but the second we stepped from the car into the Mexican sunshine, Sinclair, the entrepreneur, was back, enigmatic and vaguely disinterested in everything around us. I wondered if that distance would apply to me, but when I hesitantly waited a few feet away from him after the car pulled away, staring at him instead of where he had taken me, he turned to me with warm eyes.

"This is the reason I love Mexico," he said, and I stepped closer to read the excitement in his eyes. They were such a glorious blue that even my artist's vocabulary came up blank and so expressive they almost entirely made up for the blank mask he always wore. I thought of his wild cry as he came in the car, blushed at the thought of the driver hearing us, and then flushed with pleasure.

"Insatiable," he scolded gently, taking my hand and winding it around his arm again.

I gasped as we moved forward. "How did you know what I was thinking?"

He chuckled darkly. "You blush beautifully when you think about sex."

I tried to control my flush and failed, so I tuned out his amusement and absorbed our surroundings.

The Pacific stretched before us; a swathe of silky azure waves topped with broken fragments of golden light. Pelicans crowded around a corner of the busy dock, eager for scraps tossed by the brawny fishermen, competently slicing open the fish being pulled in by wheelbarrows from incoming boats. The mild sea breeze kept the air from reeking of putrid fish guts, and I marveled at the exotic specimens lying on the broad marble tables, their long, silver bodies and sword-like protrusions reminiscent of prehistoric creatures.

Sinclair led me through the fanfare, the intense Spanish repartee and busy dockhands with a sure hand and widened eyes. He was enjoying himself, happy to point out the different types of fish—marlin and wahoo and dorado—all so exotic, like jewels scattered carelessly across the giant slabs.

"They don't waste any of it," he explained, his voice lower than the racket but still excited. "What the tourists or professionals don't take home, the dockhands use to feed their families. Fishing is a serious sport in this part of the country. Most families have made their living from the sea for generations."

We were past the fillet station and out into the open air of the docks, walking swiftly between the boats in search of our own.

"We're going fishing?" I asked, slightly incredulous.

His lips twitched at my lack of enthusiasm. "Trust me, you'll love it."

"I really doubt that," I muttered, but he ignored me.

"I'll tell you what," he said, biting down on the corner of a smile. "Whoever catches the biggest fish dictates what we do tonight."

"Oh okay, I have this couple's package—it's a long story—but a massage might be ..." I trailed off with a gasp when Sinclair tugged me into his arms and leaned down to delicately trace the edge of my ear with his tongue.

"I had something more intimate in mind."

"Oh." I sighed. "In that case, you're on."

We were still smiling as we finally came to a stop at a boat that was not what I would have called luxurious. It was an oddly shaped powerboat with a blue awning and a small upper deck. The name scrawled across the old but carefully maintained hull was *Rosa,* and despite my reluctance, I laughed.

When Sinclair raised a brow at me, I flapped my hand in the air. "My middle name. It must be a good omen."

He frowned at me, but the arrival of a small, deeply tanned Mexican man distracted him from questioning me further.

"Antonio." Sinclair's mouth trembled as he suppressed a smile, but he did allow himself to reach down and warmly clasp the short man's hand. "*¿Qué tal?*"

"*Bueno, bueno obviamente.*" Antonio responded jovially.

He had enormous eyes that sparkled like onyx as he beamed up at me, his mouth full of crooked but bright white teeth.

"Elle." Sinclair's hand wound around my side and swept down the length of my hourglass curve. "This is my friend, Antonio, the best fisherman in all of Mexico."

Antonio chortled loudly and took my hand in both of his. "Beautiful."

My laugh was more air than sound, and we both blushed happily at each other as I thanked him. He kept my hand, tugging me along like a child as he led us onboard the *Rosa,* and gave me the grand tour of the compact two-story boat. He enthusiastically described the mechanics of the down riggers, the huge weights anchored to both sides of the stern that would drag the fishing lures to the depths of the sea where massive, almost otherworldly fish liked to swim.

Slowly, because I was unsure and deeply interested, I helped Antonio and Sinclair prepare the lines. I even took a brief turn at the wheel, but the stress of keeping the boat straight on the rolling waves had me laughing hysterically, and Antonio soon took over again.

When everything was set, Sinclair ushered me to a low fold-up chair facing the rods and handed me a Dos Equis beer before taking a seat himself. His legs were outstretched, long and partially bare in his long khaki shorts, and I devoured the sight of him like that, spread out and casual like unfolded laundry. I wanted to lie on top of him and drag his masculine scent deep into my lungs.

He stopped chuckling at something Antonio was explaining, and his features collapsed into their usual impartiality when he caught me staring. "Can I help you with something, Elle?"

He was using his coolness to tease me, I thought, but still, I blushed and focused on peeling the label from the green bottle in my hands.

"I just like seeing you relaxed. It's different."

"Relaxed? The only thing I feel around you, siren, is desire." As if to prove his point, his eyes set flame to every inch of my skin, burning me like a witch for the spell I had cast over him.

The thought delighted me.

"I think your passions bring you comfort. Me"—I cleared my throat—"I mean my body, fishing, your business deal with the failing resort. It's like that for me with my art; like having an itch, that constant stimulation, but being too comfortable to scratch it away."

He pursed his lips. "It is certainly an interesting analogy."

I shrugged because I knew I could be clunky with English; it was much easier to wax poetic in French or Italian.

"I see only one problem with that," he continued, looking out at water that matched the same striking shade of blue as his eyes. "You are unlike anything I have ever dealt with before; therefore, there can be no frame of reference, no precedent to compare you to."

I frowned at the beer in my hands. "That doesn't exactly sound like a good thing."

"The unknown; it has stalked mankind since the beginning."

"Are you trying to say I'm stalking you?"

"Is it stalking if the recipient is eager to be followed?"

We stared at each other with barely contained smiles bright in our eyes and wobbly on our lips. Eager questions bubbled in my throat, the pressure building until I was sure my lips would pop open and a stream of embarrassing neediness would erupt.

What were we doing?

Why did I like you so much?

Wouldn't it be great if this was more than a holiday affair?

Happily, Antonio's sudden shout shattered our connection, and the Mexican hastily pulled me to my feet as he dashed by to take the bobbing fishing rod in his hands.

"You take, you take!" he urged, reeling in the line rapidly.

I watched skeptically as he tugged fiercely at the trapped fish. It looked much too strong for me.

"I'll guide you." Sinclair's presence at my back calmed me, and I was instantly obedient, allowing my hands to be manipulated into the proper position on the rod.

The waves undulated under my feet, and it was hard to find purchase on the slippery deck, but I ground the soles of my shoes into the floor and squatted lower.

"Place it just below your belly button and keep the rod tilted up. You want the line tight," he coached. "Brace your feet, pull the rod up and back slightly, and then quickly reel in the slack."

The blunt end of the fishing pole dug painfully into my gut as I struggled to reel in the fish. My right arm was already weak from exhaustion, but adrenaline coursed through my veins. The hard pulse of my heart was the epic soundtrack to my big catch.

"Steady." Sinclair's strong voice grounded me. "Don't pull too hard. You need to play the fish. Coax him closer to the boat with a firm hand."

My mind flashed to his firm hands, bringing me to orgasm the night before, and I slipped slightly when the fish zigzagged to the left. Before I could right myself, he was there, his strong arms cupping my elbows and his steely chest pressed to my back. I leaned back against him, settling my bum against his groin.

"Behave," he ordered quietly as Antonio darted around the deck, preparing to net the fish while trying to drive the boat at the same time. "You wouldn't want to lose this monster fish just because you couldn't keep your focus."

I gritted my teeth. "Says the man who is distracting me."

His warm chuckle ruffled my hair, and he slid it off my sticky neck. "Do you have an elastic?"

"Left pocket," I mumbled as I frantically reeled in the tiring fish. A flash of scales a few meters from the boat thrilled me.

As did Sinclair's gentle hands as they gathered my hair and put it rather adeptly into a high ponytail. "Much better," he murmured against my damp neck, skimming his teeth from my ear down to my collar. "Easy access."

I moaned slightly but narrowed my eyes and wriggled my hips, trying to get away from him. He was so arrogant, thinking that he would win the bet, and I would spend the night sprawled across his bed completely at his mercy. More determined than ever, I pushed him away with a firm thrust of my hips and adopted the position Antonio had taught me.

"Antonio," I called. "Sinclair is a terrible tutor. Would you mind helping me?"

Sinclair's smoky chuckle sounded from somewhere behind

me, but I was glad he was giving me the space I needed to concentrate. It was so easy to become distracted by thoughts of what he could do to my body. The mere sound of his lightly accented voice whispering dirty promises into my ear was enough to...

I shook my head. *Snap out of it!*

"Is a big fish!" Antonio yelled close to my ear as he came up to adjust my grip. "Very big. Maybe the man should take over?"

"No, no, no," I growled, leaning all of my weight back to keep the fish somewhat close to the boat. How long was it going to fight me? "I can do it."

There was condescending amusement in the Mexican fisherman's voice when he said, "Okay, you do it. But this marlin is a very big, very strong fish."

I almost broke into a dance. Sinclair had said marlins were the biggest fish and the hardest to catch. Imagine the things I could make him do to me if I caught one ...

"Concentrate, Elle." As always, Sinclair sensed my thoughts, and his stern voice cut through my fantasies. "This fish could feed Antonio's family for a week."

My tongue peeked out between my lips, gently clamped against my teeth as I concentrated. Antonio's excited voice babbled in my ear as he checked my progress. I was at the stern of the little boat for forty minutes playing the fish, reeling in fast, then pulling back on the rod in an undulating motion exactly like the sea beneath my braced feet. I had never thought of fishing as a sport, but I soon realized just how taxing it was. My arms and legs felt like jelly, and the rod bit painfully into my stomach even as I shifted it around, trying to find a more comfortable position. But it was thrilling too. At one point, the marlin jumped high into the air, flashing its sapphire ridge and sharp nose. My cramped fingers itched for my camera, and I seriously considered giving up, unsure how much my weak body could take.

"Little closer, closer! Steady, steady," Antonio yelled while dangling over the side of the boat with a large net in his hand.

In one sharp jerk, just a twist of his wrist, he snagged the marlin, calling for Sinclair to help him. The rod was super-glued to my aching fingers, and I watched dumbly as the men wrangled the massive fish into the little hull of the boat. Antonio retrieved a small baseball bat-type instrument and hit the fish over the head until it stopped flailing. Despite my revulsion and the intense swell of empathy I felt for the magnificent creature, I watched rapt as they killed it and heaved it into a water cooler built into the boat. It made me uneasy to realize that I had never seen the process involved in killing the food I so easily shoved into my mouth each day.

Sinclair came over to me somewhat cautiously, and I realized that my confusion must have shown on my face. Gently, he unpeeled my fingers from around the rod and set it aside before taking my hands in his. He rubbed each finger, stroking down to the base and back up to the next finger until they tingled pleasantly.

"I'm very impressed with you, Elle." His voice was quiet but intense. "You have remarkable endurance, and not every fisherman can say they caught a 125-pound marlin."

My eyes widened comically. "I did that?"

"You did." He nodded and ducked his head to press a firm kiss to my lips. "I should have known a siren would have mastery over the sea."

His words ignited my previous excitement, and I squealed, jumping into his arms. He hesitated before his hands slid under my bottom to hold me up. I rained kisses over his face then pulled back to beam into his pleasantly surprised face.

"I'm basically a master fisherman now, aren't I?" When he didn't answer quickly enough, I leaned back to call to Antonio. "Aren't I, Antonio?"

His resulting grin was wide and toothy. "You can fish with me anytime, señorita!"

The rest of the trip was glorious. I lay down on the small upper deck in my bathing suit, recovering from my exercise in the sun. At some point, Sinclair came up to check on me and rubbed sunscreen sensuously into my skin. I dozed in and out of sleep, catching tidbits of Sinclair and Antonio's easy Spanish banter. The language was close enough to French and Italian that I could make out the gist of what they were saying, but I was happy just to drift as they chattered excitedly to each other like little boys.

Sinclair yelled with triumph sometime later, rousing me from my sleep, and I smiled. It was a privilege, I think, to see him so unbound from the tight restraints he kept himself in. Out on the sea, he was less reserved, and when he came bounding up the stairs to where I lay, I cracked open one eye to see him crouched before me with a wide, devastating grin.

"Did you catch one?" I asked sleepily.

He nodded, bouncing slightly on the balls of his feet. "I did."

"Is it big?"

His hand reached out to adjust my floppy white hat. "Don't worry, Elle, you'll have what you want tonight."

I closed my eyes and hummed. "Good."

I fell asleep to his soft chuckle.

When we returned to the docks, people waited with ancient wheelbarrows to take our large haul in so that they could be weighed and filleted. First, Sinclair ordered a picture of me with my huge marlin, strung up beside me from a pole where it dwarfed me twice over. A small smile played over his handsome features as I grinned into the camera and laughed with some tourists who peppered me with questions. Thanks to Antonio and Sinclair's sage advice, I was actually able to answer most of them, and when I returned to his side, Sinclair kissed my hair, and I knew he was pleased that I had enjoyed fishing so much.

We stayed to watch them fillet the fish, and I frowned when a large silver fish, a wahoo, I thought, was heaved onto the bloody slab. It was huge, fat and long, and with growing dread, I realized it might be bigger than mine. I twisted my head to look up at Sinclair and gasped when he stared down at me with sparkling eyes.

"You lied to me!" I accused, pointing a finger into his strong chest. "You said I caught the biggest fish."

"No." He shook his head slowly. "I said you would have what you want tonight." He leaned close into my outraged face. "And you will enjoy the things I am going to do to you very much."

I harrumphed and fisted my hands on my hips, but a smile cracked through when Sinclair barked with laughter. His head tipped back, exposing his brown neck to my hungry gaze. He was so beautiful it made something in my chest ache.

We thanked Antonio and gave him most of our spoils, but I was happy when Sinclair held back some marlin to cook up back at the resort. I dozed on his shoulder in the car, exhausted from the combination of sun and fishing, while Sinclair murmured in

Spanish into his phone. He woke me up with a gentle shake when we reached the hotel.

"Hi." I smiled up at him, blinking the drowsiness from my eyes.

He looked down at me with an almost unnerving intensity that caused my heart to pound. "Hi."

We stared at each other for a long minute until I became discombobulated by the brilliant azure of his irises.

"I have business that I have to take care of tonight." His features hardly moved as he spoke, and I clung to the passion in his eyes as my nerves started to set in. "I won't be back until late."

I waited for him to suggest a late-night rendezvous, and when he didn't, I swallowed my disappointment and nodded. "Right. Well, I could use a good night's rest anyway."

He nodded, carefully studying my reaction. When I remained expressionless, he turned away from me. "Good. I'll contact you tomorrow then."

I shivered at the coldness of his words. We had just spent a fantastic day together, and when I thought about the night before, I was instantly alight with desire. Why was he doing this? Had I done something wrong?

Through my confusion, I took a page from his book, tightening my expression and deliberately cooling my words before saying, "I had a very pleasant day. Thank you for allowing me to join you."

I turn to get out of the car, but I looked over my shoulder to see his reaction. My heart shuddered painfully when he only nodded curtly without looking at me and returned his attention to his phone.

The moment I had walked around to the entrance, the car took off. I watched it swerve onto the palm tree-lined drive until it disappeared through the gates. I hadn't felt so alone since I was nineteen, and my twin siblings left the house one after another without a word. Tears pricked the backs of my eyes, and it took me a moment to realize that I held the parcel of marlin that Sinclair had saved for us. I sucked in a deep breath. I hadn't come to Mexico to moon over a man, however handsome and devastating he might have been. I came to relax, to steel myself for the tumult of returning to my family. I didn't care if I saw Sinclair again, I assured myself. And buoyed by my lies, I entered the lobby with my chin tipped into the air like a princess.

"I'd like the kitchen to cook this for me," I said to the concierge. "I'll eat at Arrecifes at eight p.m."

"Excellent, Mrs. Buchanan. Will anyone be joining you?" he asked with a pleasantly bland smile that did nothing to help my mood.

Someone coming in from the beach caught my eye, and I turned to a brief-clad Stefan with a broad smile.

"Stefan," I called, my confidence revived by his appreciative smile. "How would you like to join me for dinner?"

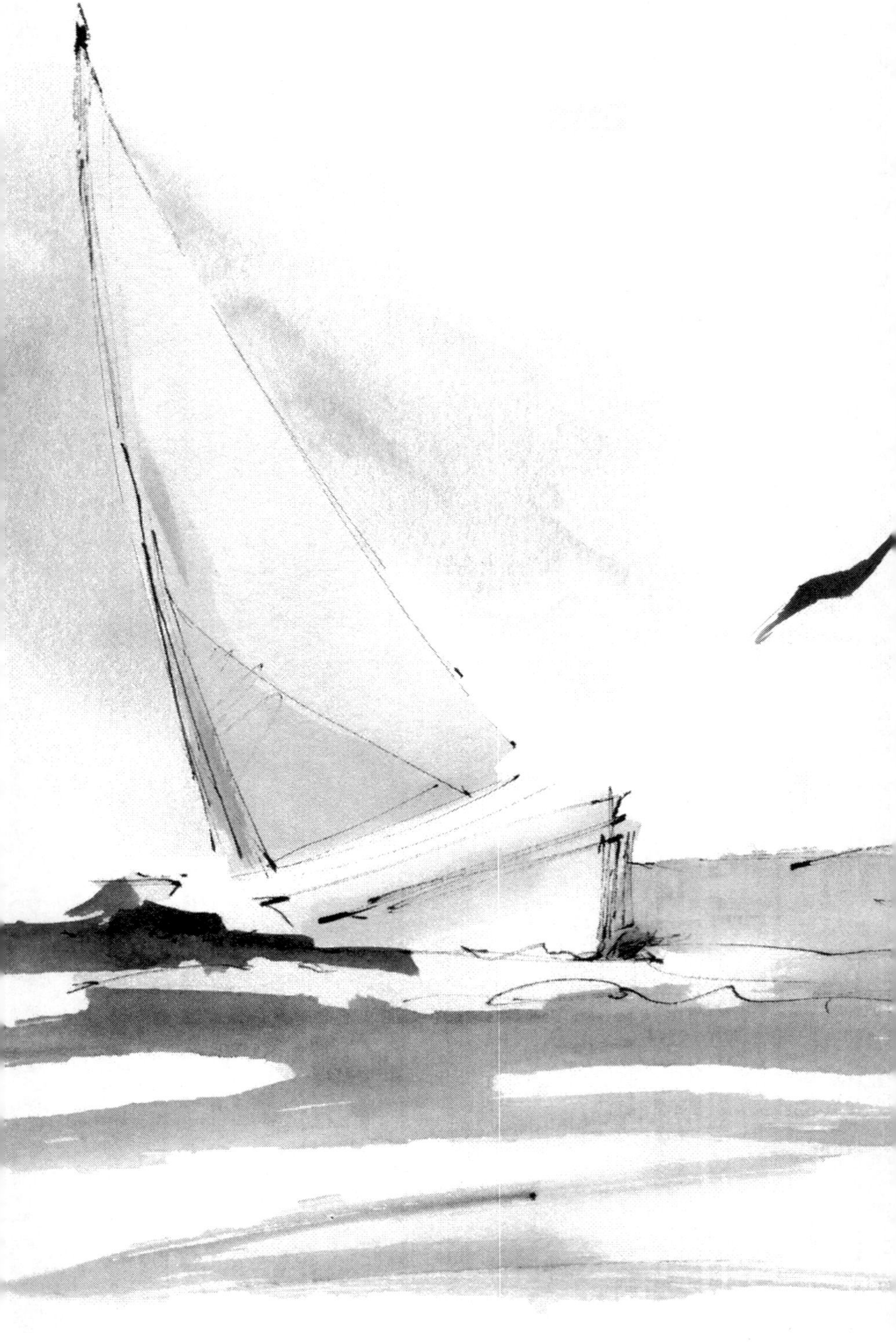

Chapter Ten

The fish was fantastic. They served it with three sauces, but the rich, spicy mole was my favorite. It was easy to focus on the delicious meal because each time I tuned into Stefan's Greek accent, I found myself thinking about another accent spoken by another man. I wondered as I pushed a flaky piece of marlin across my plate, what the business was that he had to conduct so very late at night.

"I know I opened with the dullness of sport," Stefan spoke louder, trying to draw my attention, "but I switched to the art world just for you, Giselle, and still your eyes pass through me. If I was a less beautiful man, I might be insulted."

I smiled at him, grateful for his easy charm. "I'm sorry, Stefan.

I had a tiring day. It wasn't considerate of me to invite you to a meal when I can hardly stay awake."

His brown fingers drummed against the tablecloth as he studied me. "No, I don't think it is sleep you want. Might it have something to do with the man down by the pool yesterday afternoon?"

I stared at my empty wineglass as if it was fascinating.

He chuckled as a server came to refill our glasses and take our plates. I hadn't finished my meal, but my stomach was in knots from thinking over what I could have possibly done to send Sinclair away.

"You are here alone, Giselle." Stefan reached forward to take my cold hand in his and squeezed it warmly. "I mean only to be a friend if you have need of one."

The tension that had been building in my chest loosened, and my shoulders sagged slightly with the release. I hardly knew anything about the Greek before me, but that wasn't saying much because I hardly knew anything about the Frenchman I was sleeping with. Had been sleeping with. But Stefan was kind and pleasantly vain, so I knew he would offer me insight over judgment and probably find genuine amusement in my situation.

"I'm having a holiday affair."

He nodded and sat back in his chair, his posture straight but regal, like a king lounging on his throne. "How exciting."

"Yes." I nodded, pretending to be someone confident and experienced—someone more like my sister than me—but I could tell by the shrewd brightness in his eyes that Stefan didn't believe me. "It's more complicated than I thought it would be."

"Affairs always are," he mused. "Is he married?"

My shoulders hunched near my ears as he hit the nail dangerously close to the head. "Longtime partner."

He frowned slightly and raised his glass but didn't drink from it. "I see. But this isn't something you normally do. Why now? Why him?"

And not me, his question seemed to imply. I knew he was attracted to me, but I also got the impression he could have been attracted to anyone with good looks, be it a man or woman. Stefan had the kind of fluid sexuality that was both sexy and scary in a man. I wished I could be as free as him.

"Do I sound childish if I say it was a feeling I had?" When Stefan rolled his eyes in gentle mockery, I laughed. "Fine. Well, he was unbelievably handsome, for starters. And I guess this sort of thing"—I waved my hand abstractly—"was the next step in my evolution from self-conscious frump to a somewhat sophisticated woman."

"From a duckling to a swan?"

I thought instantly of Sinclair, assuring me that the airplane was something beautiful and full of power—a swan. "I guess," I murmured.

"How is it working out for you so far? I must say, you have a glow in your cheeks, and if it weren't for the tension in your shoulders, I would say you look remarkably well."

"We don't talk about anything specific; those are the rules. But he took me to a business party and out fishing today. I feel like I'm getting to know him in a way, but when we returned to the resort, he was cold and dismissed me so easily."

I remembered so clearly the feeling of shame as he left me at the entrance. Just another person disappointed in me.

Stefan was staring at me with narrowed eyes, his lips quirked down in concern. "I could hit him if you'd like?" When I laughed, he glared reproachfully at me. "You wouldn't laugh if you knew how much I value my hands."

I wiped a tear escaping from my eye and swallowed the giggles still hovering in my throat. "I'm sorry, Stefan. That was a very gallant offer, but I think I'll pass."

"What is it that you want to do then? Are you happy to let him dismiss you?" He leaned forward, his bared teeth glinting in the low light. His face had contracted, and I could sense the sudden hostility in him. "Maybe you bored him in bed, Giselle, or maybe you shattered his expectations. Are you happy never to know? This is the problem with women, you know? They think men know everything, that we are unmoved by their charms. The truth, my French-Italian beauty, is that you bombard us with desires. And a woman like yourself should never be dismissed, even if the man in question is 'unbelievably handsome.'"

"What are you saying?"

"I'm saying, if you aren't ready to end your holiday affair, then don't let it end. Go to him, seduce him all over again." His eyes skimmed my form in frank admiration.

The idea of seducing Sinclair was deeply appealing. I could picture him before me, his dazzling blue eyes burning with desire, his head tipped back as he groaned at the feel of my mouth on him.

"There you are." Stefan smiled at me, tipping his wineglass and at last taking a long sip. "Your gumption is back."

I took a sip of wine to hide my coy smile. "Any ideas of how I should surprise him?"

Stefan grinned broadly and rubbed his hands together in glee. "Now we are getting to the good stuff."

Hours later, when the moon was swollen in the dark sky, and all the diners had long since retired to their beds or downtown prospects, I stood at the door of Sinclair's room with my fist closed and poised over the wood.

Despite Stefan's pep talk over more than a few glasses of wine, my confidence was dissipating with each breath. Sinclair had dismissed me for a reason, I reminded myself. Who did I think I was just showing up at his room in the middle of the night? What kind of woman did that?

Me, a small but remarkably powerful voice in my head cried out. *I do that!* The kind of woman I wanted to be, had always dreamed of being, wouldn't hesitate to take what she wanted.

Besides, I had spent over half an hour in my room freshening up for my seduction. I didn't own any beautiful lingerie, so I had opted to go nude beneath the thin white summer dress fluttering against my upper thighs, and Stefan's hands had artfully mussed my hair into something indefinably sexy. I remembered his words of encouragement and sucked in a final deep breath.

No one stirred within the room. I knocked again, with more force, and considered the very real possibility that Sinclair was still at work, or worse, that he was with someone else. I was surprised I even cared. Of course, he could be. What claim did I have on him as a stranger who had known him for three days and knew nothing of his origins or even his last name?

With the last ounce of my courage, I knocked once more before turning on one of my highest heels to leave. I had only taken a few steps away when the sound of the door opening behind me prompted me to look over my shoulder.

Sinclair stood in the frame clad in a dismantled suit, his white shirt untucked and slightly wrinkled and his feet bare. The sight of those naked brown feet had me swallowing past a swell of unexpected desire, but the instant I caught his eye, I almost choked on his expression. His beautiful blue eyes were bloodshot, and his features carefully guarded as if I had come to trick him out of something precious. He didn't say anything as he stared at me, his posture rigid but not hostile. I doubted my purpose for a second as he waited for me to speak, but when his thick brows rose daringly, I straightened my spine and dug deep for some confidence.

On slightly wobbly legs, I slowly walked back to him, only stopping when my high heels brushed his toes. I had to crane my neck to look up into his expressionless eyes.

"Have you eaten?"

He frowned, and I was thrilled that my question threw him off. Jerkily, he nodded.

I bit my lip in genuine nervousness and noted the way his eyes lingered over the motion. "Do you have room for dessert?"

Slowly, both to heighten the anticipation and to calm my jittery heart, I slid the flimsy straps of my white sundress off my shoulders. No one was in the hall. It was too late for returning diners, and anyone out clubbing wouldn't return home for hours yet, but still, the vulnerability of my almost nakedness as my dress slipped easily off my shoulders to pool at my feet was intense. I kept my eyes on his the entire time, watching as first shock and then excitement flared in those azure depths. I tried not to fidget as he took in my bare breasts, heaving slightly under my anxious breath, and the white cotton underwear blocking me from total nudity.

A thin hiss streamed through his clenched teeth, and he shifted uncomfortably on his feet, but his eyes left blazing trails across my skin. "Jesus Christ."

I raised an eyebrow and shakily joked, "I'm not sure he would approve."

A startled smirk twitched his lips, but he shook his head. "Elle, I shouldn't do this."

I watched his Adam's apple bob convulsively in his brown throat, and it distracted me from the itchy scratch of guilt that prickled up my spine. "You promised me seven days." I cleared my throat, but my voice remained husky with nerves and desire. "You don't seem like a man to go back on your word."

"I made a promise to the woman waiting for me back home," he countered, but his voice was quiet as if even he didn't want to hear the truth of his statement.

I nodded slowly and opened my palms, aware of every ripple of air across my bare flesh. "I know, and I respect that."

It seemed so surreal to be having this conversation in the open, wearing nothing but my modest panties.

His gaze flashed across my exposed skin once more before settling on my eyes. He stared at me for a long moment, his expression hardened with uncertainty. I kept my features open and honest, radiating the simple desire I had for him and allowing some of the other feelings—the ones I was too scared to analyze—to slip in around the edges. Finally, he seemed to find something in my face that he had been desperately searching for, and he let out a ragged sigh.

Feeling brave, I placed my hand against his slightly stubbled cheek. "I want you."

His groan reverberated throughout the still night air, and before I could move, his lips were on mine, his tongue swiping across the closed seam of my lips persuasively until I opened for him. He bent and grasped the backs of my thighs to hoist me into his arms. My frantic hands dived into his thick chin-length hair and tugged, pulling him even closer to me while the hands that cupped my bottom squeezed. Vaguely, I was aware that we were in his room now, the door kicked shut behind us and that he was moving us quickly toward the bed. When he softly deposited me on the mattress, I mumbled a protest against his lips as he moved away.

I stared up at him with pleading eyes, my body physically shaking with my desire for him. His eyes burned as he looked down at me, and I was pleased to see the swell of his dick tightening against the zipper of his slacks.

He licked his bottom lip unconsciously, making me gasp. "You are glorious."

His words infused me with sensual confidence. My heart beating erratically as I allowed my closed knees to flop open, revealing my underwear-covered center. His breath hitched, but he gently pushed my hands away when I reached for him. I watched with questioning eyes as he sank to his knees on the plush carpet and ran his hands up the outsides of my legs to my bottom so that he could tug me closer to the edge of the bed. I leaned up on my elbows to watch him as his fingers ran up one of my legs, lifting it into the air.

Whether it was the fact my seduction had worked or that I had never seen such carnality in a man's gaze before, I felt more confident and infinitely sexier than I ever had before.

I sighed as he kissed the arch of my foot.

"I think we'll keep these on," he husked as he ran his tongue lightly over the seam between my exposed foot and the outrageously tall high heels.

His eyes caught mine, and I sucked in a deep breath at the wicked intent there. Moving up my legs, he sunk his teeth lightly into the soft skin of my inner thigh while holding my gaze. My head collapsed back on my shoulders as I shuddered out a groan.

I squeezed my eyes closed as he lifted my rump to pull off my underwear and splay my legs farther apart. I might have exposed myself to him at the door, but the thought of him staring at the most intimate part of me still made me immensely self-conscious.

A finger dipped through my wet folds, and his smoky voice ordered, "Look at me."

I did as he asked; my eyes wide with apprehension as they landed on his face just an inch away from my aching core.

He blew cool air onto me, and whispered, "You are beautiful."

My entire being flushed hot and prickly with embarrassment, but his strong fingers clenched my thighs until I stopped wriggling. His tongue flicked out over the most sensitive part of me, and desire spiked through my system. Wanting to touch him, I whimpered and grasped at his strong shoulders to pull him toward me, but he resisted, and the gentle scrape of his teeth against my drenched flesh was a warning to let him continue. But the memory of him against my tongue, the unique taste of him, and the wonderful power I felt as I took him inside my mouth spurred me on.

"I want to taste you."

He froze at my words and then groaned against me. I

squealed as he lifted me into his arms and flipped around to lie down on his back on the bed. He lifted me over him easily and spun me around to perch me over his face. Panic seized me, and I started to mumble my reluctance, but his firm hands yanked my hips lower until I could feel his tongue swirl over my clit. I trembled and braced my hands on his lower stomach.

I could feel the bunch and pull of the steely muscles under his skin as he moved under me, and I followed the tapered V of his abdomen to my prize. His arousal pressed into his stomach, and when I slid a thumb over his tip, it was wet with desire. I moaned as I leaned down to lap it off him, and his thighs flexed under my palms in reaction. I was beginning to think there was nothing I craved more than the intimacy and the power that came with having him in my mouth.

I had never gone down on Mark. He had respected my reticence in doing so, and the only time I had before was with Christopher. My mind contracted around his name, and I forcibly shoved it out of my head but not before I tensed over Sinclair.

Sensing my distraction, he gently pulled me to the side and turned to lie beside me on the opposite end of the bed from the pillows. He licked his lips as he settled against me, slipping an arm under my head to support me, and my eyes followed the path of his firm mouth. I leaned in to kiss him, but he pulled slightly at my shoulders so that I couldn't.

"What happened?" he asked. His voice was still pure sex, but a flicker of concern wavered in those expressive eyes.

I shrugged. "I don't know what you mean."

Anger clamped down on his features, turning his face into that distant, cold mask. "I'm not going to sleep with a woman who keeps secrets from me."

I couldn't help but snort at that. "We don't have anything but secrets between us, Sinclair."

His frown was fierce, knotting the skin between his chestnut brows in a way that I was beginning to find strangely adorable.

"Not here. In my bed, I want you to be honest with me." Something like pain crossed his expression before he could hide it, and I wondered, not for the first time, about his partner back home. "I need you to be honest with me."

He hitched my leg over his hip and settled so close that his hard length pressed against my heat. My breath caught and released on a thready sigh. This was what I needed, I realized as I looked into his beautiful face, this intimacy. I had been without male comfort for most of my life, and to have someone like Sinclair desire me like this was beyond my wildest fantasies, my most hidden dreams.

He pressed against me slightly so that just the tip of him rested inside me. I clamped down on him, and the fire that flamed in his eyes unlocked my reticence to speak.

"I told you I wasn't a virgin," I whispered, closing my eyes so that I didn't have to see his reaction, "and I was telling you the truth."

He stilled against me and stroked my hair in silent support.

"We had a family friend, almost like an uncle, who helped us financially. We were pretty poor, especially for a while there, and he was almost like a guardian angel. When he started to date my sister, I think the family was relieved even though he was old enough to be her father. He was handsome and nice and everything." I clenched my eyes tighter until spots interrupted the memories playing across my lids. "I didn't really think anything of it when he started to seduce me."

Sinclair was so still and silent beside me that I wasn't sure what to make of it, so I slowly peeked out from under one lid. He was staring at me with the telltale muscle in his jaw jumping, and his eyes blazing so blue that I closed mine again.

"He was careful not to hurt me, and he was really kind, but we did some ..." *Horrible, disgusting, immoral, degrading?* "Unpleasant things together. No one ever found out, and when my mother and sister moved to America, they left him behind. I haven't seen him since, but"—I gestured back and forth between our bodies—"it feels strange to actually want to do some of those things with you."

"You don't have to do anything—" he started to say, but I opened my eyes and pressed my palm against his mouth to silence him.

My throat ached with sorrow, but I was grateful for my dry eyes when I whispered, "You don't understand. I want to do those things with you so badly I tremble."

I showed him my slightly quivering fingers and pressed them to his firm chest, trailing them down his skin until I reached his still semi-hard erection.

I wrapped my hands around his base and squeezed firmly. "I need this."

When I looked back into his eyes, they glowed with understanding and, thankfully, desire. He wasn't repulsed by my anxiety or my sketchy past, and I blew out a deep sigh of relief.

At a loss for what to do now, I was grateful when he said, "Taste me, Elle." When my eyes widened, he nodded, and his tone grew stern. "Take me in your hands, between your lips, and do what you want with me. Make me come."

The dominance in his voice left no room for argument, but I could tell by the gentle stroke of his hand over my hair that even though I would be pleasuring him, this was for me too. He was commanding me to step past my fears and do what I wanted desperately and secretly to do. He nodded at me, seeing the understanding in my expression.

With trembling fingers, I pushed him onto his back and straddled his thighs in order to run my fingers over the bumps and muscular curves of his torso. Sinclair was built powerfully but lean like a runner, and I traced the map of his muscles with reverent fingers. Soon, that became inadequate, and I dipped my head to sketch the texture of his abs under my tongue. His groin vibrated under my lips, and I smiled against his skin as I took his rigid length tightly in one hand.

I was surprised by how badly I wanted to take him in my mouth, but I withheld. Twisting my hand over his length slowly but surely a few times, I then flicked the head with my tongue. His fists bunched in the duvet as I parted my lips and pushed him into my mouth. It was impossible to take all of him in this position, but I tried anyway, relaxing my throat and swallowing to fight my gag reflex, but mostly, I swirled my tongue across his luscious head and even lightly scraped my teeth across the base of him.

I could feel my own desire drip down my inner thighs, and by the time he pulled me off him, I was perilously close to orgasming, and he hadn't even touched me. So, when he finally settled between my legs and plowed into me, I screamed in pleasure. I hadn't realized how I would ache for him even after less than twelve hours without him inside me. It didn't bode well for me if I was this desperate for him after only four days with our inevitable end rushing up to meet us.

He shifted the angle of my hips and captured both my hands in one of his to press them above my head. The feeling of helplessness, the texture of his coarse chest hair against my aching nipples, and the fire he stoked so skillfully between my legs banished all rational thought. I threw back my head and groaned.

Sinclair watched me with eyes on fire. His taut jaw and the beads of sweat crowning his forehead were the only other signs that he was not completely in control. He dipped his head and took one of my peaks between his lips, sucking hard. My legs tightened, crossing against his flexing buttocks until the sharp point of my heels dug into his tender flesh. He hissed against my skin and took my nipple gently between his teeth. Unbearable heat swirled through my body, and I clenched my teeth, desperate for release from the tension.

Sensing my need, Sinclair's free hand slipped down my damp

belly to the soft curls of my sex, unerringly finding the button of pleasure at my center. I gasped as he flicked me.

I was so close that stars burst across my vision.

"Sinclair, please," I begged, my head thrashing from side to side at the myriad of sensations he evoked in my body. I was so close, but I wanted—no, needed—him to give me permission to tumble over the edge.

"Yes," he growled against my breast, and with my nipple still between his teeth, he clamped down almost viciously.

I let out a hoarse scream as the seams of my body unraveled, and the brutal climax overtook me. Releasing me, Sinclair reared up and began to move for himself, pounding into me with short, hard strokes that drove me higher and higher. When he finally groaned and released inside me, I was heavy and saturated with pleasure, unable to even drop my freed hands from above my head.

He collapsed beside me, his breathing uneven and his dusky skin covered in a sheen of sweat so that he seemed to glow in the soft lamplight. It was late, and I felt more liquid than human. My lids weighed ten tons, but I so loved to look at Sinclair, especially when he wasn't aware of it. I noticed the faint stubble lining his sharp jaw and wondered idly if I would have beard burn painted across my sensitive skin. The thought of being branded by him made my recently sated desire stir its sleepy head.

As if sensing my thoughts, he smiled slightly with his eyes closed. "You are insatiable."

"How did you know what I was thinking?" I laughed.

One lid cracked open, revealing a vivid blue iris sparkling with humor. "I might not know you very well, but I do know your body." His left hand smoothed over the curve of my hip, and I turned on my side to face him. "I know how much I turn you on."

I blushed, but he chuckled and chucked me softly on the chin. "Nothing to be ashamed of. If anything, I'm flattered." His lips twisted as if he couldn't believe it himself. "I know it isn't in your nature to be so bold."

"No," I agreed, fiddling with the edge of the silky pillowcase. "I wasn't sure you'd be pleased."

He raised a brow and indicated toward his satiated organ. "Despite evidence to the contrary."

I smiled, but self-consciousness had reared its ugly head again, and it was hard to put it back to bed. Even though I might not know him very well, I knew enough about his dominant predilections to question whether he had truly enjoyed my assertiveness.

"You don't believe me," he said, and though I wasn't looking at him, I could feel his frown.

"Well, I know you like to be the one in control," I murmured.

The sudden silence was thick and electric with tension. I hadn't expected him to react so strongly to my simple observation, and when I looked up at him, he seemed frozen, staring woodenly at the ceiling.

"I didn't mean to offend," I said softly, but I wasn't really sorry because what I had said was true.

I remembered Cosima telling me about the world of sex and games, glossing over the finer details but still too knowledgeable to be inexperienced in their arts. She had mentioned domination and submission, the thrill some people got from administering punishment and controlling another's pleasure. I wasn't sure how far Sinclair's kink went, but I was pretty sure he was into some degree of BDSM.

He sighed heavily and dragged his arm across his forehead, almost as if he wanted to shield his eyes from me. "I'm overreacting. I was the one who said there should be no secrets in our bed."

A little thrill from hearing him call the bed "ours" raced up my spine.

"I ..." He rubbed a hand over his face. "I used to be involved in the BDSM scene, years ago now, but when I met E... When I met my current girlfriend, I gave it up. She wasn't interested." He laughed harshly. "In fact, she was repulsed by it."

Tenderness swelled in my chest, and I reached out tentatively to touch his arm. "Most people are afraid of things they don't understand."

He turned his head to stare at me, his expression fierce. "You don't know anything about it."

"No." I nodded slowly. "But I'd like to."

His dark brows shot up, but his eyes were stilled guarded. "You don't know what you're saying."

It was my turn to sigh. I propped up on one arm in order to look down at him.

"I do. We've already broken so many rules, yours and mine. If we are going to have a holiday affair, why not live out those fantasies? I can't say I know much about all of that, but I'm curious." I looked down at the crumpled bed sheet, suddenly bashful but unwilling to admit it.

"We aren't talking about squash here, Elle." He was angry now, his voice smooth and steely. "BDSM isn't something you can dabble in. You need complete trust and honesty in order to be safe, and you hardly know me."

And shouldn't trust me, I read in his gaze.

Yes, I thought stubbornly, *I can*.

"I'm not saying I want you to tie me up and gag me every time we sleep together." My skin pulsed with hot and cold pinpricks of lust and fear. "I'm not even saying I want to do this for you." He raised a brow at that but allowed my white lie to go uncontested. "I was shy and miserable with it for so long, declining every indulgence that came my way because I thought I didn't deserve it." I tilted my chin and tried to stop my stomach from quivering with nerves. "This is something that I want, Sinclair. Something that I need."

He stared at me for a long time until my elbow ached from my awkward position, and my skin cooled. I watched his implacable expression, searching for the tells I was now so familiar with, but only his eyes gave him away; the intense blue depths were dark with troubled thoughts.

Finally, he spoke, but his lips were strangely unmoved so that, at first, I didn't know he was talking. "It's intimate, Elle. For some, there is no turning back."

His eyes were locked onto mine, emphasizing his point. I blinked through my surprise because the thought that I may be converted to the lifestyle had not occurred to me.

He nodded, and I wondered if I had spoken aloud. "You acted on impulse, but you didn't really think this through. As a man who has become enchanted by the siren's call, let me at least warn you before you take the plunge."

"Show me." When his lips pursed to argue with me, I placed my palm over his mouth. "How will I know if I like it or not if you don't show me?"

I knew so little about what to do, so I followed my desires, folding onto my knees and scooting closer to him. Taking his angular face between my palms, I composed my features and hoped that I sounded, well, irresistible.

"I want to submit to you."

Why was saying it out loud so arousing? I felt the power of those vulnerable words pull my shoulders back and blaze behind my gaze.

He touched my chin, pinching it slightly in his fingers. I waited calmly as he studied me and felt a thrill course through me as he shuddered with acquiescence. My eyes fluttered closed as I waited for him to kiss me, ravish me in some way, but his chuckle made them spring open. He was smiling at me with something close to tenderness as he drew two fingers down my throat, hovering over my throbbing pulse.

"Not tonight, siren. As I said, this isn't a game, and if we are going to do this, then we will do it properly."

He looked into my eyes with the kind of intensity meant to scare me, and honestly, I felt a shiver of apprehension race across my skin, but before I could react, he was pulling away from me and swinging to his feet with feline grace.

I watched his small, firm buttocks as he bent over to pull on his charcoal gray lounging pants. When he turned back to me, the shutters were once again pulled down over his emotions, and his gorgeous blue eyes were only vacant pools.

"I have work to do," he stated, coolly staring at me as if I was a business associate and not his lover.

In some ways, I supposed, I was no more than an agreement, a pleasurable one certainly, but still just an equal investor in a mutual asset. The thought made me suddenly sick to my stomach.

An angry flush burned my cheeks as I scrambled out of bed and into the other room to search for my discarded summer dress.

He entered just as the cool fabric dropped down over my damp skin. I knew that he watched me as I adjusted the skirt and ran my fingers through my hopelessly tangled hair. I didn't know why he stood there when it was obvious he wanted me gone. It only made it more awkward to have him wait impatiently at the doorway to his bedroom.

Resentment fizzed across my skin, infusing me with sudden shame-fueled hatred. I turned to him, mouth open and ready to snap at him for treating me so callously, for being the most mercurial man I had ever met, but something in his face arrested me. His hands flexed restlessly at his sides, and he rocked lightly back and forth on his feet while his face—the devastating face I was coming to like entirely too much—stared at me with that wolf-like hunger I had only caught glimpses of before. But this time, after a round of passionate lovemaking, the expression was skewed by something other than lust—tenderness, maybe, and an undercurrent of regret.

As if he knew my thoughts, he nodded and cleared his throat to softly bid me good night. "Get a good night's sleep, Elle. You'll need it."

The fight left me. There was indecision in his stance, and in my heart, I wondered if it had been the right thing to come back to his room. It could have ended so amicably if I had just stayed away, but now it was too late, I was invested, and as I nodded curtly at my Frenchman, I could already feel my heart clench painfully with foreboding.

My hand was on the door handle when I felt him grasp my arm. Without turning me, he pressed himself against my back and placed a gentle kiss on the side of my face.

"Sweet dreams."

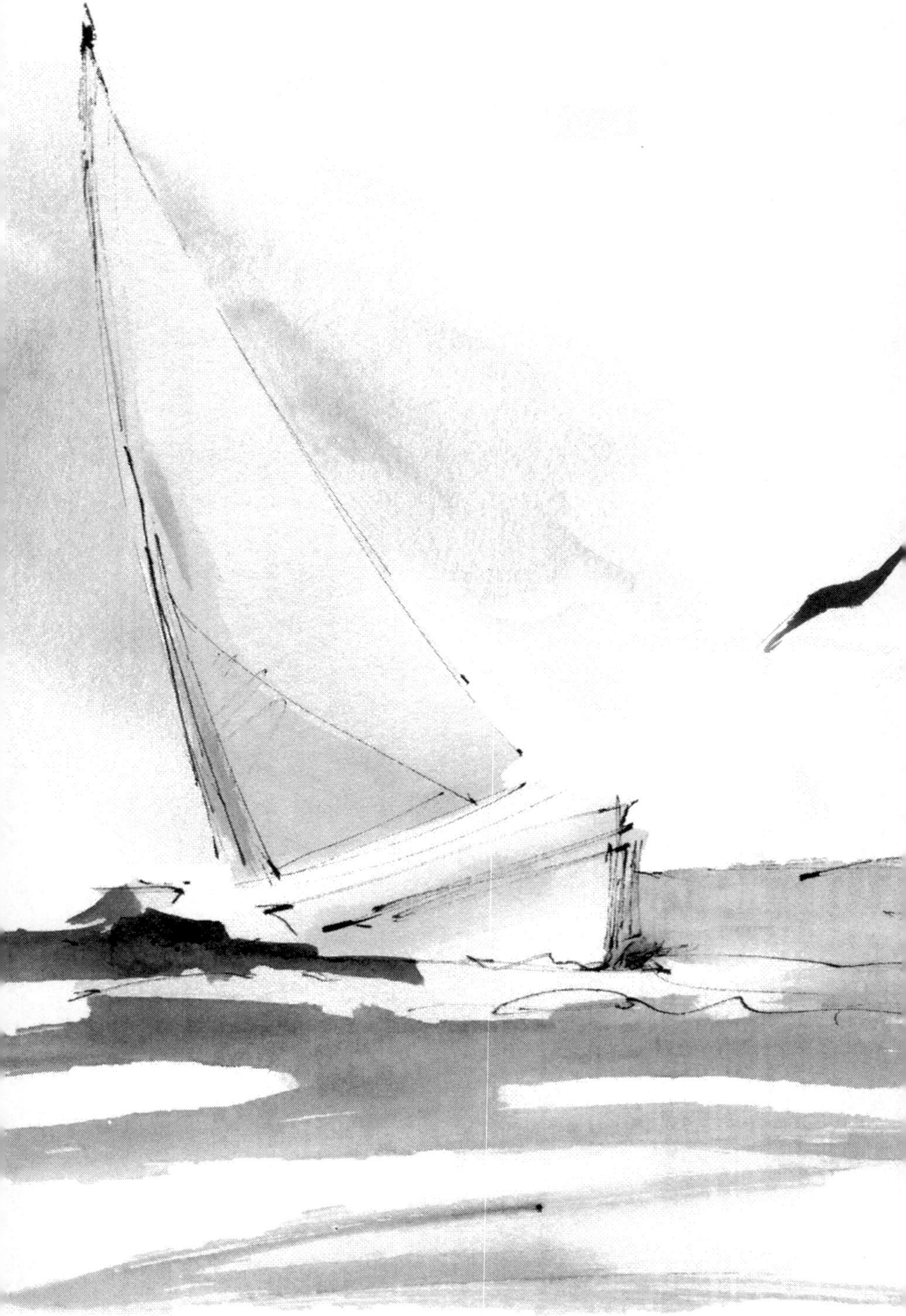

Chapter Eleven

"So," Cosima practically yelled, "how are things going with the married man?"

I hushed her even though I sat alone on the sand, and no one could hear her through the phone. The midday sun beat down on the landscape, hammering everything into gold. It had been a productive morning, swimming followed by a few hours of photographing and sketching the surrounding area. Now, I lay pleasantly exhausted in the sun slathered with sunscreen. The heat was the only thing I really missed about Naples, and despite being a redhead with freckles, my skin loved a good golden tan. Even though I hadn't heard from Sinclair, I was beyond content, especially listening to the familiar spiced tones of my sister through the phone.

"He is an enigma," I murmured, shifting sand through my hands.

"Oh no, you never have been able to resist a mystery. And I'm sure the sex is fantastic. You must have it bad."

"Cosi!" I protested through my laughter. "I haven't even told you about our sex life."

"I know." I could hear her smile. "Which tells me it's excellent. Otherwise, you would have a million questions and complaints."

Fair enough.

"I do still have a few questions." I took a deep breath and fought the flush I could feel flaming across my skin. I stood to walk to the water, hoping the cool ocean would steady me. "He is, well, he's a bit into domination."

"Oh." The single syllable was loaded with meaning. I could picture my beautiful sister pursing her lips, trying to decide how to approach this. "And are you into it, as well?"

"Yeah," I whispered. "A bit. With him."

"Well, I honestly never thought I would be having this conversation with my older sister. No offense, Gigi, but I also figured you for vanilla all the way."

"Me too. But with him, it's different. *I'm* different. I know it's only a holiday affair, but I want to please him. He is almost totally cut off from everyone, cool and remote. One minute he is so tender with me, almost as if he really likes me, and the next, he's telling me to get lost."

"He sounds like a *bastardo*."

I laughed. "No, he's too well-mannered to be that."

"Your life is your life, *bambina*, but I do have to say it. Don't do this just for him. BDSM isn't something to dabble in." Her voice was weighted, and I wondered what exactly my little sister had experienced in her short twenty-two years. She had left home so young, alone and in a business that often sexually abused women.

"Miss Buchanan?"

I looked over my shoulder to see a young waiter standing hesitantly on the sand. "One second, Cosi." I walked up the beach to address him. "Yes?"

"I've been asked to give you a message." His dark eyes skimmed over my exposed curves quickly before landing on my face. At least he had the decency to blush.

I smiled warmly at him as I took the envelope. "I'm sorry, I don't have any cash on me."

He once again noted my bikini-clad form. "No problem, *señorita*, enjoy the sun."

With my phone tucked between my ear and my shoulder, I ripped open the envelope and sighed when I read the compact script written inside.

"What?" Cosima asked impatiently.

I fingered the letter and smiled hugely. "I have to go; my Frenchman is waiting."

He had been waiting for me on the other end of the beach just off the shore in a small, sleek motorboat. A man offered to drive me out to him on the Jet Ski, but I ignored the offer, giving him my bag to take out to the boat while I walked into the ocean, eager to swim the distance.

Sinclair watched the entire time, his eyes a physical touch on my skin. I was a skilled swimmer, and the velvety brush of the azure waters against my skin gave me confidence. When I reached the boat, I grasped the ladder and paused, tipping my head back as water streamed off me. He didn't offer a hand as I swung onto the deck, and I had to hide a giggle behind my hand when I saw the lust written across his stern face. My eyes flickered down his linen shirt to his worn denim shorts and noted the bulge there. It had only been a dozen hours since I had last seen him, yet the sight of Sinclair, strong legs braced against the rocking waves and skin kissed gold under the sun, stirred something intense inside me.

"Hello, Sinclair," I said, surprised by the huskiness of my tone.

My voice snapped him out of his trance, and he strode over to me. Gripping the backs of my thighs, he lifted me swiftly, easily into his arms. His hands were hot on my bottom, and his lips were instantly on mine, sweeping possessively into my mouth. I groaned against his tongue.

"I missed you last night." His voice heated my skin as his lips skimmed across my throat and down to my shoulder, where he sank his teeth lightly.

My heart warmed like a small furnace in my chest. God, I hadn't realized how much I wanted to hear those words from him. I tipped my neck to the side, giving him greater access and shuddered as he took advantage, sucking and nipping on the delicate skin.

"Me too." I sighed, sinking my fingers into his lustrous mane. "Don't send me away again."

"No," he agreed, his hands flexing on my ass.

We made out like teenagers, his fingers traveling up and down my body, eager to touch every square inch while his mouth worked wonders on mine. When we finally broke apart minutes later, we were both panting. We were so close, staring at each other, that we breathed the same breath. Electricity crackled in the air between us until finally, I grinned. I watched his features crack and break out into a glorious smile. Giddiness bubbled in my chest until I couldn't contain it, and giggles frothed over. He began to laugh too; rich, throaty laughter that made him squeeze his eyes shut.

We were being stupid and silly, just like teenagers fresh in lust—in love—but I didn't care. My heart raced, and I could feel my skin glow. My holiday affair had just become something so much more. And though he didn't verbally acknowledge it, I knew somehow that Sinclair felt the same way.

"What are we doing out here?" I asked as he let me slip down his body to my feet. His erection pressed into my belly, and I shivered at the familiar feel of it.

"I thought you might enjoy going snorkeling with me." He looked down at me, a small smile lingering on his lips.

"You thought right." I smiled, filled with happiness.

The future, those thoughts about going back to reality where he had a girlfriend, and I wasn't bold, were pushed firmly to the back of my mind. I was determined to enjoy the rest of my time with him, no matter what.

He nodded and took my hand to lead me to a small seat beside the wheel. I realized that the resort staff had already dropped off my bag, and I quickly checked on my camera. We were the only people on the boat, and it appeared that Sinclair intended to drive it. He winked at me as he started the engine, obviously catching the surprise on my face.

We didn't speak as he drove us, but he looked over at me sometimes with that slight Sinclair smile. I studied him, pleased with his preoccupation. He stood easily behind the raised control panel, his legs braced and his hand loosely on the throttle. The wind whipped his chestnut hair back from his face, revealing features that were uncharacteristically soft and open. It thrilled me to know he was relaxed in my company, enough so to shed the hardened exterior that he wore for everyone else. Was he like this with the girlfriend? I shoved the thought aside with a frown and focused on the passing coastline instead.

"Can I take your picture?" I yelled over the noise.

Sinclair frowned slightly but relented when he looked over at my eager expression. I snapped a dozen pictures of him, too many really, moving carefully across the hull to get a full-frontal picture of my captain. I knew they would be beautiful photos, and I was happy to have a permanent piece of him to pull out after our holiday ended.

When he turned off the engine, I looked up from my viewfinder to take in the beauty of the small cove we bobbed in. Large reddish rocks bracketed a secluded white sand beach, and the turquoise water was so clear that I could see the multitudes of fish passing by our boat as if through a magnifying glass. I looked over at Sinclair with an overexcited smile.

He placed a hand against my cheek and leaned down to press a kiss to my smiling lips. "It's good to make my siren smile."

I fought the urge to swoon and won.

I shrugged. "It's okay, I guess."

He blinked and barked with laughter. Tugging me to my feet, he swatted my rear. "Ungrateful brat."

We continued our banter as he outfitted us both with flippers, goggles, and a breathing piece. I shook my head at the offer of a life jacket, and he took my hand as we stood at the stern of the boat, ready to jump in. He was so playful and open that it was hard to contain my enjoyment even though I knew better. Logically, I knew he was mercurial, and the situation was temporary, but I felt myself falling, tumbling almost brutally and certainly clumsily, in love with him.

The surf was calm and silky as we moved through the cove. Sometimes, we swam together amidst a school of yellow and silver fish, their touch like cool kisses against my skin, but after a while, we abandoned the serious snorkeling and began to horse around. Sinclair was an excellent swimmer, and when I asked him about it, he divulged that he had been a swimmer since high school and all through college, which explained the delicious cut of his lean body. We swam for over an hour before I dragged myself to the beach, collapsing in exhaustion on the caramel sand.

Sinclair laughed as he emerged from the waves, pushing his wet hair back from his forehead as he stood over me. "My siren can't be tired already."

I wanted to close my eyes, but it was difficult to take them off him. "A certain someone tired me out last night. I didn't get much sleep."

His lips curved softly as he bent down, running two fingers down my chest to collect the drops of water lingering there. "You won't get much rest tonight, either."

No, I wouldn't. The promise in his shaded eyes drew the heat of a different kind across my bare skin.

"You could be a model," I murmured, sitting up to run my fingers over the rippling mass of muscles in his abdomen.

His fingers froze at the line of my bikini bottoms, and a cold anger settled into his previous contented features. I watched his mouth twist before he sighed and dropped to the sand beside me.

His shoulders were rounded as he stared out at the ocean, and he let me take one of his slack hands in my own. "I was a model actually."

My eyes widened comically. I was thankful his gaze remained riveted on the sea.

"My foster mother discovered me; she was my agent before she became my mother." He shrugged as if he didn't care, but I could feel his sadness seep into my skin where we touched. "I only did it for a handful of years. When they discovered I had a sharp mind too, they decided that could be put to better use."

I shifted on the sand until I sat behind him, my legs spread wide by the sheer width of his body between my thighs. He tensed as my arms slipped around him in a gentle embrace, but when I pressed a kiss to his salty skin, he sighed raggedly and relaxed.

"Parents shouldn't make their children sad," I said because I could remember the despair that my father, Seamus Moore, always left in his wake.

"You are very sweet and very correct, but that does not stop it from happening."

"What did they do to you?" I whispered, almost afraid to press him when he was being so inexplicably open.

He was quiet for a long time and utterly still but for two fingers that slid back and forth gently over my forearm.

"Nothing so bad. They used me mostly to position themselves in society. Sometimes it was as easy as making friends with the right sons of important men or modeling to help make enough money to support my father's campaign." His knuckles swept up my wrist and over the back of my hand so that he could link our fingers. "Sometimes, it was about seducing the right person. As I said, it wasn't so bad."

"That's not funny, Sin."

"No." He pressed a kiss to our combined hands. "*Mais comme des gens disent, c'est la vie.*"

But as people say, this is life.

"Not anymore," I said with more ferocity than I intended.

"Not anymore," he agreed. "Perhaps it is easier to understand my need for control now."

It was. My heart ached with the influx of love and sympathy. If there had previously been any hope of emerging unscathed from this affair, it was gone.

"Are you still in touch with them?" I mumbled against his salty shoulder.

"It's complicated."

"Why do I have the feeling most things with you are?" I

teased, poking him in his unyielding stomach in an attempt to lighten the mood.

He lifted one of my hands and pressed it to his slightly smiling lips. "Just be grateful you are rid of me in four days."

"More like three," I retorted flippantly even though my chest tightened dangerously. "And for all you know, I could be as complicated as it comes."

He snorted, an undignified sound that was so at odds with his sophisticated persona that it made me laugh. "I highly doubt that. Your straightforward innocence is one of the reasons I find you so irresistible."

"Irresistible, huh?"

He bit gently into one of my fingers. "No man can resist the taste of this skin." His tongue darted out to soothe the fading pain, inciting a sigh from me.

I was tempted to cave to his seduction, but if he was going to speak freely, then this was too good an opportunity to pass up.

I pressed my cheek to his back once more, and murmured, "My family has been broken for a long time."

Sinclair pulled my arms closer around him so that I was flush against his back. His lips against my open palm urged me to continue.

"My father was a drunk and a gambler," I said as if that explained everything. Why my sister had run away, why my brother had moved soon after to America, why my eldest sister hated me—all of it.

"Is he ...?" His body tensed so that I felt like I was hugging a wooden board. "Is he the reason you weren't a virgin when we met?"

It took a moment for his question to settle in. I shuddered but shook my head vigorously. "In a way. If you're asking if he sexually abused me, he didn't. But maybe if he had been around...?" I shrugged.

We were quiet for a few minutes, just holding each other. We were both sticky with salt and sweat from the brilliant afternoon sun, but I was so happy my blood fizzed and danced like champagne. It was hard to tell what Sinclair was feeling, especially when I couldn't see his face to search for his tells, but it was probably better that way.

Three days. Only three more days with this brilliant and beautiful man. My arms tightened around him.

Sensing my mood, he gently reached back to swing me around to his front, settling me over his lap. The feel of his large hands spanning my waist delighted me.

"Are you mad?" I asked, reaching up to run a hand through his silky hair. Under the blazing Mexican sun, it was an astonishing shade of copper.

He lifted his knees so that I could rest my back against them and leaned back on his hands, presenting his long, flat torso to my other wandering hand.

"For?"

"Well, we haven't exactly adhered to your rules. Dunkard fathers and exploitative foster parents aren't business talk or sex."

The left side of his mouth quirked as he said, "No, not exactly. But if you haven't noticed, I gave up on the rules relatively quickly." When I pursed my lips, he shook his head as if I was dense. "Sleeping beside you, taking you fishing, fucking you last night after I promised myself I wouldn't ..." His hand slipped up the curve of my waist, over my breast, and up into my tangled hair. "I think it's pretty obvious I can't control myself around you."

I snorted. "You're never not controlled."

His eyes flared, and I gasped when he sat up and sank both hands in my hair, holding me tight so that even if I had wanted to, I couldn't move.

"Challenge accepted," he murmured darkly before slanting his firm lips over mine.

I moaned into his mouth, opening eagerly for the feel of his hot tongue against mine. My nails raked up his back and locked around his neck, tugging him closer as I wrapped my legs around his torso. I rocked over his erection so that the fabric of my suit rasped against my clit.

His hands plucked at the sides of my string bikini and tugged it off quickly so that his fingers could find me, already weeping with desire for him. There was desperation to our movements, a neediness that inflamed me. It didn't surprise me that I was already aching with want. When two fingers played through my damp curls and swirled at my opening, I groaned and ground down on them. He trapped my bottom lip in his teeth, warning me to stay still as he teased me.

"I don't want to come without you inside me," I panted into his mouth before skating my teeth along his jaw, tasting the salt of the sea and of him against my tongue.

His jaw tensed under my lips, and he quickly undid the tie to his swimsuit, exposing his cock to my waiting fingers. I placed him at my entrance and wiggled over the tip, waiting until his dark eyes met mine to slam down hard onto him.

We both groaned at the sensation. There was some pain, but it only contrasted the pleasure, heightening it. Sinclair took my hips in his hands and tilted my pelvis, hitting a new angle inside me that made my legs tremble. Somehow, I was already close to an orgasm.

Seamlessly, Sinclair rolled me onto my back, spreading my legs open with his palms on my inner thighs, his thumbs teasing me where we were joined together. He was watching himself plunge in and out of my slick depths, his eyes glazed with arousal and two streaks of pink slashed high on his cheekbones. I had never seen anything more attractive.

I shuddered when he picked up the pace, and one thumb found my clit. He circled it firmly, pushing me into a sudden and intense climax that wracked my entire body. I cried out long and low, repeating his name like a chant. I was still out of it when he tilted my hips and began to plow into me, scraping against the sweet spot deep inside me with each thrust as if he was desperate to claim all of me. His features were warped with pleasure, and the sight of him lost in rapture, knowing that I was capable of making him lose control, made me dizzy.

"Elle," he groaned, bottoming out inside me and burrowing his face in my neck as he came.

Afterward, we lay in the sand. His body was too hot and heavy on top of mine, but when he tried to move, I whimpered in protest and linked my legs with his. I could feel him smile into my shoulder, and when he raised himself onto his forearms, I was rewarded with the sight of his smug satisfaction.

"Now, did that seem very controlled to you?" he asked, playfully tweaking my nipple.

I scrunched up my nose. "No. In fact, that was almost barbaric."

He laughed and licked a bead of sweat between my breasts, smacking his lips. "I told you, the taste of you is intoxicating."

"Mmm." I tightened my inner muscles against his softening length, watching his mouth open and his eyes unfocus slightly. "As is this."

When he began to harden again inside me, it was my turn to gasp. "You're insatiable!"

He nodded solemnly. "I only have three days left to enjoy this body, you better bet I'm going to take advantage of it."

I closed my eyes against the dual sensation of panic and desire that bloomed in my chest when he dipped his head to take my nipple in his hot, sucking mouth.

Three days. Only three more days with him.

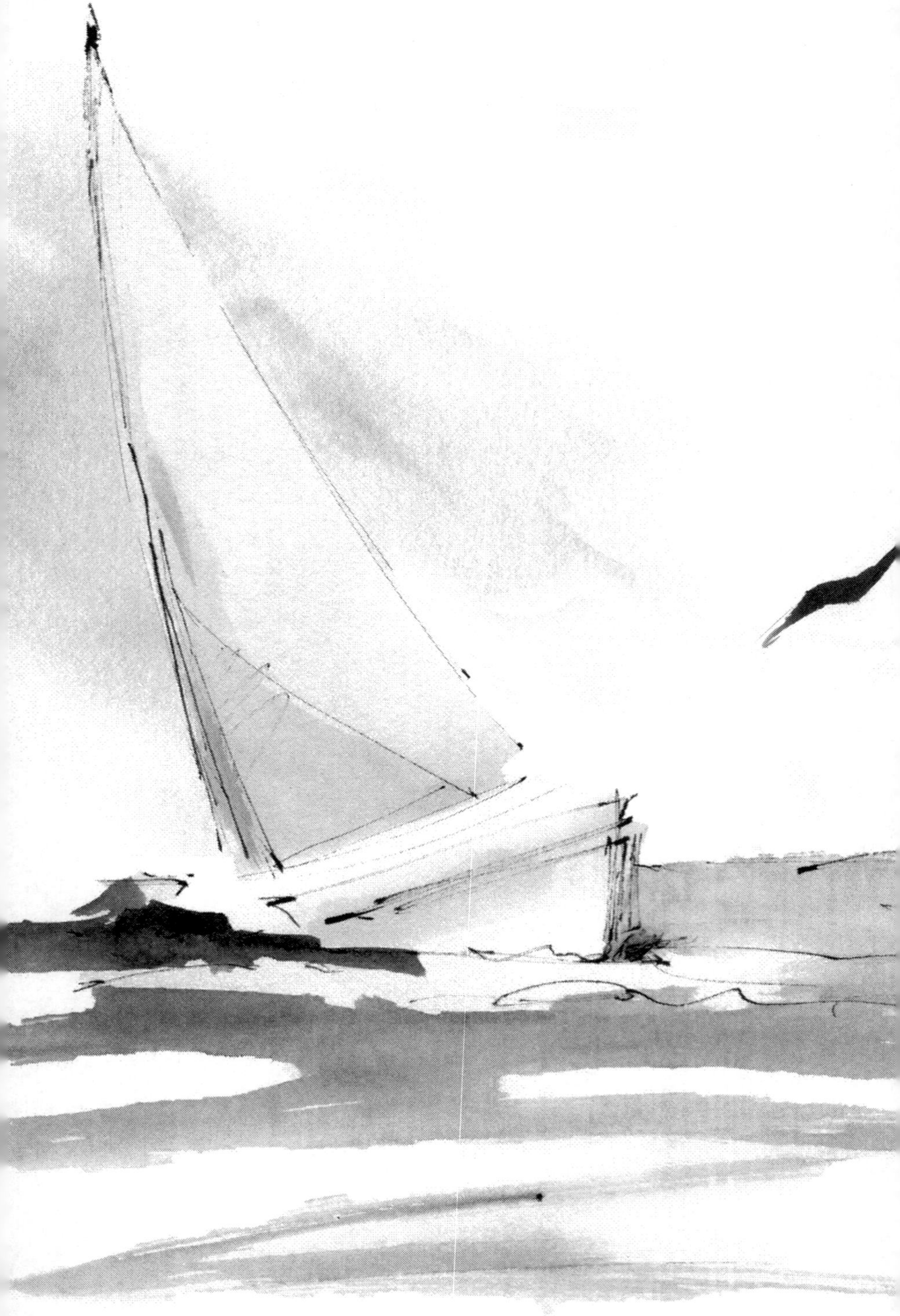

Chapter Twelve

I sat on the deck of Sinclair's expansive resort suite, wrapped up in an overlarge fluffy white robe with my feet tucked underneath me and my freshly washed hair curling dry in the light breeze off the ocean when Sinclair's phone rang. We had been suspended in the kind of natural silence that usually takes years to form, only occasionally breaking from his work and my painting to smile like fools at each other.

The entire day had taken on a slightly hazy, almost dream-like nature. After taking me again on the shore, we swam back to the boat and returned to the resort. He had spoken on the phone while we crossed the grounds to his room, but he caught my hand in his, tucking his fingers into mine so I wouldn't feel ignored. I blushed when heads turned to watch us, their eyes lingering on Sinclair with varying degrees of lust and envy. He squeezed my hand when he caught my wide-eyed stare roving over them all, and the side of his firm mouth twitched in a private smile just for me.

After a quick shower where we mostly refrained from inappropriate touches, he led me to the patio without hesitation, swinging open the French doors to reveal a large wooden easel laden with a fresh canvas and the basic tools of my trade. When I had turned to him, my mouth slack with surprise, he shrugged and suggested that because he had to work, it was only prudent that I had something to occupy myself with too.

Now, I sat before the canvas with a soft lead pencil and a nearly completed outline of the Frenchman sitting across from me. It was a three-quarter profile to showcase the strong cut of his jaw and the slashing lines of his high cheekbones. I hadn't even brought his face to life with color or depth, but I could feel the intensity of his eyes and the texture of his twitching lips as they struggled to hold back a smile under my fingers as I feathered them over the canvas. There was a gaping space to the side of his slightly parted lips where I knew a woman's face would appear, head tilted at a desperate angle, mouth open beautifully but tired like the fading bloom of a rose, unfurled and red. I closed my eyes to imagine the heat in her gaze, her flaming sexual intent. Though he appeared to be the aggressor, dark and overwhelming in blacks and shadows, it was she, this woman on the very precipice of desire, who brought the passion into focus.

The sharp trill of the phone cut through my imagination, and for a moment, I wasn't sure where the noise was coming from. Sinclair frowned at the cell phone vibrating on the table beside him, the white light from his computer screen casting his features in stark relief.

I knew immediately who it was when he looked up at me with compressed lips.

I tried to shrug casually as I returned to my work. "You should get that."

His eyes were hot on the side of my face. "I'll leave."

"No. I don't mind if you stay." I turned to look at him even though I was worried he would see the sadness in my eyes.

He looked hard at me before nodding curtly and sweeping across the touch screen to answer the call.

"Darling," he answered.

My lips twisted involuntarily. Darling? That didn't seem like a pet name Sinclair would use. But I guess it suited his buttoned-up personality.

"The four thirty," he confirmed. "I understand. I'll catch a cab in ... No, it's important you are at the party when she gets there, and I really don't care." He paused, and I snuck a look at him. He tugged at a longish lock of hair, a nervous gesture that made him seem vulnerable, and when his eyes met mine, they were foggy with confusion and strain.

I stood, aware that my movement toward the door made Sinclair tense up.

When I returned to the deck a few minutes later, he was still speaking with her. His head snapped up, and I could tell he wanted me to look over at him, but I reclaimed my seat with a calm expression and took up my palate, swirling a cerulean blue with a dab of bright chartreuse in an attempt to replicate the electricity of Sinclair's blue eyes.

"I'm looking forward to meeting her," Sinclair was saying, his voice cool and modulated. "I know it will be hard on you, but seeing your family happy will more than make up for it ... Yes, I know. You'd be surprised by how resilient family ties are to the passing of time."

Was it just me, or could the girlfriend sense the sorrow in his tone? I wondered how much she knew about Sinclair's particular brand of sorrow; if she took special care to distract him on Father's Day, what they did together on Christmas, and if he was close with her family. These questions sloshed between my ears like leftover seawater, making me nauseous and unbalanced.

"I don't know, darling."

There it was again. *Darling.* I tried to picture her, conjuring up someone with golden hair and a golden smile, tall of course, with legs for days and perfect breasts. If we met or if, God forbid, she found out about me, she would sneer at the sight of me. *This*, she would say, *is who you chose?*

"I have to go now, but please try to enjoy the meeting. It's not often you get to meet a Clinton."

A Clinton? Oh great, so Darling was not only beautiful, but she had a glamorous job that was also intellectual. I sighed heavily, indulging in my self-pity for one more minute before resolving to obliterate it completely. Sinclair wasn't mine, and it was unfair for me to take my frustrations out on him over that fact.

So when he came to stand behind me, close but carefully not touching, I leaned back into him and tipped my head back to smile.

"Hi."

His eyes were guarded. "Hi."

"Sit down," I urged, glaring at him when he hesitated to do so. Only when he was seated did I follow him across the deck and fold onto his lap.

He stared down at me in surprise, but his arms wrapped around me instinctively, and after a moment, he relaxed, sighing into my hair.

"I wish you hadn't heard that."

I wish you hadn't had to take it.

"It was fine, Sinclair. I know how this is ... How it ends."

His arms tightened around me almost painfully, and he only let go when I wriggled uncomfortably. I wanted to move on, to keep my promise to myself and enjoy the moment with him while I had it, but niggling questions about his girlfriend continued to plague me.

"A Clinton, hey?"

He adjusted in the chair, pulling me closer and tilting me so that I was more comfortable. One hand stroked through my hair, and he watched as the sunshine caught the strands and turned them into fire.

"She's a new associate at a top law firm and fairly political." He waited to see if I wanted to hear more and continued when I nodded. "She works most of the time."

"What's she like?" I asked quietly, paralyzed with apprehension.

He pressed a kiss to my crown. "Elegant, composed, extremely intelligent. When we first met, through her glamorous sister, I couldn't believe they were related."

"I know what that's like. My sisters and I couldn't be more different."

I thought of the inscrutable Elena, composed and tragic like a queen forced to abdicate her throne, and Cosima, sunlight incarnate. I'd been envious of them for years, striving to emulate every one of their formidable attributes.

"I can imagine. You are unlike anyone."

My heart contracted, and I had to bite back a moan. "It hurts me when you are so sweet."

He snorted but pulled back from me to stare into my face. "I'm hardly sweet. I don't have time to be nice, remember?"

I nodded, but I could tell he was surprised and maybe even a little disconcerted by my comment. "I still don't really know what you do, you know."

"No, you don't."

"Do you want to give me a hint?"

"Maybe." He leaned forward, bending over until his lips were just an inch from mine. "But that information comes with a price."

"What if I'm willing to pay?" I darted forward to nip his lip playfully and laughed against his mouth when he caught my lips in a punishing kiss.

Things were just heating up when the bell to his suite rang. When Sinclair didn't immediately pull away, I pushed at him and stood, righting my robe as I moved inside.

"I'm not done with you yet, Elle," he called from the deck as I reached the door and let the waiter in with the cart of aromatic Mexican food.

"I know you are new to this," he began to explain, his voice drifting closer as he made to come inside, "but disobedience will result in punishment."

I'm sure I was the exact shade of my flaming hair when Sinclair rounded the French doors and saw the flustered young waiter and me standing awkwardly side by side. His cool eyes swept over the scene without emotion, and I gasped when he casually leaned against the doorframe and crossed his arms, one eyebrow raised.

"I ..." I cleared my throat as my eyes darted back and forth between Sinclair and the young man. "I ordered food."

"I can see that." Sinclair nodded, the picture of banality with his bare feet peeking out of unbuttoned jeans and his overlong hair curled chaotically around his handsome face. "You need to keep your strength up for what I have in mind tonight."

My throat worked convulsively to swallow my shock. The waiter appraised me with a new kind of interest, his dark eyes lingering over the deep V exposed by the robe. Despite myself, I found desire surge through my blood. When I looked back at Sinclair, he nodded as if he could see my arousal from across the room.

"Pay the man, my siren. Where are your manners?" he reprimanded softly as he padded over to me and took the receipt from the waiter.

He watched me as he signed it and tugged me into a silken

embrace, his arms wrapped around my form so that I could feel his entire length even through the thick robe. He sunk deep into the kiss, tantalizing me with deep strokes of his talented tongue while a hand pushed my robe daringly low on my shoulders, exposing the tops of my breasts. Forgetting myself completely, I submitted to his possession and moaned quietly as I melted into his arms.

When he finally pulled away with a slight but very smug smile, I had to blink rapidly for a minute to reorient myself.

"Oh," I squeaked when I saw the waiter shift uncomfortably, adjusting a very discernable bulge in his pants.

Mortified, I dashed into the bedroom and closed the door on Sinclair's deep chuckle as he addressed the poor young man. I closed my eyes and banged my head lightly against the wall to dislodge the lingering desire cluttering my thoughts. How could I have been so … slutty? I could feel the dampness between my legs, slicking my thighs as I rubbed them together. I had been so turned on by Sinclair's possession, by my exposure to another man. What if I hadn't freaked out? Would he have taken it—me—further? The idea of being laid bare before a stranger as Sinclair manipulated my body brought on a molten wave of desire.

"Oh my God," I murmured, sinking to the floor before the bed with my head in my hands.

That was how Sinclair found me minutes later. Immediately, he swooped down to pick me up and took me out into the main room, where he had set up the small table on the deck with some candles and our food. I was mute as he settled me in the chair and turned on the soothing twang of Spanish guitar over the speakers. He maintained the silence as he served us, and I was grateful for the space to calm my whirring thoughts. Even though I enjoyed the food immensely, I was hot and cold with shame throughout the meal.

It wasn't that big a deal, I knew. So what if we had made out in front of an audience of one, and Sinclair had made a few innuendos? No big deal. But I was so inexperienced with both sex and being in the spotlight that I didn't know what to make of my embarrassment and, even more so, my excitement.

When I reluctantly gave up on the creamy rice pudding after only three bites, Sinclair tugged my chair closer to his and pulled me onto his lap. He loosened the front of my robe, ignoring my sudden tension, and softly began to stroke my neck and shoulders.

"Talk to me."

I sighed deeply. "I don't know what to say."

"There is no right or wrong thing to say here, Elle. I just want to know what you think about what happened?"

"I ..." I sighed again. "I liked it."

He tilted my chin up so that I could see his smile. "I thought you might. You like it when I make the decisions. When you aren't responsible for the shame of your sexual desires."

I hesitated but nodded. My hand was resting on his chest over his heart, and I found a much-needed sense of calm in his steady pulse.

"What I would do with you if I had more time." He shook his head, but his voice was wistful and amused. "But as it is, we only have three more nights. And I have plans for this one. As I remember it, you owe me a fantasy."

I gulped as our fishing bet came back to me. My skin tingled with desire in anticipation of Sinclair lighting me on fire. It was astonishing how ready I was for him all the time; I constantly felt in danger of bursting into flames.

His fingers skated down my neck and squeezed gently. "Your pulse is racing. What are you hoping I will do to you?"

I stared up into his achingly handsome face while ideas stampeded through my mind. My lips parted, and he dipped his thumb into my mouth so that I could gently nip at it.

"Tell me."

Banked fires stirred in his eyes, and I was suddenly determined to ignite them, to take hold of the passion he felt for me and coax it into a livid blaze. I knew what this man liked. I might have only known him for five days, but I knew how to touch him, how to tease him. My submission was imminent, but that didn't mean I couldn't first take pleasure out of seducing him.

"I want you"—I paused, watching the flicker of surprise in his eyes at my boldness and the way I lightly tugged his roguishly long hair—"to undress me."

Immediately, the rope holding together my robe was pulled into his hands, and the fabric gaped open across my chest, not quite revealing my pebbled nipples. I watched his eyes dip into the hollow between my breasts and his Adam's apple bob as he swallowed hard.

"Do you see how my body reacts to you?" I breathed, too timid to speak in the husky tones I imagined would better suit my sensual words. To make up for it, I swept one hand from my neck, between my breasts, to the top of my curls. "Feel how wet I am. Dip just a finger inside me."

He did as requested, one long finger tracing the folds of my drenched sex. I swallowed my moan, determined to remain in power for as long as he would let me.

"Take your clothes off and lie down."

His eyebrow quirked, but he did as I asked, slowly pulling his white T-shirt over his head to reveal the stretch of his lightly tanned abdomen that always made my mouth water. He undid the clasp of his linen pants, staring at me with blatant desire as they dropped to the floor to reveal his hardened length. All moisture left my mouth.

He lay down without touching me, but I didn't care. As soon as his back hit the bed, I straddled his lean thighs and notched his cock against my center, sliding along it slowly, methodically. His hands fisted in the bed sheets at his side, and I was thrilled with his discipline. When he was slick with my moisture, I shimmied down farther and took him firmly in my hand, my eyes on his as I languidly licked a path up his shaft.

"Elle," he groaned, his legs shifting restlessly as I drew circles across the tip of him with my tongue. "Careful."

I was so turned on, especially knowing that my heady power was given only out of graciousness, that he could and would rip it away from me in a second. Eagerly, I drew my lips over my teeth and took him to the back of my throat. I echoed his strangled moan with one of my own, reveling in the salty, manly taste of him.

Until then, I hadn't been able to take him fully inside my mouth, but as I pumped the rest of his length, damp with my salvia, I knew that I had to.

"Elle," he growled again in warning. "I am not coming in your mouth."

I hummed in agreement, which only made his hands come to my shoulders and clench firmly. I was still in control but barely. Before I lost my nerve or Sinclair took the situation out of my hands, I swallowed his length down my throat and moaned in triumph, careful to breathe through my nose.

"Jesus Christ," he barked, jackknifing into a sitting position. His hands suddenly gripped my hair, both forcing me off and farther onto his cock.

I fought his hold and tentatively swiped my tongue along the base of his shaft before rising slightly for breath and lowering again. He allowed me time to find my rhythm, and in less than five minutes, I was rewarded with the first taste of his warmth in my mouth. I pulled back to take the rest on my tongue, laving him gently even after he had finished and collapsed on the bed.

I crawled up to lay beside him, just an inch apart but not touching. Even satiated, the thin wedge of air between us hummed with tension as if our molecules were magnetic, pulling inexorably and almost painfully toward the other's.

"Don't get too comfortable."

I shifted to look up at him. His eyes were closed, but his voice had deepened, darkened into the velvet ropes that bound me to his will.

"In two minutes, I'm going to get up and leave the room. You will completely disrobe and wait for me on the bed. Do you remember how you were positioned on the bed our first night together? I want you like that."

My muscles twitched with memory, and before he had even fully left the room, I was shedding the rest of my clothing and falling into position on the end of the bed. My bum was high in the air, propped up by my folded and spread legs while my hands gently grasped my ankles. Even though my dampening sex was fully exposed, there was a certain comfort in being so contained, small and perfectly parceled for Sinclair to unwrap at his leisure. I could smell us on the sheets, and even though it was harder to breathe, I pressed my nose into the silky fabric to inhale deeply.

After a few minutes, my breath and pulse slowed slightly, and I fell into an almost meditative state. All my senses heightened, from the greedy throb of desire at my core to the abrasion of the sheets against my aching nipples.

I pictured the things he might do to me. My imagination conjured whips and chains, strange instruments of pain and torture that would set my teeth on edge as he forcibly extracted pleasure from my body. A shiver slapped the small of my back and vibrated up my spine.

The door opened with a soft breath, but Sinclair didn't say anything as he moved into the room. I almost jumped when something soft trailed between my legs and up over my back. The sensation didn't last long, and I realized as he tied it firmly and carefully around my head so that our skin didn't brush that it was a blindfold. He smoothed a hand down my spine, his fingers splayed in a possessive move that made my teeth rattle with a deep shudder.

"I'm going to tie you up, Elle." His cool voice was as glossy and impassive as a still water lake. "Would you like to know why I'm doing this?"

I whimpered as another tie brushed over my weeping sex on its descent to my ankles, which he gently secured to each wrist so that I was in a kind of depraved yoga pose.

"Use your words," he reprimanded.

"Yes, please."

He had barely touched me, and I was already a tight wire suspended over a dizzying abyss.

"You need to be punished for making me come in your mouth without permission."

The last tie was secured, and he moved away from me to somewhere else in the room where I could hear him prepare something.

"You need to understand how to control yourself."

Without warning, a resounding smack rang throughout the room. The pain was so shocking that it actually took a moment for my bottom to erupt in fiery pain. A cry rose in my throat, but I swallowed it with a barely discernable gargle.

He blew across my stinging right butt cheek, and crooned, "You are not a good girl, are you?"

I wasn't sure if I should answer, but just as I opened my mouth, his hand came whipping down on the other side of my ass. This time, I cried out.

"No, I know you are not." Another delicious wave of cool air wafted across my aching skin and sent tingles shooting straight down to my sex.

Again, his hand went swinging down on me, releasing endorphins and sweet-edged pain. I gasped into the sheet and moaned.

"A nice girl doesn't get turned on by a spanking," he scolded, his fingers dipping into the pool of desire beneath my burning bottom.

He dragged one knuckle down over my clit, and I jerked in my bonds at the roar of pleasure it released. With one hand still on my center, he spanked me again, pushing me further into an unfamiliar basin of shimmering pleasure. My fingernails dug into the thin skin of my ankles as I tried to find the ground beneath my floating body, but the sharp tingle of pain only elevated me further.

"How many do you think you deserve? Ten, twenty? Your ass is already a beautiful shade of pink."

I groaned, desperate for him to go on but incoherent with pleasure. My brain was too busy trying to process the waves of desire pounding down on me to form actual words.

Two fingers sank into my heat at the same time that his other hand landed.

"Ahhh!" I screamed.

My entire body was coiled so tightly that there didn't seem to be any space between my skin and bones, my blood and muscles. I was reduced to quaking flesh, an organism entirely dependent on pleasure to survive.

"Sinclair."

"You may not orgasm."

"Ugh!"

"*Silence*," he ordered in French. "*Si tu restes juste comme ça, je te donnerai ce que tu veux.*"

If you stay just like this, he said, *I will give you what you want*.

I gritted my teeth.

Two slaps landed in quick succession.

"You took me in your mouth without permission."

Slap.

"Splayed your naked body on a public beach for my pleasure."

Slap.

"You begged me to dominate you, to take your pleasure and make it all mine."

Slap, slap.

I was panting heavily now like a feral animal, and my wetness was coating the inside of my thighs, pooling on the silk sheets.

He paused for a long beat, his fingers still inside me and his thumb poised just over my clit.

"You seduced a taken man."

My racing heart tripped over itself, and I lost my breath completely. Shame swirled with my desire until they formed something new, something brighter and more powerful. It built in my pulsing body until my tongue throbbed with my confession.

"Yes," I groaned. "I did."

"Good girl," he crooned.

He pulled his fingers from my clenching sex, and I opened my mouth to scream at him to put them back, but his words interrupted me.

"Would you do it again? Seduce a taken man, give him your sweet pussy and let him make you his?" he asked.

The blunt edge of his erection brushed against me, and I bucked back against my bonds in a desperate attempt to get him inside me. I was so close to orgasming. All I needed was one of those beautiful gusts of his cool breath against my heat, and I would have shattered.

"Don't make me ask you again."

Slap, slap.

I groaned raggedly, too aroused to worry if I sounded sexy or not.

"Yes!" I hissed. "I would do it again, and again and—" My litany was cut off with a hoarse shout as he thrust inside me to the hilt.

My sightless world erupted in pinwheels of brilliant color as I fell completely into the darkness, free-falling past the bold shards of my devastating desire. I vaguely felt Sinclair's fingers tighten on my hips, his length dragging deliciously, almost too roughly against my firing nerve endings and his almost silent shout of release before I blacked out.

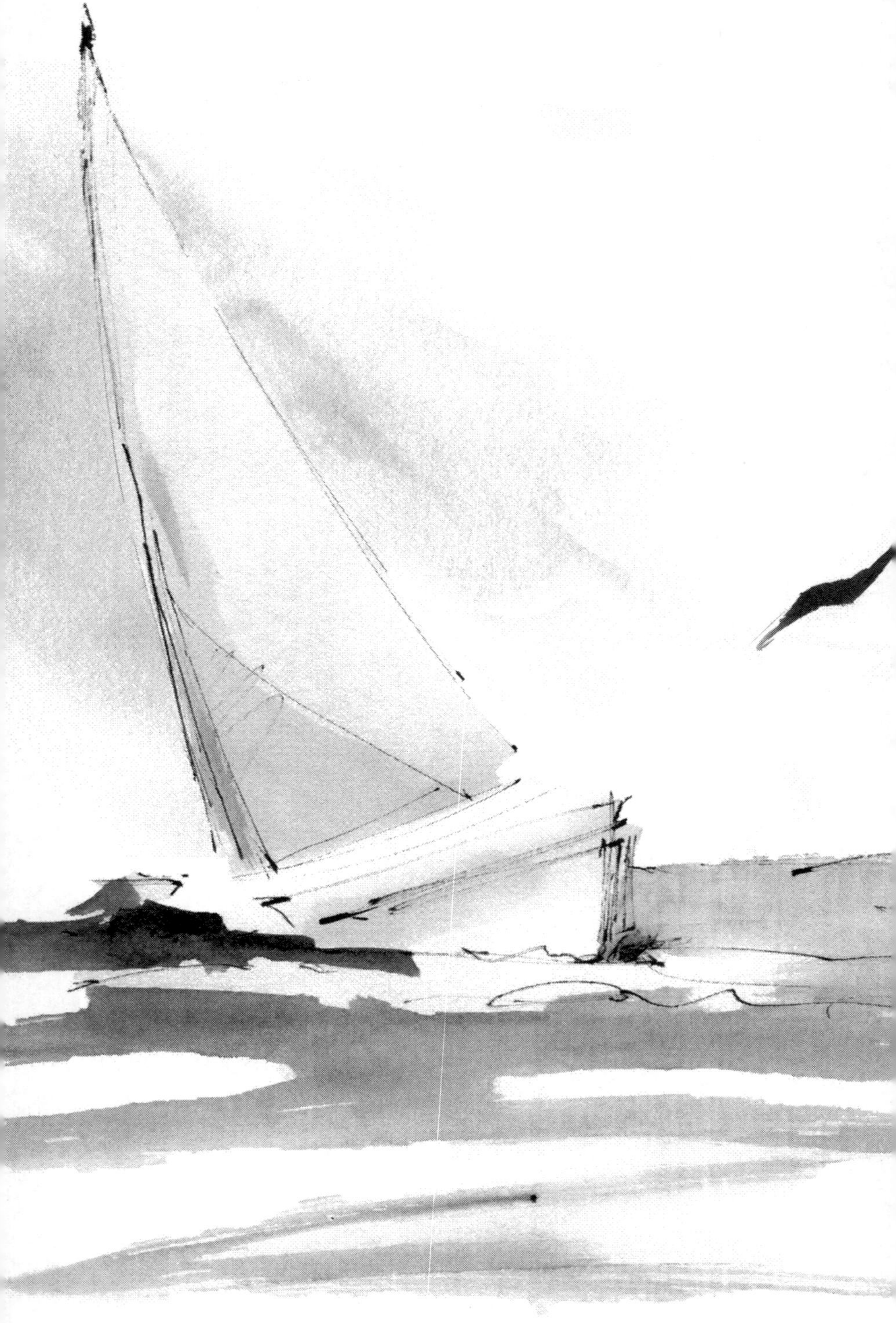

Chapter Thirteen

I fidgeted in my chair, trying to take the pressure off my pleasantly sore backside. Though the café had padded chairs, I could still feel the warm pain, and each movement I made forced my thoughts back to last night and the things Sinclair had done to me.

I looked up from my half-eaten bagel to find him staring at me with a raised brow from across the table. He was speaking with Richard Denman and Robert Corbett about the resort they were in the process of securing; a place twenty minutes down the beach that had been abandoned due to financial strain. Sinclair had shown me pictures yesterday, and I had to agree with his instincts; the thick slice of land right on the white sandy beach was well worth the price.

I took a sip of my latte and deliberately allowed the foam to kiss my top lip. As I watched him, my tongue made a slow sweep across my mouth. His other eyebrow joined the first, marring his usually fathomless expression. I laughed softly and broke eye contact, turning to the left to see Candy observing us. Immediately, I ducked my head and fought the blush crawling across my skin.

Her hand found mine on my thigh and squeezed lightly. "You look as though you've enjoyed your trip, Elle."

"I have, very much." I nodded but refused to meet her eyes.

There was no doubt in my mind that she knew about my holiday affair with Sinclair, but I didn't want to make her any more uncomfortable with the knowledge of it.

"So has Sinclair."

She nodded her head toward the Frenchman now locked in a heated debate with Duncan Wright. Well, Duncan was heated, speaking animatedly with his hands while his mouth twisted around his frustrated words. Sinclair just sat there with his hands placed loosely on the table, posture straight but professional, not hostile under Duncan's anxious focus. I scoured his face for clues and found nothing but calm.

"You leave tomorrow, right?" Candy continued, and I finally turned to her. "Time flies."

I tried to breathe through the sudden depression gripping my throat and shrugged. "It will be good to see my family."

"Uh-huh." She slanted me a long look, waiting for me to say something more. When I didn't, she sighed and turned fully to face me. "Listen, I've been working this whole trip, and I'd love to take a break to do some shopping. Would you go to town with me this afternoon?"

Immediately, my eyes sought Sinclair. He had mentioned going to the failing resort to look around with some building inspectors and Richard Denman, who I found out was a revered architect from Chicago. I had been invited along, but after learning that Margot would be there, I had begged off.

"It will be fun," Candy trilled. "I promise."

I laughed at my hesitation and shook my head to clear it of the Frenchman. I had no obligation to Sinclair; he was busy, and though I should have been photographing, I figured I could do that in town.

"I would love to."

Candy nodded curtly. "Good."

I had my purse and my camera, so we decided to head out right after breakfast, but I lingered, trying to get a private moment to say goodbye to Sinclair. I knew it would only be a few hours until I saw him next, but being away from him still made me slightly anxious. I groaned into my hand.

God, I had it bad.

"What are you moaning about?" His trademark small smile brightened his handsome face as he looked down on me. "Personally, I can't think of anything to bemoan. I am in Mexico on a beautiful day the morning after sleeping with a gorgeous woman."

His words wooed me, and I stepped so close to him; we were almost pressed together. I knew the others stood just to the side, but Sinclair didn't seem to mind. In fact, his grin widened, and he pressed my hips to his with a firm hand on my lower back.

"You'll miss me this afternoon."

It wasn't a question, but I nodded anyway. "When will you be back?"

His thumb inched under my shirt and rubbed over the bare skin at the base of my spine. "Not soon enough. In time for dinner."

I smiled at the domesticity of his comment, unsure if he realized it or not. "No worries. If you are late, we can skip right to dessert."

"Mmm, lavender and honey. My favorite." He leaned close,

bending down to look me straight in the eyes. I thought he would kiss me, but he only smiled, his firm lips parting to reveal nearly perfect white teeth. "Be safe and have fun, siren."

I swallowed and braced my feet farther apart, afraid that I would float into the air on cloud nine. "Will do, sir."

He chuckled and lightly brushed his hand over my bottom as he let me go and stepped away.

"Are you done hitting on my lady, Sinclair?" Cage demanded as he stepped away from a shell-shocked young woman who stared after him and slung an arm around my shoulders.

I laughingly shoved him away with my hip, but he held on, his face collapsing into sorrow. "Look what you've done, turning her against me."

Candy hit him none too lightly on the back of his head with a binder. "Let her go, you oaf."

Cage winced, rubbing the back of his skull. "You guys are no fun."

"I assure you, that's not the case." There was a trace of humor in Sinclair's cool tones.

His colleagues blinked, shocked by his innuendo. Robert Corbett cleared his throat and shifted uncomfortably, but Richard Denman grinned broadly at me and winked. Sinclair was the one to break the silence by raising a condescending eyebrow at his dumbstruck friends and winking—actually winking—at me as he walked past us to the waiting car.

"Wow," Candy breathed, a hand to her lower stomach. "I'm surprised I'm still standing."

I flushed but didn't try to contain my laughter.

"What have you done to that man?" Richard clapped a hand to my back, his silver hair gleaming in the sunlight. "Whatever it is, keep it up. I haven't seen Sin so light at heart ..." He frowned and then threw his head back to chuckle. "Ever."

Their compliments were slightly awkward. I had wondered what Sinclair was like with Darling back at home; if he was so charming, so passionate. It seemed that I now had an answer, but it only led to so many more haunting questions. Like would I ever see him again after I got on the plane tomorrow?

Cage, surprisingly, didn't say anything. Instead, he squeezed my shoulder and released me, taking a step back to study me. He was wearing distractingly bright green spandex swim shorts, and the sight of his muscular thighs and the bulge in the thin material momentarily distracted me. After a second, he grabbed a piece of paper off the receptionist's desk and scribbled something on the back of a card before pressing it into my palm. Distracted by his sudden departure, I tucked the folded paper into my purse without reading it.

When the men and an unseen Margot had left, Candy and I decided to walk to town. It was a half an hour trek in the hot sun, but we were both up for it, and it gave me the opportunity to photograph the small stretch of local boroughs before we hit the market. Candy kept up a constant stream of pleasant conversation, happily pointing out things I might find of interest, and she flat-out giggled when I insisted on taking a picture of an old Mexican man wearing nothing but a long pair of dusty shorts. He was sound asleep and practically rolling out of his seat before a small but carefully maintained pink house.

"How long have you been doing photography?" she asked me, wiping off the crown of sweat beaded on her forehead.

"My sister bought me my first camera when I was sixteen." I could still remember the feel of the secondhand Canon in my hands and the hard click of the shutter as it closed over an image. I still had the camera, carefully wrapped in my suitcase because I hadn't wanted to risk shipping it to New York with the rest of my meager things from Paris.

"Did you train?"

The mouth of the marketplace loomed up ahead, and the colorful cacophony made my finger twitch over the lens of my camera.

"Five years at *L'École des Beaux-Arts* in Paris, mostly in painting."

"Wow. I've always loved art. Obviously, working with Sinclair, it's a prerequisite. But I cannot paint to save my life unless you count splatter painting."

I laughed, but my mind was caught on her earlier comment. "Sinclair likes art?"

She frowned at me over the rim of a large ceramic pitcher she was inspecting. "Well, he should. He owns one of the more prestigious art galleries in the city."

What city? I bit back my question and nodded. "Right."

She must have caught my sigh because suddenly her hand was on mine.

"Listen, Elle. I know we don't really know each other, and under other circumstances, I'm sure the classy cultured artist would have nothing to do with the dumpy businesswoman." Her smile was sharp with self-deprecation. "But I feel as if we are friends. And as a friend, I can tell you that I've never seen my boss like this. He's lightened. Usually, he walks around like a living sculpture, beautiful and untouchable, but you make him come alive."

Tears stung the back of my eyes. "Why are you telling me this?"

It was brutal to hear about his possible affection when I knew it would end tomorrow. Besides, no matter what other people might have said, I knew that Sinclair only wanted a holiday affair, no personal attachment and no strings. But God, it felt good to pretend, if only for a minute, that he felt something more than lust toward me.

Candy's grip tightened over me. "Because I think you should tell him how you feel. If you have feelings for him, fight for him. I like his girlfriend"—she paused, and guilt flashed across her strong features—"but that doesn't mean I can't see what is so clearly happening between you and Sinclair."

I shook my head and pulled my hand away from her. "Stop."

Her dark eyes were wide with sincerity, but she held up her palms in surrender. "Fine. I had to say it, but I understand if you are too afraid to act on it."

I flinched as her arrow found the bullseye. The new Giselle wasn't timid, or afraid, or meek. But—I bit my lip and took another step away from her—that didn't mean I was stupid.

She sighed deeply and picked up the pitcher again. "So what do you think? Too garish?"

We spent the next few hours tripping around downtown Cabo San Lucas; all talk of Sinclair clearly off the table. Instead, Candy told me about her start in business, interning for large corporations and subsisting on ramen noodles and business lunches before she met Sinclair at a conference. They had hit it off right away in the Q&A session of a famous real estate broker who they reduced to a blubbering mess after ripping into his flimsy business model. She laughed as she recounted the story, and so did I, imagining them tag-teaming the poor man.

I told her little about my past beyond Paris, and if she noticed my evasion, she didn't let on. It was difficult to explain my splintered family and the fear that had driven me first from Italy and then my beloved Paris. It felt strange not to tell her about my siblings, though. Usually, when someone questioned me, I automatically spoke of their more glamorous lives, casting my own dull existence into shadow. Instead, we talked about art and France, both of which Candy was an expert in.

By the time we decided to head home, the light was syrupy as the sun began to sink in the cerulean blue sky, and Candy was laden with shopping bags.

"I can't believe you didn't get that bracelet," she said between each labored breath. "Seriously, Elle, it was gorgeous."

I sighed, picturing the Mexican silver and turquoise cuff that we had seen in the jewelry store. It had been a beautiful piece of jewelry, but I couldn't afford it. The credit card Cosima and Sebastian had given me practically burned a hole in my pocket, but I refused on principle to use their money for anything less than essentials.

"Starving artist," I said by way of explanation, though that wasn't exactly the truth either.

"You don't look it." Candy eyed my curves with good-humored envy. "I'd give my right arm to have a figure like that."

"It took me a long time to be okay with it," I admitted, running a hand over the exaggerated flare of my hip. "I have two tall, thin sisters."

Images of Cosima in *Sports Illustrated* flashed through my mind, but I repressed my old habit of comparing us, burrowing it deep beneath the confidence that Sinclair had newly gifted me.

Candy pursed her lips. "Damn, there are more of you?"

I laughed and felt warmth suffuse my chest as she linked her arm with mine. It felt good to be lighthearted and girlish, to laugh too loudly at Candy's impressions of Cage and snigger together over details of her last lover who had a thing for woman sucking lollipops.

"No, seriously," she had said, eyes wide. "I ended up with three cavities."

I had never really had many friends unless you counted my family. Brenna was my only true friend, and I couldn't even remember the details of our relationship in the beginning. After she had invited me for coffee the first time, who had called whom next? Either way, it had always been easy, and I realized that I felt the same unself-conscious ease with Candy.

We were laughing when we entered Sinclair's suite using the spare key card he had given me. I pretended not to notice Candy give it a significant glance, and happily, the low murmur of chatter in the room distracted her.

Obviously, the inspection had gone well because the men involved each clutched a flute of frothing champagne, and they all cheered when we entered.

"You got it?" I asked, breathless from the excitement crackling in the room.

Sinclair dropped the unopened bottle he'd been holding—which Cage caught hastily—and strode over to me before I could even blink. He hefted me in his arms and beamed into my face. "Oh yes, siren, we got it."

I squealed and hugged him, too aware of the others to do anything more. Cage, apparently, shared no such qualm because he was on Candy, his lips slanted over hers before she could protest. When he finally broke away with a loud smack and a cheeky grin, she was the color of a vivid sunburn.

"You ass," she snapped.

Cage only chuckled and turned to me, trying to plant a kiss on me as well.

When Sinclair raised an eyebrow at him and hugged me closer, he only shrugged and murmured, "Spoilsport."

I ignored him. "Are we going to celebrate?"

"We are." Duncan adjusted his glasses and indicated his champagne flute.

"Santiago and Katarina are coming." Sinclair spoke in his normal muted tones, and though everyone could hear him and see us, I knew he was absorbed by me. "Do you want to go out with them?"

"Dancing?"

His eyebrows rose over twinkling eyes. "You like to dance?"

I shrugged, thinking about our first night together when we had moved sinuously across the dance floor. "I'd like to dance with you."

His arms tightened around me before he loosened his hold. I slid down his body, feeling his half-hard bulge press against my stomach when I finally landed on my feet. He was still staring at me with the small smile I was coming to think was just for me.

Cage coughed loudly and took a long chug from the champagne bottle he had caught from Sinclair. "Are you sure you want to go out? We can get out of here if you want to"—his eyebrows waggled—"stay in to celebrate. In fact, if you really beg, I'll stay for that party too."

Candy dug an elbow into his ribs. "You're such a child."

"Prude."

"Asshole."

I smiled at their exchange, still looking up at Sinclair. His face was relaxed, his hands loosely clasped around my waist. I caught Richard's eye over Sinclair's shoulder and watched him nod his approval, lifting the flute in a silent cheer.

"Cage is right," I murmured, rolling onto my tiptoes into order to speak against the corner of his jaw. "We did have other plans for tonight."

He groaned, his hands flexing on my hips. "Don't tempt me, minx." He leaned down, running his tongue along the delicate shell of my ear. "I could take you right now, in front of all these people, and you wouldn't say no, would you?"

A shudder wracked my spine, and his dark chuckle was warm in my ear. I shoved him away playfully and battled with my blush.

"Sinclair," a feminine voice snapped.

I turned to see Margot standing in the open door to the suite, momentarily distracted by how lovely she was in her vivid green dress with her silky blond hair gleaming. She was staring at us with haughty indignation as if I was some whore who had lured Sinclair to the dark side.

He tensed, but his voice was cool when he addressed her, "Yes, Margot, no one will force you to go if you would rather stay here. Alone."

She bristled and took a few steps into the room, oblivious to the ominous silence that had descended as everyone watched the exchange in rapt attention.

"I know you better than this," she said, waving her hand disdainfully in my direction. "You don't do messy. Cut her off now before she deludes herself into thinking this is anything more than a holiday affair."

Each word struck me in the chest like a poisoned dart. I took a step back, right into Sinclair, who clamped an arm around my waist.

My skin burned with shame, but when I tried to wriggle free, he leaned down to growl, "Stop it."

"Stop being such an Ice Queen. Can't you see he's happy?" Candy said, her teeth bared.

Margot raised one pale brow and looked me over, cataloging everything from the rubber flip-flops at my feet to the volume of my humidity-infused hair.

"She leaves tomorrow. Can't you see the consequences?"

"Enough." His voice cracked like a whip. "You will not ruin the night for everyone, M. Is that understood?"

Her throat worked as she swallowed, and her eyes were wide as she tried to silently appeal to his logical side, but I could tell by the weight of his arm across my stomach that he wouldn't yield.

Strangely, I felt bad for Margot. Even though I hated to think about it, she was right. Even if I made Sinclair happy now, was it worth the guilt he would feel returning home to his girlfriend? I wasn't so sure.

I placed a hand on his arm and gently removed it, deciding to give them a minute to speak without the awkwardness of my presence.

"Come on, Candy, help me pick out what to wear?"

I extended my hand to her and smiled when she happily interlocked out fingers, shooting a withering glance at Margot as she did so.

"Your things are in the bedroom." Sinclair spoke softly, but I heard him even from across the room as we opened the door to leave for my room.

"Excuse me?"

I didn't turn around, but I could tell by the sudden silence that everyone was as confounded as I was.

"I said your things are in the bedroom."

Finally turning around, I glanced helplessly at our audience. He had a girlfriend, for God's sake. What was he doing announcing to them that we were sleeping together? Obviously, we hadn't been completely discreet, especially tonight, but still.

My frantic eyes found his, and I opened my mouth to speak but clamped it shut again when I saw the stern expression on his face. He was daring me to protest over his lack of respect for my privacy or my individuality. *I own you*; his words from the drive to the marina echoed in my head. I swallowed past the rising fear that he did, and he would continue to own my heart long after we left this place.

He sighed, tucking his hands in his pockets as the shutters slammed down over his features. "Go get dressed, Elle. We will wait for you."

I stood there for a minute as he turned to talk to the men, ignoring the last ten minutes of public affection and humiliation as if it had never happened. Margot watched me curiously with her head cocked to one side as I hesitated.

"Are you okay?" Candy whispered.

"I'm just not used to being controlled," I hissed, even though this seemed like the millionth time this week that Sinclair had done so.

"What are you going to do about it?"

I pursed my lips as Cosima's accented voice echoed through my head and urged me to follow her example. I picked out the tiniest dress in my arsenal, one that Cosima had bought me for Mama's restaurant opening two years ago, and held it up for Candy with a smile.

"I'm going to make sure he doesn't regret it."

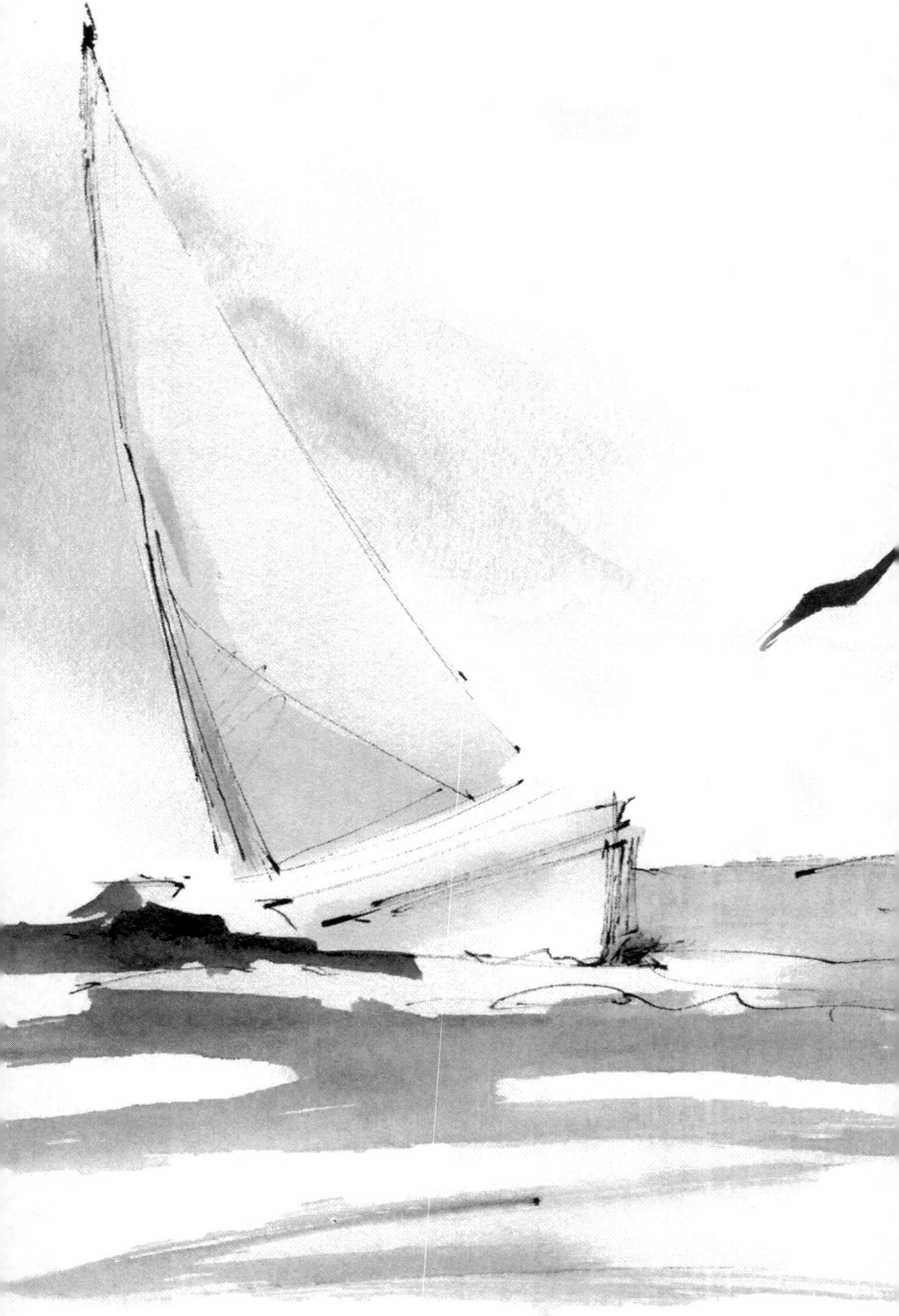

Chapter Fourteen

The dance floor vibrated with the pulsing beat of the techno music blaring through the five feet speakers surrounding the dance floor at the Pink Kitty nightclub. Scantily clad dancers ground against each other, their bare skin glistening in the blue and pink lights flashing overhead. My long hair was tangled and damp against my exposed back, so I lifted it from my skin, wishing fruitlessly for a breeze to pass through the open front of the club into the back where we moved to the throbbing beat.

My eyes sought out Sinclair over at the bar talking to Santiago and Candy. I had politely implied that if he could distract those two, then maybe Cage and Kat would dance together. He had raised those strong brows but done as I requested, and now Kat stood close to me, laughing as Cage danced around her with the flair of the expert performer he was.

Smiling to myself, I pushed through the crowd, desperate to get some air. My feet were sore from dancing so long in my only pair of high heels, a ridiculously tall pair of nude pumps that I had purchased in Paris when Brenna invited me to the premiere of one of her movies. Sinclair had seemed to like them, though, if his dark promise to fuck me with nothing else on was anything to go by.

When I had emerged from the bedroom, everyone but Sinclair had left to wait for us in the lobby. He apologized with a twisted smile for Margot's inappropriate behavior. I didn't correct him—our behavior was far more inappropriate than her concern—mostly because the way he looked at me in the short, tight white dress I wore was enough to distract me from the truth.

The cool air hit my sticky skin as soon as I pushed open the heavy door to the fire escape, and I breathed a sigh of contentment as I lifted my hair from my neck.

"You've got a beautiful smile," a hot voice breathed into my ear.

I scrunched my nose against the foul smell of the stranger's breath and tried to step farther down the stairs so that he could get by. When he didn't move, I turned to look up at him, finding a vaguely attractive frat boy leering down at me.

"Thank you," I said coolly, drawing my arms across my chest to hide my ample cleavage from his gaze. "My boyfriend thinks so too."

The deception fell from my lips too easily, and for a second, I allowed my mind to go there, to imagine what it would be like to be Sinclair's girlfriend. I wondered if he would call me darling and give me space to express my independence, or if he would be the man I knew him to be now, deliciously possessive and spontaneous.

"Come dance with me, babe."

The man's voice rudely interrupted my daydreams, and I looked up at him sharply, noticing that he had closed the distance between us and now stood only a step above me.

"I'm good, thanks."

I turned to walk farther down the steps, thinking I could make my way around to the front of the club where there would be more people, but his arm snagged me just as I was taking a step. A squeak punctuated my fall as I slammed into the railing, and the air collapsed from my lungs. Taking advantage of my position leaning over the iron banister, he pressed into my back and slowly righted me so that I was flush against his front.

He groaned. "This is nice. What do you say we skip the dancing, and I take you back to my hotel?"

My heart was beating painfully hard, but I knew how to think through the fog of panic, thanks to my experiences with Christopher.

"As I said, I have a boyfriend." My voice was surprisingly calm, and I was thankful for it. Some men did this for the thrill of the fear, I knew.

I attempted to step free from his arms, but they constricted around me like a boa.

"We don't need a hotel." He spun me around and clamped down on my lower back, pushing my hips tight against his arousal.

His head descended, and I frantically fought for a way out of this situation. My arms were held tight at my sides, and without leverage, there was no way I could dislodge a man almost a foot taller and eighty pounds heavier than me.

So, I did the only thing I could.

When his lips slanted over mine and his greasy tongue stabbed into my mouth, I bit him. Hard. The taste of blood blossomed against my tongue, and his hoarse cry rattled my eardrums. He shoved me away, and I stumbled on my stupid heels, falling back with a crash against the railing. Pain exploded in my head as it cracked against the metal, but I stood as quickly as I could, fighting the wooziness. The pervert was bent over, his hands folded over his heavily bleeding mouth.

"You fuckin' bith," he mumbled and took a menacing step forward.

I kicked off my shoes, leaving them on the landing, and took off down the rest of the stairs. I could hear him lumbering after me, but I knew I was quicker because he was crippled by pain. I stepped on something painful as I tore around the corner to the front of the club, but I ignored it, stopping only when I saw a large Mexican bouncer. I bounded into him, and he caught me without question, pushing me behind him when he caught sight of the man trailing behind me.

"Ignacio." The bouncer nodded at another man guarding the door, and he took off toward the creep who had assaulted me.

Finally, the bouncer turned to me, his large face creased with concern. "Are you okay?"

I nodded, but my body was shaking, and I could still taste his blood against my teeth.

"Can you tell me what happened?"

There was shouting down the street, but the bouncer took me gently by the shoulders and bent down so that his large brown eyes were all I could see.

"I need you to tell me what happened. Can you do that?"

The cool air off the ocean made me shiver and gave me the wherewithal to shake my head and request the one thing I really needed. "My boyfriend is inside. He's tall with reddish hair and really pretty blue eyes. Can you get him?"

He stared at me for a minute before nodding tersely and moving me to the stool that he probably sat on when the line was slow. I started when he slipped a coarse blanket around my shoulders, but he smiled kindly at me and moved away a few steps to speak into his walkie-talkie. I could hear the man I'd bitten groan as the other bouncer dealt with him, but I didn't look over at them. I knew I would cry if I did, and I wanted to be stronger than that. So, I sat on the stool and dragged deep handfuls of air into my lungs, counting to seven before I released each breath.

A few minutes later, my group burst through the door to the club, and Sinclair was suddenly before me, crouched on his knees in order to look up at me.

"Elle," he croaked, two knuckles skating down my cheek to the corner of my mouth. They came away with blood on them, and I realized that he thought it was mine.

"His," I explained through my chattering teeth.

His eyes were large, the color of wet blue velvet, and his voice was unbearably soft when he said, "*Désolé, ma sirène.*"

I swallowed a sob and wrestled one hand out of the blanket to clutch his damp button-up. "Hold me?"

I was in his lap before I could blink, nestled in the cradle of his arms with his firm lips pressed to my forehead. The bouncer was speaking with Candy and Richard Denman, both of them yelling at him for answers.

"Stop," I called and cleared my throat when my voice didn't carry as well as I wanted it to. "Stop asking him questions."

They turned to me, blinking widely, struck dumb by my insistence and probably my awful appearance.

The bouncer bent down before me, and I realized that despite his impressive bull-like size, he had a handsome face made sweet by large eyes the color of melted chocolate. "Can you tell me what happened now?"

I nodded and took a deep breath, drawing comfort from Sinclair's arms as they squeezed gently around me. Santiago, Kat, and Cage all appeared while I told my story but quickly turned away to speak with a policeman who had shown up, interacting in rapid-fire Spanish. Sinclair's body grew increasingly tense as I recounted the incident until I felt like I was sitting in a cage. When I finished, the bouncer asked me a few questions before going to join the conversation with Santiago and the policeman.

I looked up at Sinclair, but he gently pressed my head back to his shoulder, and I knew it was because he didn't want me to see the anger on his face.

"Cage, get her some water to wash that cretin's blood out of her mouth. Candy, I want you to take her home now. Go straight back to the resort and take her to my room," Sinclair said, once again the cool and controlled businessman.

I was mute as he placed me carefully on my feet and moved a few steps away. The sudden distance was like alcohol in an open wound. Why was he leaving me?

Cage reappeared with a plastic cup of water I used to swish out my mouth, spitting the pink liquid into a street grate as I kept an eye on Candy stalking after Sin.

"What are you doing?" Candy hissed, her large teeth flashing as she bared them at her boss. "You should take her back."

He shook his head but didn't look at me. A muscle in his jaw spasmed, and I watched his fists clench and unclench as he fought to remain calm. For some reason, the sight of him made me want to weep.

"Do it now, Candace," he ordered before turning around and striding over to the conversation with the police.

Candy turned to me, her angry eyes dulling with empathy as she took in the miserable sight of me. With a gusty sigh, she placed an arm around my shoulders. "Come on, Elle. Let's go back."

We were silent in the cab, but she held my hand the entire time. I didn't cry, but my body was weak with the effort to hold in the tears, and my left foot throbbed brutally from a deep slice on my instep. The stupid incident, coupled with Sinclair's continued hot and cold attitude, the fact that I was leaving tomorrow and he would go back to his darling girlfriend, sent the careful walls compartmentalizing my life crumbling down.

When we reached Sinclair's suite, I hesitated in the doorway. He had ordered Candy to take me home, and my heart throbbed as his words echoed in my head.

"Come on, I'll make you some tea while you take a shower, okay?" Candy placed a hand on my back, and I winced when she pressed into tender skin from where I had fallen backward on the stairs.

My head and heart pulsed in painful tandem, and I was grateful to her for leaving me to my own chaotic thoughts.

"You don't have to stay," I still offered.

She looked at me like a headmistress, her expression deeply at odds with the tight blue dress I had encouraged her to wear. "Don't be selfish. I want to be here with you."

I ducked my head and nodded, warmed and shamed by her gesture. I quickly made my way to the bathroom and shucked my clothes, waiting until the temperature was close to scalding before stepping into the spray. I brushed my teeth twice, then let the water pound the thoughts out of my head and pressed my cheek to the tiles as sobs finally wracked my aching frame.

I didn't know where Sinclair was or why he hadn't taken me back to the resort. He could have been angry with me for disappearing alone, and I wouldn't have blamed him; it was incredibly stupid of me. It was our last night together, and I had ruined it.

Otherwise, my encounter with the drunken horn dog at the club didn't disturb me as much as it might have. I was used to men taking what they wanted, and their aggression didn't surprise me anymore. Which was why, I think, I was so deeply enthralled with Sinclair. He was such a contradiction to the little I knew about men. He struggled to do the right thing, to remain in control and logical despite the desires that burned brightly within him. He was a deeply passionate man beneath the calm resolve, and I admired him for it even though I was the one to take that calm from him. The pain increased in my chest when I thought about what I was doing to the woman who loved him back home and to the man Sinclair struggled so hard to be—a good man with morals.

Self-loathing bloomed in my chest until I almost couldn't breathe. Everything awful that I had done in my short life welled up from my memory banks and flooded me. It was a strange and bone-numbing feeling to realize you were the villain in your own life story.

Later, after I had finally expelled all my tears and the water had beaten my body and psyche free of all hurt, I lay in the king-sized bed with Candy sound asleep beside me. She had insisted on staying until Sinclair came home, but he had been gone for over two hours now. I turned my head to look at the glowing face of the alarm clock.

2:43 a.m.

I sighed, bone-tired but unable to sleep.

I bolted upright when the door to the suite opened and closed a few minutes later. The sound of male conversation wafted in through the open door, and I strained to make out what they were saying.

Candy stirred beside me, and I quickly turned on my side, my heart galloping as I feigned sleep. I felt her sit up and the gentle scratch of her gaze on my face before she slipped out of bed to join the commotion in the living room. As soon as she had gently closed the door behind her, I was up and at the door, cracking it open noiselessly for better audio.

"It was fucking stupid, Sin," Cage was saying as he took a seat on the couch.

"And you know when Cage says something is stupid, it's really idiotic," Candy added dryly as she curled up sleepily on the couch.

"It was fucking necessary," Sinclair snapped as he poured himself a snifter of brandy from the bar. "You know the police wouldn't have done anything."

Cage shrugged as he snagged the drink from Sinclair, who

promptly poured himself another, but his voice was tight when he said, "You didn't need to beat the guy to a bloody pulp."

"And you didn't need to help."

I covered my mouth to muffle my gasp.

Sinclair poured more brandy into his now empty glass and prepared another one for Candy before he went to sit beside her. She waved her hand at the glass, dismissing it as she uncurled from her position.

"This is a talk between men, I think." She placed a hand on his shoulder and squeezed tightly. "Not a long one, I hope. It's late, and that girl in there needs you."

She smiled with her mouth closed tightly over her teeth as she moved toward the door. Her hand was on the handle, gently swinging it closed behind her, when she muttered, "And don't underestimate how much you need her too."

Sinclair's back was to me as he stared after her, and I had the pleasure of watching him peel off his blood-soaked shirt and throw it onto a nearby chair, every movement jerky with anger. I had never seen him so thrown off, and despite myself, attraction sizzled over my skin as his naked back came into sight.

After a few moments of silence, Cage leaned back against the cushions, his leather pants creaking, and slanted his friend a look. "We have a problem here."

I watched Sinclair's jaw work as he chewed his thoughts over. Finally, he tipped his glass back and drained the scorching liquor. He placed it on the table and braced his hands on his thighs.

"I know."

"What are you going to do about it?"

They must have really hurt the creep if they were talking so seriously about the consequences. I shivered and rubbed my bare legs together.

"I honestly have no idea." He thrust both hands into his hair and tugged harshly. "How did I get myself into this fucking situation?"

"Do you really want me to answer that? Because I've been wanting to say some things for a while now."

"Since when have you censored yourself?"

"Fair point." Cage nodded. "*D'accord*. I think you're in a relationship for the wrong reasons. Yeah, she's smart and beautiful, and your parents love her, and you guys get along well, but that's not what love is."

"And you would know?" Sinclair barked, but immediately, he shook his head. "Sorry."

"*Mon ami*, I'm not exactly a relationship guru, but I've known you for years, and no matter what you try to tell yourself, you can't control everything. Hell, you shouldn't be able to. You and Elle …" He shook his head, and I sucked in a deep breath. "It's the first time I've seen you cut loose like this. She's good for you."

"She can't be."

"Bullshit."

"I don't know anything about her." He stood in an explosion of movement and began to pace back and forth. "Where she lives, who her family is … nothing. And she sure as hell doesn't know anything about me. If she did …" He shook his head as his voice petered off.

"If she did, she would be just as into you," Cage asserted. "She's a strong girl, Sin. Look at how she reacted tonight. She gave that guy exactly what he deserved and didn't even break down."

This seemed to take the wind out of Sinclair's sails. He sat down with a ragged sigh. "She's too good for me."

"Probably," Cage agreed easily. "But any girl worth being with always is."

They were silent for a few minutes, each lost in their own thoughts. I stood against the wall just inside the bedroom and struggled to unravel the thread of my thoughts. Did Sinclair feel even half as much as I did for him?

"She scares the fuck out of me," Sinclair muttered. I had never heard him swear so much.

"You've never been one to back away from fear."

"I knew the minute I saw her that she would do this," he said, and I felt a pang in my chest for causing him so much undue pain. No matter what he felt, I knew I would be getting on the plane alone tomorrow.

"I think that says more than enough about your connection with her. For once, take something *you* want. Not what Willa and Mortimer want. Not what you think society expects you to have. You've made it. You're successful as fuck and respected. You've earned a little trouble, especially when it comes in as beautiful a package as Elle."

Sin was quiet, staring into the bowl of his glass as if he could divine in the brandy for answers. "I have obligations."

Cage sighed dramatically. "Why do people tie themselves to things that make them miserable, hmm?"

My Frenchman didn't seem to have any response to that. Instead, he leaned back against the cushions and expelled an exhausted breath.

"I'll leave you with her." Cage unwound his large body from the couch, flipping his long braid over his shoulder as he did so. He leaned down to clap Sinclair on the back and brought him close, touching their foreheads together for one long minute. I held my breath at their intimacy. Who was Cage Tracy, lead singer of France's hottest band, to be so close to Sinclair, a man whose icy barriers seemed nearly impenetrable?

When they broke apart, Sinclair was calmer, his shoulders relaxed. He followed his friend to the door and stood in the middle of the living room for a few minutes after Cage left, tugging a hand through his tousled dark red locks until they were in utter disarray. I longed to go out to him, wrap my arms around his trim waist, press my breasts to his naked back and slide my hands over the moguls of muscle crossing his stomach.

But the truth was, I had no place in his world. It was just as it had been all my life. I was a meteor in a universe of floating stars as bright and beautiful as diamonds, secure in their function and place while I zoomed by.

A noise from the living room alerted me to Sinclair's movements toward the bedroom, so I scrambled back into bed and tried to breathe calmly through my clattering heart. I knew I had to talk to him even though I had no idea what I would say, but I kept my eyes closed when he came into the bedroom and paused just beside the bed, looking down at me.

His fingers brushed a few stray hairs away from my face and lingered against my parted lips. I wondered if he knew I was faking sleep, but I kept my breathing even just in case, and a minute later, he turned and padded softly into the bathroom. The light spilled into the room from the open door, and I opened my eyes as I listened for the sound of his movements. When I heard nothing, I got up to investigate.

He stood with his arms braced on the sink, his chest bare, and his head dipped so that long strands of glossy mahogany hair obscured his face. I hovered in the door for a moment until I was sure he could sense me by the slight shiver that rippled through his stiff shoulders.

Slowly, he tilted his head to the side to look at me. When our eyes met, I gasped. I felt our connection as painfully as if an anchor had rooted its sharp, sure hooks deep in my heart, linking our two souls with a thick, unyielding chain. It was not a delicate hold or a whimsical emotion. Love gripped me tightly, wringing me out until I wasn't sure I breathed.

Sinclair's eyes were large, but his expression guarded as I took the few steps necessary to reach him, then bring my hand to his face and trace the sharp angle of his cheekbone. After a second, he let out a short, sharp breath and turned his head to press a kiss into my palm. The gesture almost undid my fragile state, unzipping what would surely be a sloppy mess of emotions, but the sight of his raw, bleeding knuckles distracted me.

I tsked as I took one of his hands in my own and turned on the tap to wet a washcloth resting on the marble counter. He watched me carefully as I gently pressed the hot cloth to his scrapes.

"No chastisement?" he asked.

"Disappointed?"

"No, surprised. I assumed you would be a pacifist."

My eyebrows rose, and I purposely placed my tongue between my teeth after reminding him, "I bit the bastard's tongue."

He held the corner of his smile back so that it was adorably lopsided. "That you did. I hope you don't mind that I added a few ... touches to your masterpiece."

"Oh?"

"Just a black eye, maybe some purple near the jaw." He shrugged. "Black and blue are really his colors, you know."

It was my turn to fight my smile, laughter bubbling up and escaping before I could help it. Sinclair being uncharacteristically playful was impossible to resist. "I agree."

We grinned at each other like idiots, my hands now holding each of his. I looked down when he did to see his fingers twine slowly with mine, and when I met his gaze again, those electric eyes were bright.

"Will you do something with me?"

My belly fluttered with desire despite myself, but he laughed and shook his head. "Get your mind out of the gutter, Elle, and help me with the blankets."

Curious, I dutifully followed his orders as we deconstructed the bed, pulling off the heavy blanket and pillows to move them out onto the balcony. He pushed the two lounge chairs together and set up our makeshift bed, presenting it to me with twinkling eyes.

"Bored of the bedroom?"

He walked around to me and ran his knuckles down my cheek before pushing my hair over my shoulder. "Would you like to know the first thing I noticed about you?"

I was oddly breathless, so I just nodded.

"It was all this creamy skin. I imagined what it would smell like." He leaned down and ran his nose along my jawline. "Lavender and honey. What it would taste like under my tongue." His tongue smoothed over the shell of my ear before he nipped the lobe. "Even though you were ill, I could imagine how it would look in the sun and underwater. I had all these fantasies."

He tipped my chin up and rubbed a thumb over my pouting bottom lip. "I wanted you under the stars."

"Why are you doing this?" I whispered.

Something flickered across his eyes and was gone. He cocked his head in question.

"Why are you making it impossible for me to walk away with a whole heart?"

A light shudder ran down his spine, and I knew it wasn't from the balmy sea breeze.

"I told you I would hurt you," he murmured.

I flinched, and his hands slid down to my arms so that I wouldn't turn away. "You did. I guess I'm the villain in this love story then."

His eyes blazed in the low light. "You are not a villain for caring. I gave you no choice."

I snorted and tugged my arms from his grip, needing space.

"There is always a choice. And I'm not mad at myself for making it." Anger flared through the heartache, and I stepped so close I was almost standing on his toes. "I would make it again."

I could see the insecurity in the quirk of his unsmiling mouth, and I badly wanted to eradicate it, to burn away all of his considerable self-hatred and replace it with my love.

"Let me love you tonight." I took his frozen face in my hands and tried to smooth away the distress. "Let me pretend that I'm allowed to love you, that I'm yours. That tomorrow, instead of getting on a plane alone, I'll go back to a life we share."

My boldness left me shaky but strangely confident. I could feel my old dull and sensible skin slide away completely, leaving me raw and new and shiny. Even if he rebuffed me and told me to leave right now and never see him again, I would have this—the new me—and that would be enough.

I listened to the breath of the sea on the shore and of Sinclair's against mine for an interminable time until he sighed deeply and pulled me against him. One hand pressed to my lower back, and the other cradled the back of my head as his fingers threaded through my damp hair. Though it was only a hug, and I still had no idea how he really felt about me, somehow, it was enough.

I pulled away and pressed a hand to his chest to let him know I wanted him to stay there. When I was sure he understood, I began to slowly undress him, tugging off his expensive scuffed shoes and deftly undoing the catch to his pants that had so eluded me the first night in his bed. When he was gloriously naked, I started to pull my own clothes off, but he caught my wrist in his hand and shook his head.

"I like you in my clothes," he said, taking the hem of his T-shirt in his hands, "but it covers too much of this skin."

I let him pull the fabric over my head and tried not to quiver when he took a step back to stare at me with burning eyes. I could feel his gaze all over my body, caressing the generous curve of my breasts and tickling the gentle slope of skin down to my heated core. The power of his appreciation bubbled in my blood until I felt woozy like I had imbibed too much champagne.

He groaned and reached for me, tugging my body into his arms with a strong pull that robbed me of breath. It was my turn to moan when he fused his lips to mine, stroking me with hot strikes of his talented tongue. I was ready for a rough fuck, something dirty that would make me flush with embarrassment and lust, but he changed the angle of the kiss, pulling back to suck lightly at my bottom lip, then the top. His hands held me delicately, as if I weighed nothing, and when he pressed a knee onto the makeshift bed to lay me down. My descent was so gentle I felt like I landed on a cloud.

I had wanted to show him how much I loved him, but he was on top of me, sweeping long strokes of his broad fingers up and down my skin and planting gentle sucking kisses next to my aching core and heavy breasts. He was worshipping me with his body, playing mine like the finest instrument, and I wondered if this was his way of telling me how he felt. If he was loving me with his body in the only way he knew how. When he finally placed an open-mouthed kiss on my pulsing center, I unraveled long and slow like a ball of yarn rolling across the floor.

When I opened my eyes a minute later, he was looking down at me with an inscrutable expression and mildly frantic eyes. I didn't know what was bothering him, but I knew how to help him. Grabbing his ears to pull him in for a long, tangling kiss, I opened my legs and wrapped them around his pelvis, tipping my hips in order to open myself to him. He pulled back when he was poised at my entrance, panting slightly, his eyes unfocused but intent on mine. Only then did he slowly push inside me, not stopping until he was as deep as I could take him.

Eyes locked, he moved inside me, long, slow thrusts that had me feeling every inch of him. It was hard not to feel wholly owned by him at that moment, caught up in his arms, thrust down on his erection, invaded by him with all my senses. Even the sixth, that elusive sensory element that was more spiritual than visceral. Every time he slid inside me, his head kissing the every end of me, I felt stamped by him. It was a mark I knew I would wear inside me for the rest of my life even if I never saw him again. Even if I never had his smoky scent in my nose, his lean muscles under my hands, his gleaming red-brown hair hanging around us like a curtain as he kissed me.

I started crying, silent tears that leaked from the corners of my eyes and slide into my hairline. Sin didn't hesitate as he made love to me, dipping down to lick the trail from cheek to temple. When he kissed me again, it was bright with salt.

"I want you to remember this," he ordered in that cold voice that encased burning intent. "I want you to remember the feeling of me in this tight pussy, the way we fit together my edges against all your lush curves. I want my body imprinted on yours forever."

And my heart? I wanted to call out in anguish. *What about that?*

Instead, I lurched up to catch Sin's lips in an all-encompassing kiss, and then, when the slow, massive crest of a tsunami-like climax loomed over me, and Sin's thrust increased with his own need to come, I breathed into his mouth the truth of my heart, "Forever."

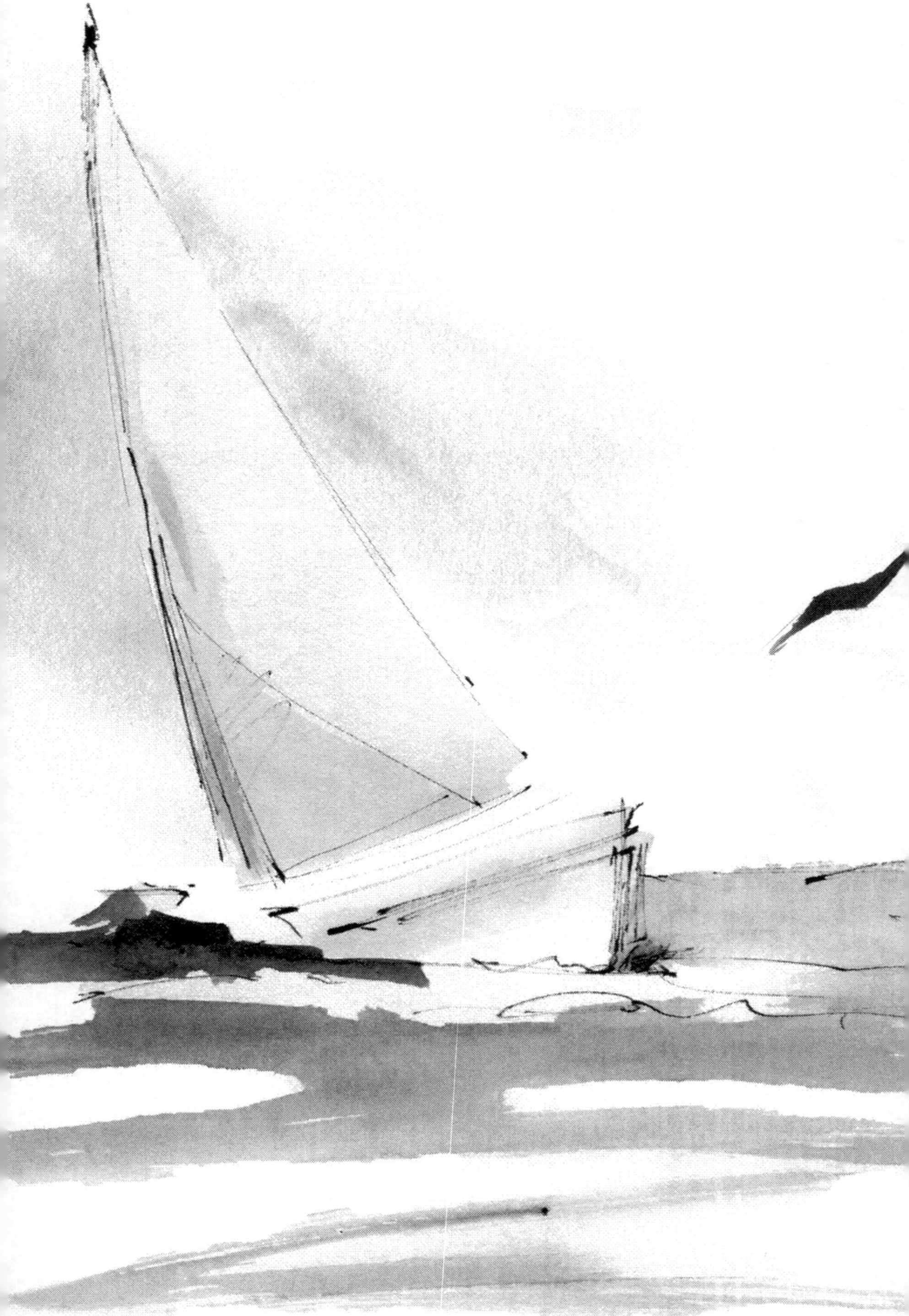

Chapter Fifteen

I woke the next morning with the gentle ocean breeze tickling a lock of hair against my cheek. The sun was just cresting over the horizon, spilling handfuls of glitter over the calm cerulean sea. I would have sat up to watch it properly, but Sinclair was a heavy weight plastered to the right side of my body. Carefully, I turned my look at him, aching at the sight of his peaceful expression and the softness of those hard features in repose. Daringly, I traced my fingertip gently over the straight reddish brows, down the strong line of his nose, and over the defined, scruff lined edge of his jaw.

It was impossible not to feel stirred by him as both a woman and an artist. If he had truly been mine, I would've spent years drawing the planes of that handsome face, discovering how it morphed in shadow and sun, as it evolved over the years with deeper creases in those hollowed cheeks and across the broad forehead. I wished I had the time to memorize every random freckle and mole, every inch of that beautiful darkly gold flesh so unique on a man with mahogany hair.

But I didn't.

This was my last morning with my Frenchmen, and I was determined not to be morose. I had one day left with him, and I would relish every perfect moment.

Carefully, I slid out of our makeshift bed so I didn't disturb him and then tiptoed back into the room to call for breakfast and plan our day with the concierge. While I waited, I showered and readied myself, still pleasantly shocked and amused that Sin'd had all my things brought to his room. It was over-the-top bossy, but I continued to find myself endeared by the quality instead of annoyed as I maybe should have been.

The truth was, Sin's dominance brought me peace and made me feel safe. I could recognize that more clearly in the wake of my assault the night prior. It felt good to know he was taking care of me, ordering Candy as my keeper while he dealt with the aggressor the way the smothered alpha male in him needed to. I'd never had anyone, but Cosima stand up for me before, and it felt unbelievably poignant to know that this man would after only six days of knowing me.

What might he do for me after years?

I pushed the thought out of my mind as I smoothed sunscreen into my tanned, freckled face and product into my curling damp hair. It was easy to choose my skimpiest bikini, a high-cut vivid blue color that reminded me of Sinclair's eyes that cupped and plumped my heavy breasts to best advantage. Satisfied he wouldn't be able to keep his hands off me, I donned a loose lavender linen cover-up and answered the knock on the door for room service.

He was still asleep when I carried the massive tray out to the terrace, and I took delight in placing it out of the way so I could straddle his hips and wake him up by peppering kisses all over his face.

"Good morning," I sang lightly as his lids fluttered open to reveal those deeply pigmented blue eyes. "Time to wake, sleepyhead."

His brow furrowed as he stretched beneath me, almost dislodging me in the process. I giggled as he grabbed my hips to keep me secured. "What time is it?"

"Nearly eight o'clock."

His brows lifted. "I can't remember the last time I slept so late."

I laughed. "It's hardly noon, Sin, I think it's okay. You didn't get to sleep until three in the morning anyway." I smiled shyly as him, aware of his warm grip sliding up my waist. "Besides, I liked watching you sleep."

"Ah, yet another clue to the mystery of Elle. You are a closeted somnophile," he teased.

I was grateful for his good mood and playfulness so I leaned into it, nipping at the tip of his nose, my hair a curtain around our smiling faces. "Not yet. But I'm discovering I might have a masochistic streak."

"Ah," he said somberly, one hand moving over my hip to grasp my bum cheek hard in his grip, making me hiss. "Maybe we should spend the morning exploring that."

"Nope," I crowed happily, flopping onto my side off him to grab for a piece of bacon on the tray. "You're always making plans, so I thought today, it was my turn."

He arched a brow as he sat up, the covers falling from his beautifully carved chest in a way that had me frozen with the bacon raised halfway to my mouth. Catching my look, he twitched his lips in that small, wicked grin, and he leaned forward to steal a bite of bacon from me.

"Excuse me," I accused, but laughter suffused my tone.

He ignored me, chewing his bacon then reaching for a cup of black coffee on the tray, but I detected the hint of a smile behind the lip of the rim as he brought it to his mouth. "So, what does the siren wish to do today?"

"We're going to go snorkeling, then get massages in a cabana on the beach and have an early dinner on the beach so we can get an early night." I blushed as I thought about what we may be retiring early to do together.

Sin considered me carefully. "I don't like the thought of another man's hands on you. In fact, it makes me irrationally angry. Do you see what you do to me, Elle? You make a sane man mad with passion."

It was hard not to take his words as a sublime compliment. No man had ever spoken to me in such a way, as if he was helpless against my pull, willingly throwing himself in my thrall.

It was heady, but it wasn't about the power for me.

It was about the vulnerability it expressed in a seemingly invulnerable man.

Maybe it was about power dynamics, I thought as I remembered how beautiful I felt when I submitted to Sin's demands. I made myself vulnerable sexually in ways both new and profound to me, and Sinclair was doing the same emotionally. The ebb and flow of our relationship seemed as timeless as the tide over the sand, and I wondered how I could ever recover from such an elemental connection.

"I've lost you," Sin murmured, studying me with keen eyes.

He had red-brown stubble roughening the skin at his jaw, around his firm mouth, and it made him look roguish and tousled, the well put together gentlemen that he normally presented a far cry from this morning's relaxed man.

"Not yet," I quipped, but the joke was stale and fell with a thud between us.

"Elle," he breathed on a sigh as he sat up to reach for me.

I didn't meet his eyes as he grabbed a loose curl spiraling over my chest and moved it through his fingers like a silk ribbon.

"Admittedly, this has become more complicated," he confessed softly before using his other hand to tip my chin so I was forced to look at him. When I did, his gaze was so clear, I could map the striations of different blues in his irises. "Let's have today. Teach a man set in his ways to relax and let us have some fun. Tomorrow at breakfast, we'll talk, yes?"

It was like a life raft tossed into the storm of emotions threatening my composure. I clung to it as I clung to him, reaching up to wrap my fingers around his wrist so I could bring his hand to my mouth for a soft kiss. Our gazes locked over our joined hands, and I smiled at him, giving us both some grace from turmoil.

"*Je suis d'accord*," I said, agreeing with yet another of his proposals. "Let's go."

We went snorkeling. I'd never been before and diving into the deeper waters between small mountains of coral where unknown creatures lurked was slightly frightening, but it felt right to push my boundaries when I was with Sinclair. He had proven last night that he would protect me and he had proven every day of the last six that he was eager to expand my horizons.

As if sensing my nerves, Sin held my hand as we pushed off the boat we'd rented and descended into the clear turquoise waters.

"Follow me," he said, that fleeting boyish excitement making him so much younger than his thirty-one years.

It was easy to follow his lead. I tried not to take too much symbolism from the way he guided me through the waters, deeper and deeper, farther from the boat, holding my hand the entire time as he pointed out the myriad of species that flashed and floated by us. Whenever we breached the ocean to breath and take a break, he explained the varieties, parrot fish, angel fish, yellow pork fish, and brilliant blue damsel fish the color of Sin's vivid irises.

It was breathtakingly beautiful.

I'd been born by the ocean in Napoli, a town as defined by the ocean as it was by its famous pizza, but I had never explored the waters from below. We were poor without the opportunity to do so, but also, the bay of Napoli was polluted beyond repair.

This was a sacred oasis. A hushed kind of reverence existed between Sinclair and me as we swam for hours in the bay. It was clear that he was deeply moved by the ocean and its inhabitants. As we floated on our backs, staring up at the almost blindingly bright sky, he recalled fishing trips he'd been on, and his company's focus on environmental sustainability.

It was the most I'd ever heard him speak at one time, and when we decided to drag our exhausted selves back to the boat, he seemed surprised to still be recounting a story to me.

"I'm sorry," he said, slightly startled. "I've been talking nonstop."

"I wish you'd go on," I told him honestly because I'd long ago given up any chance of being coolly aloof with him. "I love to hear you speak. You have a lovely accent and vocabulary for someone whose first language isn't English."

A shadow crossed his face as he'd helped me into the boat and turned to ready it for our return to the resort.

"As do you."

I recognized it for the subject change it was and sighed lightly as I took my seat and tied a lavender scarf around my hair so it wouldn't turn into Medusa-like dread locks in the wind.

"My father was a native English speaker," I explained but didn't go on.

This was one time when I was happy for our rule about revealing too much of our lives. Talking too much about Seamus always depressed me.

Sinclair left it alone, and we didn't speak again as we motored back to the resort for our massages.

In fact, the cool Frenchman was back in full force as he checked into the spa and followed our masseurs down the beach to the private section used exclusively for the spa. It was getting late in the afternoon, and we were the only couple on the sand. It should have been romantic, but he hardly looked at me as we were left alone to disrobe and make ourselves comfortable on the table.

I wanted to say something to break the strange static energy emanating from Sin, but I didn't know what to say, and I couldn't find the words before the two male masseurs returned.

Happily, he was incredibly skilled at massage, and I was soon emptying my mind to make room for the languid pleasure of having my sex-sore and previously assaulted body worked over by knowing, strong hands. Lulled by the massage, the lyrical rush of water against the shore, and the soft strains of guitar music funneled through hidden speakers, I soon drifted into a kind of half-sleep.

So, I only faintly heard the conversation that took place in Spanish over my head. I didn't speak the language, and I figured the masseurs were allowed to banter while they worked.

I didn't even flinch when my masseur moved away for a moment, thinking he was retrieving more oil.

It was only when another minute passed that I thought to lift my head from the hole in the bed, but just as I did, a soft touch to the back of my crown had me lowering again.

I obeyed the silent comment and relaxed into the rough, strong hands as they moved from the small of my back, framing my spine, all the way to the nape of my neck. Once there, one hand collared the column tightly, working thumb and fingers into the tight muscles.

It was a firm, almost possessive grip that sparked something low in my gut and turned the massage from passively pleasant to heighteningly erotic. It was hard not to squirm as those firm hands cupped the outside of my ribs, thumbs rolling down until they reached the dimples in the small of my back and then began slow, strong circles over them.

A moan escaped my mouth, followed by a long sigh as I melted further into the bed.

"That's it," a smoky voice said close to my ear as the man massaging me leaned over my back, hands still working. "I am the only man to make you moan. You should remember that, my siren, even when you leave this place."

I startled slightly at the sound of Sinclair's voice. "Where are our masseurs, Sin?"

"Dismissed."

"Sin!"

"With a very healthy tip," Sinclair amended with humor in his tone. It disintegrated in the heat of his next words. "I told you this morning I had a difficult time imagining another man's hands on you, bringing you pleasure. It seems the reality was even worse. I would have paid even more than I did to banish him and take his place."

I was a dazed mess of flattered, aroused, and bemused, but with Sin's hands still working over my body, I quickly succumbed to arousal. He chuckled low as I squirmed when he ran this thumbs under the sheet covering my bottom up onto the high swells.

"I don't think we need this anymore, do you?" he asked rhetorically as he tugged the sheet off with one hand.

The cool breeze whistled through the gap in the curtains of the cabana and smoothed over my suddenly feverish skin. I gasped as Sinclair moved lower, his hands unyielding against the dense flesh of my bum as he massaged it.

"Such a gorgeous ass," he hummed appreciatively, the way one would after sampling good wine.

When I tensed as his thumbs dipped between the crease and pulled me open to his gaze, he hushed me softly. "Relax, my siren. There is no part of you that isn't beautiful and tempting to me."

I shivered lightly as he pulled my cheeks apart, my hole exposed to him.

He groaned at the sight as he continued to knead my bottom, opening and closing my cheeks like a perverted game we were both enjoying entirely too much.

"If I dip my fingers down just here..." he muttered darkly, a finger running from the inside of my crease down to the wet leaking from me like an overturned jar of honey. "Ah, yes. I shouldn't be surprised anymore to find you so ready for me. All you need is my voice in your ear, isn't that true, Elle?"

A whimper was my only answer. I'd never known a massage could be so sensual that the mere press of his hands into my muscles could ignite such a burning need to climax.

"Please, Sin," I whispered, no longer surprised that he could raze my inhibitions so completely to the ground.

We were in a loosely concealed cabana on a public beach within sight of the resort beachgoers only twenty yards away.

Yet, I was willing to bare myself to him completely. To fold and bend and contort into whichever shape might please him best because in pleasing him, I was pleasing myself, knowing he would bring me only toe-curling satisfaction.

When he moved away from my core, I groaned in protest, but he only hushed me and worked those steely fingers down my legs all the way to my toes, where he wrenched gratification even out of my pinky toe.

"Flip over," he said finally in a rough voice that abraded my skin until it pebbled into goose bumps.

It felt good to know he was affected too, and when I turned onto my back, I caught sight of the glorious erection tenting the white towel affixed around his hips. I went to grab it, but he clucked his tongue at me. I waited patiently as he moved around the table to my head and then leaned up as he gripped the headrest and took it out of the table.

"Drop," he ordered, waiting until my head fell backward, my upside down gaze fixed to his groin. "Move forward so there isn't as much strain on your neck."

I obeyed, scooting forward so that more of my shoulders were over the edge of the table. The adjustment brought me perfectly in line with the lower half of his groin.

My mouth watered, and I wondered mildly if I had an oral fixation.

Sin stepped forward so that the rough toweling over his dick brushed my lips. I stared up at him into his burning blue eyes and sucked in a breath at the savage desire there.

"I had a feeling you would like playing behind such a flimsy veil," Sinclair taunted me, almost cruelly, yet I was utterly aroused by it. "You love the thrill of discovery. Of someone finding you consumed by me and the pleasure I can bring you. Do you want to be consumed now, Elle? Do you want to take my aching cock between those sweet lips and into that tight throat while I play with your gorgeous breasts?"

I was panting, sweat beading on my forehead, saliva pooling on my tongue. Reduced completely to flesh and womanhood.

"Yes, please," I whispered hoarsely, licking my dry lips and catching the towel in the act.

Sin jerked his hips forward slightly. I couldn't resist the impulse to cup his shaft through the material, tonguing it until it was warm and wet over his hot flesh.

When he'd had enough, he unhooked the towel so that it fell to the floor at his feet. He kicked it away, gripped the base of his erection in one fist, and painted the wet tip along my lips. The smell of him, musky and briny, invaded my senses and made my head swim.

"Open," he commanded, and I was obeying before he could finish the word.

His flesh was silken heat across my tongue as he tunneled instantly to the back of my throat, then paused while I worked to swallow around him. The position made it shockingly easy to take him into my throat on a smooth glide and I hummed in contentment around him when he was seated to the hilt.

"That's it," he said in that kingly tone that implied my pleasure was his to own. "I know how much you love my cock in your mouth."

I did so much it was almost worrying. I felt close to climax, just feeling the texture of his shaft between his lips and up over my tongue, from the salty taste of him exploding over my taste buds. When his hand, still slick with oil, found my breasts and began to roughly massage the flesh and play with my nipples, I groaned long and low in warning.

I'd orgasm in seconds.

Playing my body like a maestro, Sinclair sensed my impending climax and thrust harder between my lips. He caught my nipples between his knuckles, and twisted until twin bursts of pain radiated through my breasts and arrowed straight to my sex.

I gasped around his dick, bracing into orgasm, and then... nothing.

Sinclair was suddenly sliding from my clutching mouth and hauling me upright before twisting me around to face him. I was puddy into his hand, limp with longing, and when he finally had me as he wanted me, butt perched on the end of the massage table, legs hooked over his arms, he notched his head at my sex and thrust inside me to the hilt.

Air exploded from my lips of a garbled cry as he started a punishing pace, the force of his thrusts pinning me ot the table. I clutched him closer, fingers slipping on his oiled shoulders, nails scratching when I lost purchase so that I was clawing him. He didn't seem to mind. Instead, he grunted and forced me even closer, the end of his cock hitting the end of my channel in a way that had pain splintering into pleasure.

"God, the thought of filling you up with my cum," Sin rasped before he claimed my mouth in a ferocious kiss that completely eradicated my composure.

I came.

I came with his tongue in my mouth, his shaft in my swollen pussy, his body all around me, and his heart so close to my own, separated only by our flesh and bone, and our flimsy promise that tomorrow we would forget each other completely.

I sobbed at the savagery of my climax, only vaguely aware of Sin chanting something over and over until he came himself on a ragged groan.

We held each other after that for long minutes, the breeze swirling around us, the light growing hazy outside the linen curtains as the sun dropped and broke open on the horizon like a spilled yoke.

I had Sinclair's softening breath in my air, his hand moving lazily through the ends of my curls, along the warm expanse of my lower back. His heart pounded against my chest as he held me close, and I closed my eyes to count the beats.

Filled with acute longing and something I couldn't swallow that felt a lot like love, I clenched him hard to me and borrowed my nose in his neck. He let me. He let me because I liked to think, he felt the same desperation for me, the same pain at our inevitable parting.

He didn't say a thing until my hold loosened, and then he pulled back to drop a small kiss to my forehead. When we locked eyes, his were carefully guarded.

"Well," I said, clearing my throat as I attempted to gather my shattered willpower to me once more. "That was certainly the best massage I've ever had. What do you I owe you?"

Sinclair blinked once, then a smile tore across his chiseled features, and he laughed at the roof of the tent, clenching me in a hug that vibrated with his mirth.

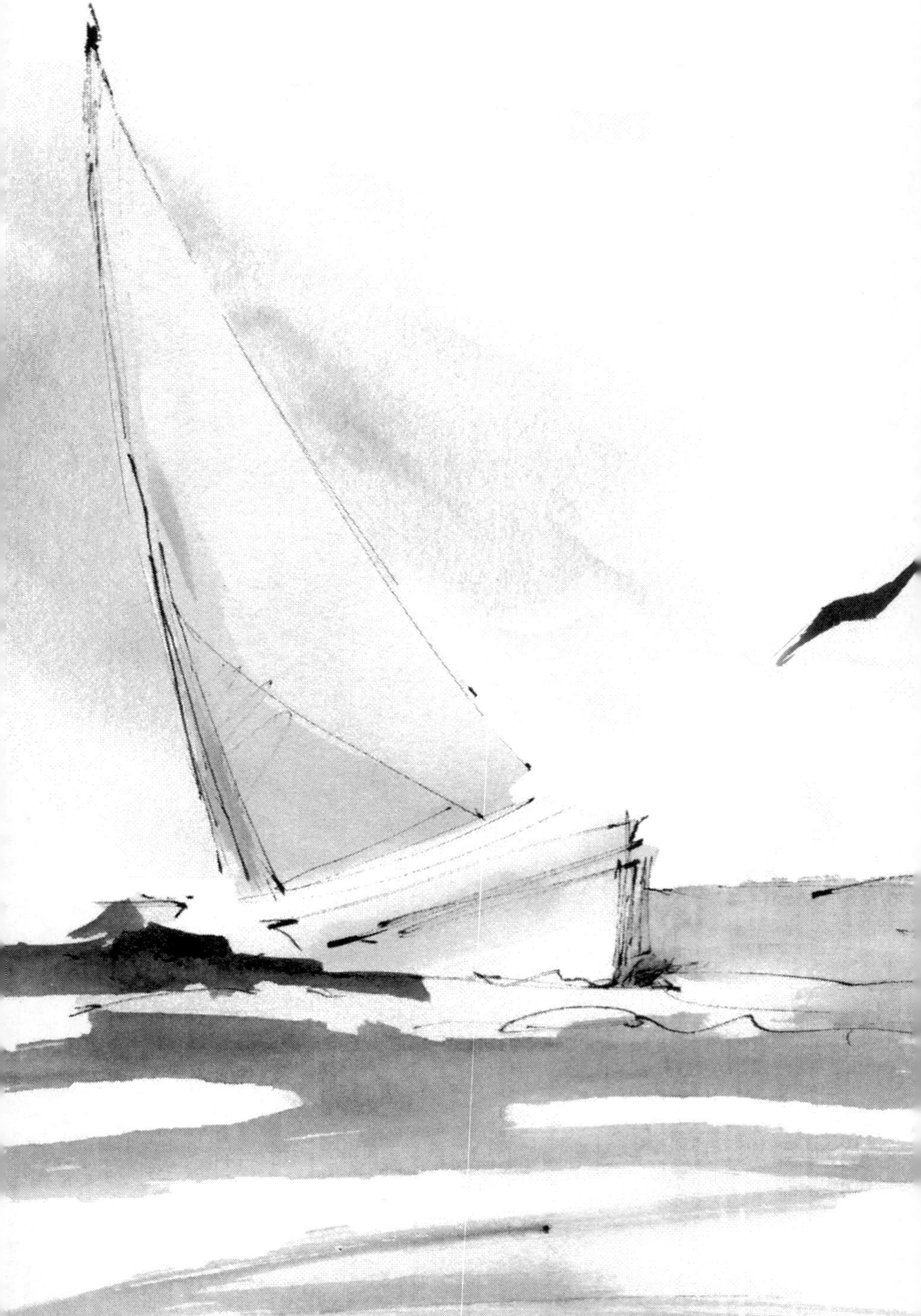

Chapter Sixteen

I was laughing so hard, my belly ached, and tears leaked from my eyes. In fact, I was laughing so hard I rolled away from Sinclair so he wouldn't see the way my eyes crinkled, and my skin went red with the effort of my rolling giggles. Happily, there was no one on the private beach the resort had ferried us to for our romantic dinner for two. Behind us, palm trees swayed, their branches rattling softly in the wind while the lit candles on the small table laid out with our meal guttered gently.

"Yes, Elle," Sinclair drawled coolly from beside me on the blanket we had spread out over the sand on the white beach. "It was highly amusing."

"I think," I gasped between chuckles. "It may have been the

funniest thing I've ever seen."

There was a soft laugh, and then Sinclair was rolling me back toward him and pinning me down with his large, lean body. His gorgeous face loomed over me. The hard planes cracked through with that small smile that seemed to illuminate the entire sky.

"He was just speaking the truth," he told me pragmatically.

I laughed harder.

The masseur Sinclair had so perfunctorily dismissed from the cabana had greeted us back in the spa when we were done with a knowing smirk and said, "Maybe *señor* can massage *me* some time. The lady is glowing."

Sinclair's response to the innuendo had been a shocked blink and a minute shrug of his shoulders as he feigned humbleness over his sexual gifts.

I'd kept my laughter contained until now, recounting the situation with him over the candle-lit dinner we had just sat down to enjoy at sunset.

"And would you massage him?" I teased.

He ran his nose down the length of mine, then shrugged a shoulder. "I am only interested in women, but I have no fear of male praise emasculating me. I am flattered."

It was my turn to blink in shock. Sinclair was so typically masculine and so buttoned up in some ways that it was often difficult to discern where the reserved gentleman began and the roguish deviant began.

"Though, it should be said," he murmured as his nose trailed off the cliff of my jawbone down to the hollow of my neck where he breathed me in as if I was some fragrant bloom. "Massaging anyone after having my hands on your gorgeous body would be a serious letdown."

"Oh, stop it." Praise still made my skin prickle like fire ants crawled over it. Compliments were for impressive boss ladies like Elena and gorgeous, loving superstars like Sebastian and Cosima.

I was ordinary.

Even my body, curved and plush, was normal compared to my siblings' lithe grace.

But Sinclair's sudden, fierce scowl had me reconsidering that.

"Listen to me," he demanded, his voice cold and powerful as he righted himself enough to grip my chin and pin my gaze with his. "You are nothing short of a siren. I do not care what passes as beauty in some magazine or movie. This is *real* life, and in it, there is no reality in which you are not a living, breathing dream of stunning perfection. If you do not believe my words, believe my actions. Would I be so helpless against your pull, so willing to deviate from everything I've ever stood for if you were not so lovely?"

My eyes burned so hot that they blurred. It took me a moment to realize I was crying and then another to realize I'd stopped breathing.

"But, Elle," Sin whispered, moving even closer so that those blue eyes were my world, and I was utterly submerged in their depths. "It is not so much this hourglass body or the flaming curls of your hair that hold me so captive. It is the soul shining in your eyes and peeking from your sweet, shy smile. You have so much to give the world. It is remarkable to me that you should not see that. I have known you only a week, and I am blinded by it."

"Stop," I whispered, and if I flipped a switch, the last of the sun slipped over the horizon, and the entire sky dimmed.

"No," he said adamantly, his hand on my chin moving into the back of my hair so he could fist it just tight enough to bring my scalp alive with tingles. "No, I hope you never stop hearing my voice say those words for as long as you need to hear them. Even when I am gone."

"When you're gone," I croaked, crying hard even though I didn't want to show him such weakness.

It couldn't be helped.

I was a goner for a man I should never have known.

A man who was never mine to have.

Determination set his jaw, his eye dark with intent as he pulled back to sit beside me, leaning back on his hands.

"Undress," he told me coolly, but his eyes? They burned. "Show me that beautiful body."

My fingers trembled as they went to the buttons on my thin floral dress as I fumbled to undo them. I watched Sinclair as he watched me, loving the tension in every inch of his posture as he held himself back from ravaging me. It was that contrast between his verdant desires and ironclad control that I found so endlessly arousing.

"Watch yourself," he coaxed, the words a sinuous coil of smoke wrapping around me like a drug that made me light-headed. "Look at that golden skin, freckled and smooth. I want to taste each one with my tongue."

"You should," I agreed eagerly.

I was very freckled. It would take him a very, very long time.

His lips twitched into a smile as fleeting as a shooting star. "Be good for me, Elle, and you'd be surprised what I would do to you."

A little shiver rippled through my shoulders as I undid the last of the long row of buttons and pushed the parted fabric open. I wore a gathered white bikini underneath that had always reminded me of seashells.

"A siren, indeed," he murmured, then went to his knees to move between my parted thighs.

I watched with my heart beating hard in my throat as he used one finger to slowly, achingly slow, draw one bikini strap down my shoulder and then the other. The light tickle of his flesh against mine drew my skin into tight bumps. It was so delicate, a whisper, yet it vibrated through me like a gong strike.

"You are the most magnificent woman," Sinclair admitted, almost to himself.

Jealousy flashed through me before I could quell it, and of

course, it was my bad luck he was observant enough to catch it.

"You want to ask if I think you are more magnificent even than her," he noted, his voice devoid of feeling.

I cursed him for his infallibility. For once, I wanted to be so unmoved.

"I want to ask a lot of things," I confessed with a blithe little shrug.

I didn't fool him.

Sin sat back and pulled my legs over his as he faced me, then tugged me up into his lap. My hair made a dark curtain around us as I leaned my forehead against his and stared down into his eyes.

"Maybe one day, my siren, I will let you ask them," he said opaquely.

I tried not to let it give me hope.

"But for now, you must know, the only two people in the entire world to me are you and me," he promised.

And then he sealed that promise with a kiss as lush as spring rain in a blooming garden. I had no choice but to respond, melting into him, wanting to give him every inch of me one last time before it was too late.

Because he could skirt around the inevitable, but we both knew the truth.

This was the end of us.

The termination of a relationship that we had only begun to sketch into something I knew in my bones could be have been the masterpiece of my life's work.

I swallowed the tears that surfaced and dived deeper into Sinclair's molten embrace.

The energy built between us, a desperation that hummed and sparked like electricity against our skin. I tore his linen shirt as I pulled it from those broad shoulders, needing his flesh under my hands, and he threw my bikini top first, then my bottoms far down the beach as if the sight of them insulted him.

I was wet when his fingers found me and slid like a brush through paint from my clit to my entrance.

"Please, sir," I begged, embarrassed of my cries but beyond that, lost to the current between us. "I need you now."

"Do you ache for me?" he asked in that cold voice that made me shiver. "Do you need me to fill up this tight pussy and remind you that I am the first man to take it?"

"Yes," I hissed sharply as he began to fuck me with his long, nimble fingers.

"Ride them for me, and I may let you ride my cock later," he promised.

I tossed my head back on my shoulders as I set my hips to the ancient rhyme of the sea on the shore, rocking back and forth, up and down. The friction was sweet and building, clenching my womb, my legs, and toes, sending sparks to my swollen breasts. I felt filled with the fire of our passion, but still, I wanted more.

Reading my restless need or perhaps feeling his own, Sin used his fingers, still wet from my sex, to quickly lube the head of his swollen dick then slotted it at my entrance.

"Watch me," he barked almost harshly.

The second our eyes locked, he impaled me, thrusting up into me at the same day he brought me down onto him with both arms wrapped tight around my torso, a hand clenched in my hair to pin me down.

I screamed at the resulting burst of pain-tinged pleasure and immediately set my hips to a punishing pace. There was this gluttonous need in me to come as if I could baptize him with my orgasm and claim his spirit for my own.

Sin grunted softly, sweat beading on his forehead, dampening the thick russet hair I ran through my fingers.

We watched each other, mirroring the expressions of the other.

Joy, lust, ecstasy, desperation and even fear.

I wasn't sure who felt what or when, only that on that beach joined together like two halves of a shell I felt we joined in perfect union, and it made me want to cry.

You were meant to be mine, I wanted to say and didn't, the words burning my throat.

A whimper escaped, a noise Sin recognized as something other than lust.

"Tell me," he ordered softly, reading my mind in that way he had, pressing his forehead to mine as he rolled his hips.

I gasped.

"Tell me," he repeated, withdrawing from me completely, leaving me achingly empty.

I rolled my hips down to bring him back to me, but his pained expression made me realize what he wanted from me. Still, I waited until he thrust into me again, all the way. He waited for me to speak, keeping me on the edge with those long, smooth strokes until finally, when I was quivering and whimpering with need, I whispered the truth that had been scorching my tongue for days, since almost the first moment I saw him.

"I love you."

He slammed back into me with a guttural moan, triggering my orgasm and his own. I clutched him to me, unwilling to relinquish the feel of his body against my own. He murmured something against my hair and pulled me into his arms as he rolled over. I wrapped one leg between his and tucked my head under his chin, bringing as much of my body into contact with his as I could. Because I already knew that in a few hours, as soon as the sun rose, I would be walking away from Sinclair forever.

The End.

The Secret (The Evolution of Sin, #2) is available now!
Turn the page for an excerpt

The Siren (The Evolution of Sin Trilogy, Book 2)
Excerpt

Is it possible to keep a life-changing secret from your family and friends when it is burning you alive from the inside out?

One week.
It shouldn't have been possible to fall in love with a man I barely knew while on holiday, but I fell so hard I was still seeing stars when I made my way to New York City to begin my new life.

Armed with newfound confidence, I was ready to distract myself from Sinclair by tackling the new challenges that awaited me in the city, reuniting with my estranged family, and launching my career as an artist in earnest.

Although I was heartbroken at the idea of never seeing the cold and dominating Sinclair again, I was braced for it.

That is, until Sinclair showed up in the last place I ever expected to see him, and my carefully guarded secret affair is suddenly in danger of being discovered by those it could hurt the worst.

The Siren: Chapter One

The waiting area in front of the arrival gates was crowded with people waiting for loved ones, and before I was even fully past the sliding glass doors, a wonderful voice, rich and decadent like a spoonful of chocolate ganache, called out to me.

"Giselle, *mi amore!*"

Cosima Lombardi was one of the lucky ones. Easily the most beautiful person I had ever seen, she crossed the crowded space on strong strides, her waist-length onyx hair floating behind her and attracting the glances of everyone in the terminal. Oblivious to it, she enveloped me in her long, thin arms and pressed me close to her body so that I was flush against her famous curves. This was the way a woman like Cosima Lombardi hugged—no boundaries, and no embarrassment, just passion.

She pulled away only enough to regard me with startlingly long-lashed eyes the color of melted butter. "I've missed you, *mi amore.*"

It was still hard to believe a woman like this could be my sister.

"I missed you too, Cosi." I dragged in a deep breath of her

spicy scent and instantly felt at ease. "But you didn't have to pick me up. I thought you had some work thing tonight?"

As one of the hottest young models on the fashion scene since Karl Lagerfeld championed Cara Delevingne, she was constantly working.

She swished one caramel hand through the air, the gold bangles on her wrist just as musical as her mild Italian accent. "My sister comes before work, Gigi. You should know that. I haven't seen you in seven months and two weeks." Her frown was fierce, and it was obvious to me why photographers loved her face as devotedly as they did.

"Excuse me." A teenage girl, no older than fifteen, approached us with barely concealed excitement, dragging her embarrassed father behind her. "Are you Cosima Lombardi?"

My sister smiled genuinely at them and extended her long-fingered hand. "Hello, darling."

She winked at the awkward father and leaned over to give the strange girl a kiss on each cheek.

"Wow," the teenager gushed, and I smiled as my sister obligingly took a picture with both father and daughter.

There was no one in the world I loved more than my sister, and it felt good to watch the people who approached her for her face and fame become enchanted with her warmth after interacting with her.

I was still smiling when she returned to my side and pressed a kiss to my cheek. "I'm sorry about that. Now, tell me absolutely *everything* I've missed in the past seven and a half months."

The shadow of Christopher crossed my thoughts, but I stubbornly refused to acknowledge it. There were only two other people in the world who knew the truth about why I was returning to New York after years abroad, and I intended to keep it that way, no matter how much I loved my sister.

"Your life is much more interesting, Miss *Sports Illustrated*."

Cosima laughed at my teasing, and it felt good when she took my arm in hers to march me over to the baggage claim.

Still, I found myself casting my gaze about the airport in search of a certain man with electric blue eyes. I knew that my own were probably still red from crying on the plane, but Cosima was too excited to see me to notice the telling signs.

"It was very weird," Cosima was saying. "The fact that people pay me just to pose for a camera is still strange to me. Do you know how much I got paid for that shoot?"

"Do I want to?" I winced, thinking about how much my studies at *L'École des Beaux-Arts* cost. Though I had been slowly climbing my way to success in the Parisian art scene, uprooting my life to cross continents was bound to take its toll, and I was reluctant to rely once again on my sibling's generous financial support.

"Probably not," she agreed cheerfully and casually reached out to smooth my wayward hair. "Let's just say it was enough to put a down payment on an apartment!"

It still surprised her, I knew, that her face could buy such an opulent life for herself and our family. I would never understand what it had been like for her, running away to Milan from our small town in Southern Italy in order to raise enough money for us to leave our impoverished life behind. Sometimes there was sadness in her eyes that I knew no one would ever reach.

"That's amazing, but you know I'm not surprised. You work so hard."

She made an unattractive sound and easily swept my luggage from the carousel. "Modeling isn't work. At least, not compared to what you do. I loved the print you sent me for my birthday. It's in the office of my new apartment."

We pushed out into the parking lot, and I was hit with a burst of bracing air. Greedily, I gulped in deep breaths because I knew the quality of the city air would be far from this clean and far from the pastry-scented, Seine-flavored breeze of my beloved Paris.

"I'm thrilled that you're home, Gigi, but I think I should warn you." Cosima peeked at me from the corner of her eye as she handed my bags to a cab driver. He was an older East Indian man with a particular smell and lovely brown eyes who stared at my gorgeous sister with nervous appreciation. "Elena is going to come down on you like the hammer of God for not coming home in four years."

"I saw her two years ago," I protested weakly, but I couldn't meet her eyes as we got into the yellow cab because I knew that was a lame excuse, and so did she.

"I know you two have ..." Cosima struggled for diplomatic words, but they did not come easily. "A distance between you, but you are sisters, and it hurts her that you never come home."

"I'm home now." But I leaned my head against her thin shoulder and sighed because I knew even though she was talking about Elena, she was really speaking on behalf of the whole family. Four years was far too long, especially for a family as close as ours. "And I brought Elena her only vice, Bonnat chocolates."

Our eldest sister was one of those women whose work was their life, which was the main reason, I think, that she liked America so much more than our native Italy. She had enrolled in law school as soon as the twins had enough money to bring her over from the motherland and now, only four years later, she was articling for one of the top firms in the country. For her to take time out of work for a man was a pretty big deal.

"So I guess she and this guy are pretty serious," I said with a massive yawn.

Cosima clucked and took my hand in her bronze one. We looked so dissimilar that no one ever believed we were related. The twins, Cosima and Sebastian, were mirror images of each other while Elena hovered somewhere in the middle with deep reddish-brown hair and stormy grey eyes similar to my own.

Cosima snorted inelegantly. "They've been together for nearly the entire time you've been gone. Elena wants them to adopt a baby."

"What about marriage?" I sat up, startled.

Marriage was a huge thing for our very traditional Italian mother; I couldn't imagine her reaction to a baby born out of wedlock.

"Daniel doesn't believe in marriage." She shrugged, but the sadness flashed in her eyes, and I wondered what she knew about the mysterious Daniel. "Mama might not understand that, but she loves Daniel enough to forgive him for it. Besides, it's already hard enough for Elena. You weren't here, but she had a meltdown when they realized she couldn't have children."

I pursed my lips and looked out the window at the passing blur of lights in the night. Elena had always wanted to be a mother; of all of us, she was the most traditionally Italian, lusting after the family life at the cornerstone of the culture. It was ironic, I had always found, since she was the least maternal person I knew. Despite my reservations about my older sister, I felt deeply ashamed that I hadn't been there for her.

"Ah, the city." Cosima tugged my hand. "She won't welcome you, *bambina*, but I promise you, in time, you'll come to love her."

I sighed and rested my head against the stale smelling headrest to watch the vibrant lights of New York City come at me. I had a feeling Cosima was talking about more than the city. I hadn't realized until now just how much I had missed in the past four years, and maybe, how hard it would be for me to come home.

My anxiety fled the moment Cosima and I pulled up to Mama's townhouse on the border of Soho and Little Italy. It was an old brick affair with black trim and red flowers in the window boxes. Mama had lived there since she and

Elena had moved to America four years ago, but I had only been inside once, when Cosima had flown me in for Mama's restaurant opening.

As soon as Cosima opened the door, the pungent smell of Mama's Italian cooking and the warmth of many bodies hit us. We shuffled through the small entrance area and into the long living room where, to my slight horror and surprise, a small gathering of people stood yelling, "Surprise!"

I laughed in delight at Cosima as she propelled me into the many waiting arms. "I can't believe you did this!"

"Giselle."

My mother's voice, the thickly accented, heavy sound of it, froze me in my tracks, and without knowing why, tears came to my eyes. Hers was the only face I saw in the crowd, and I realized with sadness that I had forgotten what she truly looked like. The twins had inherited her coloring—the inky waves, the golden eyes, and caramelized skin—but her figure, a classic hourglass like Sofia Loren but softened with good food and kind age, was like mine. A silent sob escaped me when she wound me up in her warm arms, and the scent of rosemary and sunshine enveloped me.

"Giselle, my French baby," she murmured over and over as she held me, her fingers pulling gently through my tangled hair.

"Mama," I breathed once, before tucking my face into her hair.

We stood like that in the middle of a room full of people for a few minutes before I could compose myself. Though we had talked almost every day on the phone or by email, it felt unspeakably good to be with my mother again. As with my other siblings, she was everything to me, and it astonished me—now that I was home—that I could have ever been comfortable staying away.

"Quit hogging her, Ma." A rich voice, the male equivalent of Cosima's but deeper and darker, resounded throughout the room, and with a shriek of joy, I threw myself from Mama's arms into Sebastian's.

He chuckled as he caught me and lifted me easily into his arms. "You've grown, *mia sorella*, and your hair ..." He tugged a piece. "I think this is the first time I've seen you red since you were twelve."

I pulled back and smiled into his ridiculously handsome face. "God, I missed you."

Mama tapped me on the bottom and tsked at my use of God's name, but Sebastian and I only laughed as he placed me once more on the floor.

Seb had visited me last year in Paris while he shot a movie, and it still wowed me that my two younger siblings were doing so well in their respective careers. Two years ago, Sebastian had starred in a low budget indie movie about an impoverished Italian immigrant in New York during the '20s. It had won three awards at the Cannes Film Festival, and now, my baby brother, the same person who used to run naked through the grimy streets of our home in Napoli, was a burgeoning movie star.

"I missed you too, *bambina*." Though I was older than the twins, they both called me baby because I was decidedly shorter than their towering heights.

"I like it better this way." Elena stepped forward, suddenly in front of me, her hands awkwardly extended for an embrace. "Your hair, I mean."

My oldest sister shared my coloring but little else; her auburn hair was darker than mine, a red so black it was the color of wine, cut short and chic around her angular face, showcasing a creamy expanse of freckle-free skin and almond-shaped eyes the color of storm clouds. Her body was lean and small boned where mine was softer, curved like the other women in our family, and I knew, as her eyes fell over my breasts and tucked waist, that she felt a pang of isolation at seeing me again. Whereas I took comfort from knowing that we looked at least vaguely similar, Elena saw only the things in me that made her different. She was the spitting image of our father, and we all knew that was hard on her. But I'd always found her heartrendingly beautiful anyway, somehow sharp and romantic all at once.

And though she was also the smartest person I knew, and despite my deep respect for her, our embrace was awkward. Something between us had wilted years ago, and I was still unsure how to recover it.

"You look beautiful too, Elena."

We both took a large step back after our hug, but the twins and Mama filled in around us.

Though I was tired and still mildly queasy from the long flight, it felt good to spend time with my family and the close group of friends they had made over the years. I met Sebastian's girlfriend, Sophie, who I had recognized immediately as being a model for Calvin Klein and a good friend of Cosima's. It wasn't serious, Seb assured me later as he refilled my wine glass, but she was a good lay.

There were also my mama's three best friends, all chefs like herself, and Cosima's old roommate, Erika, a Dutch model with cheekbones that could cut glass, and Elena's assistant, Beau, whom I had known for years and was closer to than I was Elena.

"So," Cosima began as she caught my arm and spun me through the doorway into a dark room off the main hall.

I had only visited the house once, on my only trip to America after the twins had officially moved Mama and Elena here three years ago, so the layout was still unfamiliar, but I thought we were in the guest bedroom.

"Tell me how things ended with the Frenchman," she said before she flicked the light on and gracefully collapsed on the deep red covered bed, patting the space next to her so that I would sit.

I sighed and placed my head next to hers on the pillow,

comforted by her spicy scent and the way she casually took my hand in hers. "I left."

"Oh?"

"I left before he woke up this morning. I just couldn't say goodbye. What was I going to say? Thanks for the hot sex and amazing adventures. I love you. Catch you never?"

I held myself still in the ensuing silence and resisted the urge to turn over to look into her expressive face for her response. Cosima was careful with her words—when she wasn't in a temper—and I knew she was meticulously sifting through them like individual grains of sand.

"I was worried you would love him. You didn't tell me much about him. I don't even know the mystery man's name, but I know you." Her thumb swept back and forth over my palm. "And intimacy for one so passionate cannot be untangled from love."

I scoffed. "You're the passionate one, Cosi."

She propped up on one elbow in order to glare down at me. "Can there be only one passionate woman in this family?"

I pursed my lips but said nothing.

"Exactly. Now tell me why you left like this. You took away his chance."

"His chance to what?" Break my heart in person?

"To ask you to go home with him."

She said it as if it was a simple choice, as if it was only natural that he would want to take a complete stranger home with him.

"He didn't know anything about me." But I winced even as I said it because I knew it wasn't true.

"You can know a person without knowing the trivialities."

"I don't even know where he lives. That's a pretty big omission."

She snorted inelegantly, and I couldn't help but smile at her. Before Sinclair, I had never loved another human being like I loved Cosima. To me, she was the essence of beauty and life, full of volatile emotions and overwhelming love.

"You would have liked him."

Her expression softened, and she smoothed a piece of hair away from my face. "I'm sure I would have."

We both turned to look at the door as it creaked open, revealing Elena who blinked owlishly at us cuddled on the bed before muttering an unintelligible apology as she closed the door.

"Get in here, Elena," Cosima scolded and jumped up to tug her forcibly into the room.

Our eldest sister looked uncomfortable but allowed Cosima to maneuver her so that we lay in a row with Cosima at our center, connecting us but tactfully giving us the space we needed from each other.

"We were talking about men."

"Ah."

"Giselle had a little fling in Mexico."

"Really?" Elena's brows almost touched her hairline. "That doesn't seem like you."

Anger rushed through me like a brush fire before I settled it with a deep, careful breath. "It isn't, but I'm glad I went through with it. I want to be more bold."

"There's a thin line between bold and reckless," Elena said in her schoolmarm's voice, the same tone I had heard countless times as a child and the same tone I still heard every time I faced a potentially thrilling situation, always cautioning me to stay safe.

"Oh, come on, Lena. It's only a harmless fling." Cosima winked one of her golden eyes at me. "And besides, you of all people can't blame a girl for falling for a pretty face."

"True."

"Daniel was a model for a few years." Cosima laughed at the expression of prudish disapproval on our sister's face. "That's how we met."

I remembered Sinclair's terse expression when he brought up his own short-lived modeling career, and even though I didn't know his foster parents, a flare of hatred burned up my throat. I was grateful to Mama for not pressuring Cosima into the profession, but that didn't mean my little sister didn't carry invisible scars on her pretty gold skin.

"Wait till you meet him. Over the past few years, he's become even sterner." Cosima made a face, comically constipated looking, before dissolving into laughter. "If Elena didn't make him have bran cereal every morning, I'd think he was having serious issues."

I laughed, scooting from the bed as I did so. I indicated pouring some wine and moved toward the door when I got their nods of approval. It was rare that a conversation amongst our family didn't include a bottle of wine.

"Very funny." Elena smiled indulgently at our favorite sibling. "I should get out there. He'll be here soon."

"Where was he this time?" Cosima asked, idly running a hand through Elena's short, elegantly curled tresses.

"Mexico," she said as I closed the door behind me and made my winding way back into the large kitchen at the front of the house.

It was an open space punctuated with a large wooden island over which Mama's prized copper pots and pans resided on a sort of rustic trellis. The cabinets were an unfinished birch, and the gleaming countertops were cool under my questing fingers as I sought out the clay pitcher of red wine Mama kept filled at all times.

I smiled at the sounds of laughter from the main room, and for the first time that night, I relaxed enough to stop worrying about Sinclair. The decision to leave him without a word would plague me for the rest of my life, I knew, but at least for this first month in a new city, surrounded by my loving family, I would have plenty of opportunities to take my mind off it.

I was pouring out three glasses of wine when I felt the prickle of awareness race up my spine. There was the soft fall of shoes crossing the wooden floors, and then the heat of another body pressed close to my back. Somehow, though I didn't know how it could be possible, when I turned around to face the stranger, it was my Frenchman.

"What are you doing here?" he snapped, his eyes blazing.

He looked at ease in the space. His crisp shirt was still pristine and tucked into his charcoal grey pants, but it was open at his throat to reveal a deep slice of brown skin, the cuffs were rolled hastily over his forearms, and his jacket hung across his shoulder casually as if he had just taken it off to relax. Even though I had just seen him this morning, the sight of him in my mama's kitchen threw into stark relief just how absurdly good looking he was.

"Well?" he growled when I didn't immediately answer.

I couldn't believe he was here. My mind spun wildly, trying to confirm his presence. It seemed more probable that I was imagining him. I had the strongest urge to reach out and run my fingers through his glossy reddish-brown hair.

"What are you doing here?" I whispered, afraid he would disappear.

Confusion crossed his face but something like horror came over his features, and he croaked, "Elle... Giselle Moore."

The Secret (The Evolution of Sin #2) is LIVE now!

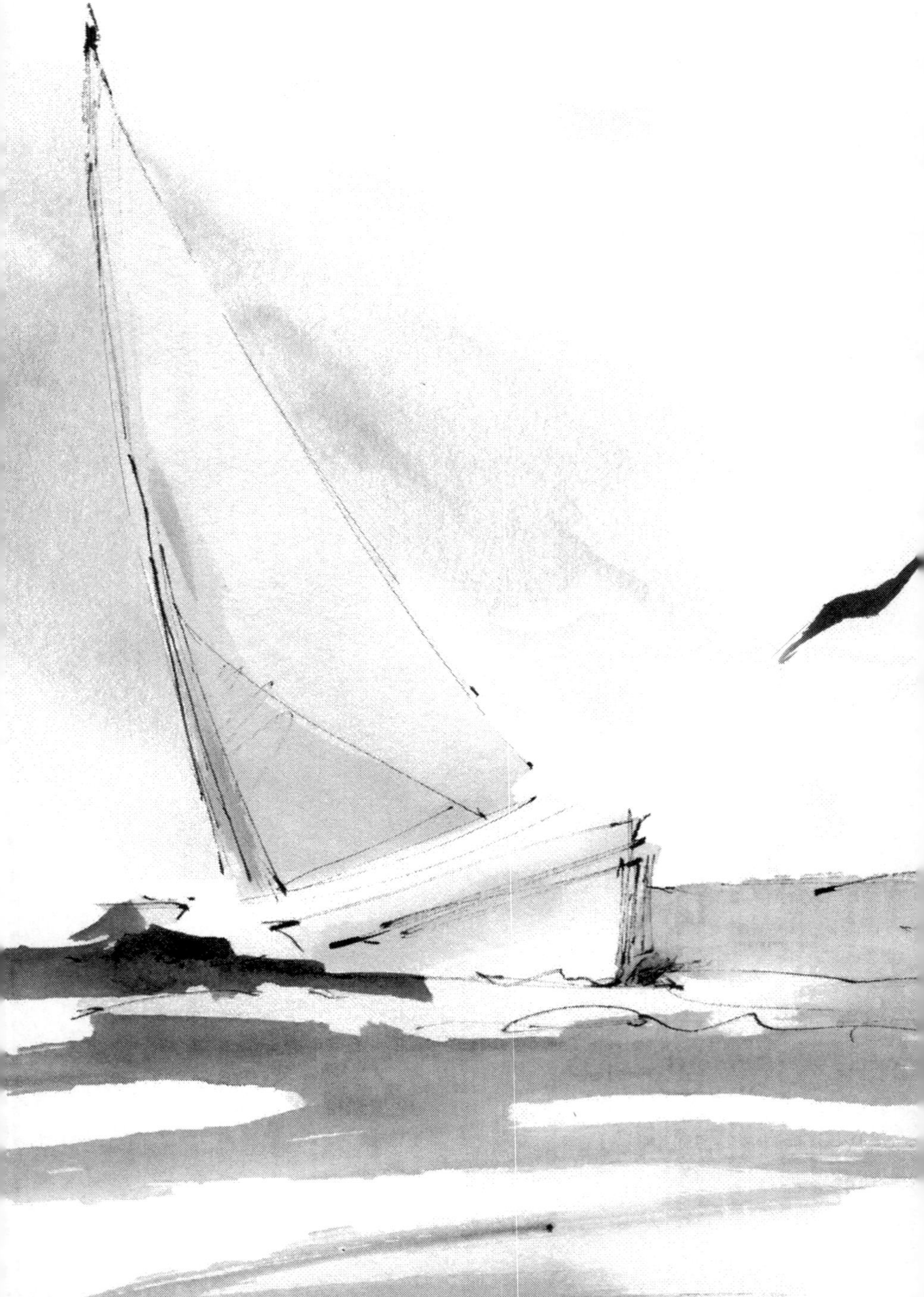

Thanks etc.

I couldn't have written *The Affair* without the loving support of my best friends. Many thanks go to Najla Qamber of Najla Qamber Designs for the gorgeous cover, Mark My Books Publicity for the blog tour, and those bloggers who took the time to read and review my book. All my love goes to my first beta readers Cassie Fite, and Angela Plumlee. Finally, a multitude of thanks goes to Patricia Essex my superstar editor, without whom I would be utterly lost! Also, thank you to Jenny Sims from Editing4Indies for giving this book new life.

Thank you always, to my love, my best friend, and the inspiration for every love story I will ever write, my man, H.

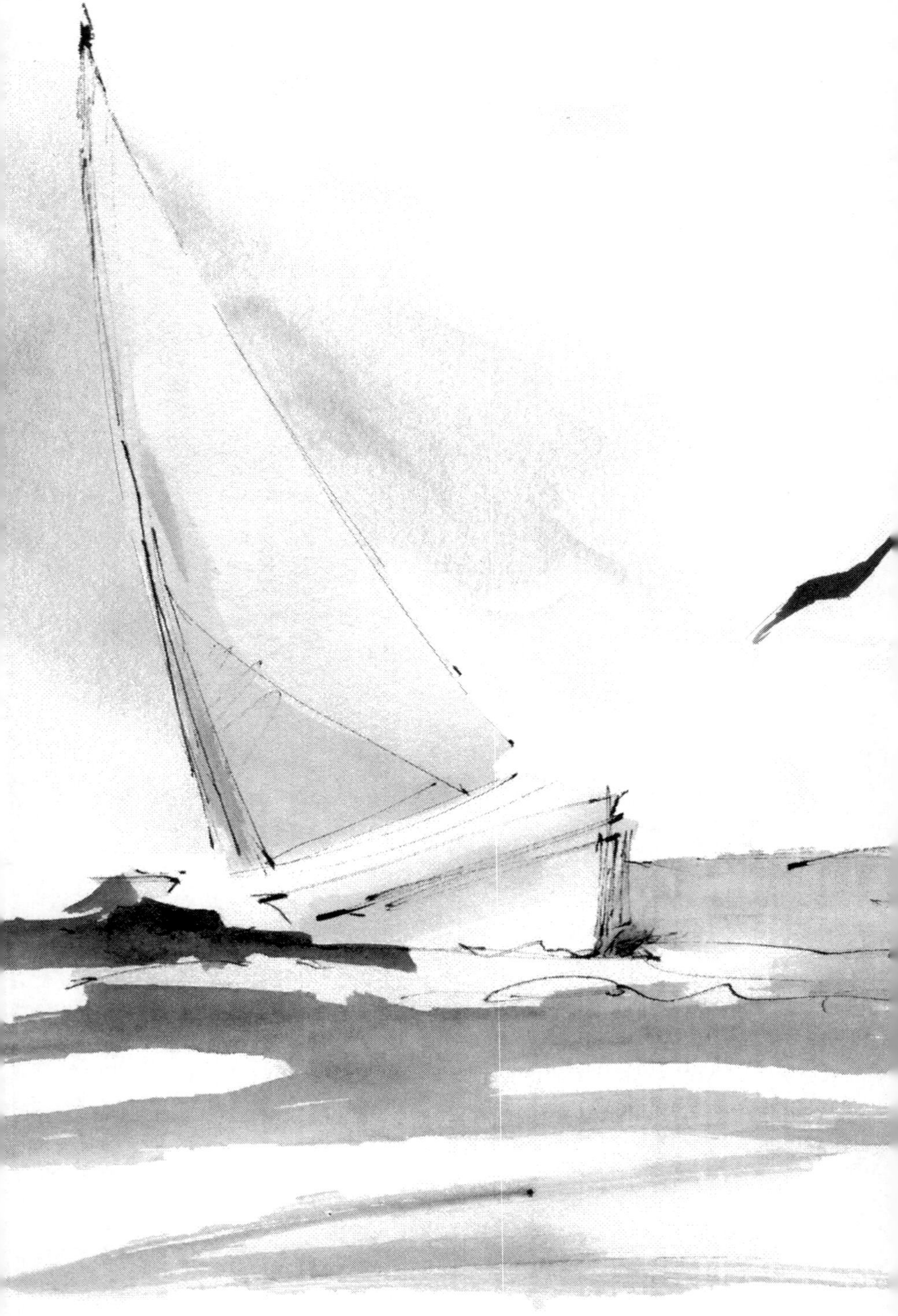

Other Books By Giana Darling

The Fallen Men Series

The Fallen Men are a series of interconnected, standalone, erotic MC romances that each feature age gap love stories between dirty-talking, Alpha males and the strong, sassy women who win their hearts.

Lessons in Corruption

Welcome to the Dark Side

Good Gone Bad

Fallen Son (A Short Story)

After the Fall

Inked in Lies

Fallen King (A Short Story)

Dead Man Walking

Caution to the Wind

Asking for Trouble

A Fallen Men Companion Book of Poetry:

King of Iron Hearts

The Evolution of Sin Trilogy

Giselle Moore is running away from her past in France for a new life in America, but before she moves to New York City, she takes a holiday on the beaches of Mexico and meets a sinful, enigmatic French businessman, Sinclair, who awakens submissive desires and changes her life forever.

The Siren

The Sinners

The Evolution Of Sin Trilogy Boxset

The Enslaved Duet

The Enslaved Duet is a dark romance duology about an eighteen-year old Italian fashion model, Cosima Lombardi, who is sold by her indebted father to a British Earl who's nefarious plans for her include more than just sexual slavery... Their epic tale spans across Italy, England, Scotland, and the USA across a five-year period that sees them endure murder, separation, and a web of infinite lies.

Enthralled (The Enslaved Duet #1)

Enamoured (The Enslaved Duet, #2)

The Enslaved Duet Boxset

Anti-Heroes in Love Duet

Elena Lombardi is an ice cold, broken-hearted criminal lawyer with a distaste for anything untoward, but when her sister begs her to represent New York City's most infamous mafioso on trial for murder, she can't refuse and soon, she finds herself unable to resist the dangerous charms of Dante Salvatore.

When Heroes Fall

When Villains Rise

Anti-heroes in Love Boxset

The Dark Dream Duet

The Dark Dream duology is a guardian/ward, enemies to lovers romance about the dangerous, scarred black sheep of the Morelli family, Tiernan, and the innocent Bianca Belcante. After Bianca's mother dies, Tiernan becomes the guardian to both her and her little brother. But Tiernan doesn't do anything out of the goodness of his heart, and soon Bianca is thrust into the wealthy elite of Bishop's Landing and the dark secrets that lurk beneath its glittering surface.

Bad Dream (Dark Dream Duet, #0.5) is FREE

Dangerous Temptation (Dark Dream Duet, #1)

Beautiful Nightmare (Dark Dream Duet, #2)

The Elite Seven Series

Sloth (The Elite Seven Series, #7)

Standalone

Serpentine Valentine (A Sapphic Medusa Retelling)

Coming Soon

My Dark Fairy Tale (A Mafia Romance)

The Moon & His Tides (The Impossible Universe Trilogy, #1)

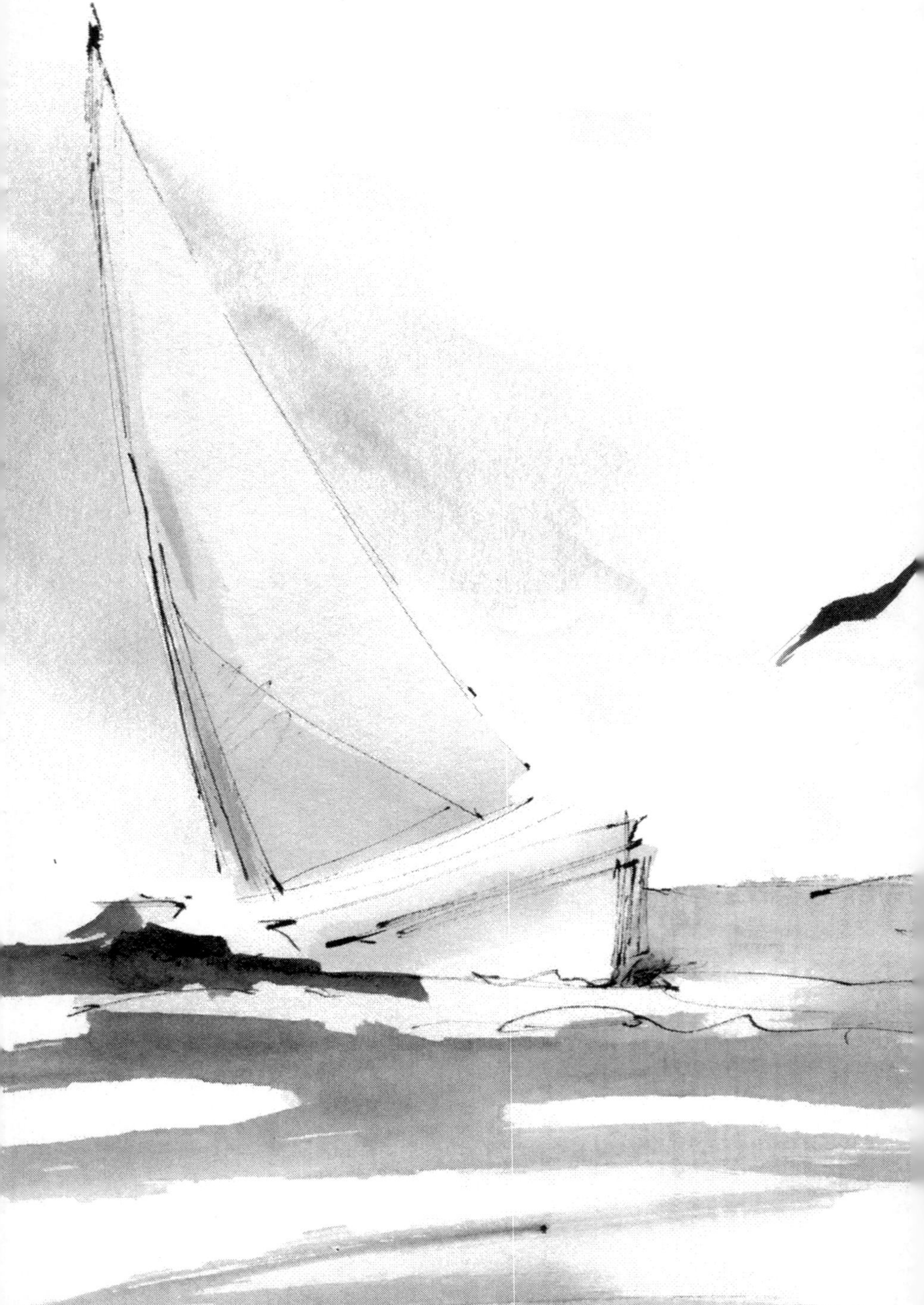

About Giana Darling

Giana Darling is a USA Today, Wall Street Journal, Top 40 Best Selling Canadian romance writer who specializes in the taboo and angsty side of love and romance. She currently lives in beautiful British Columbia where she spends time riding on the back of her husband's bike, baking pies, and reading snuggled up with her cat, Persephone, and puppy, Romeo.

Join my Reader's Group
Subscribe to my Newsletter
Follow me on IG
Like me on Facebook
Follow me on Youtube
Follow me on Goodreads
Follow me on BookBub
Follow me on Pinterest

Made in the USA
Middletown, DE
10 March 2025